ABYSS

Tricia Rayburn is the author of *Ruby's Slippers* and the Maggie Bean trilogy. Despite fearing all creatures of the deep, she's still drawn to the water and makes her home in a seaside town on eastern Long Island in America. You can visit her online at www.triciarayburn.com.

ABYSS

A Siren book

TRICIA RAYBURN

faber and faber

First published in the USA Simon and Schuster in 2012
(as *Dark Water*)

First published in this edition in 2013
by Faber and Faber Limited
Bloomsbury House,
74–77 Great Russell Street,
London WC1B 3DA

Typeset by Faber and Faber Ltd

Printed in the UK by CPI Group (UK), Croydon CR0 4YY

A CIP record for this book
is available from the British Library

ISBN 978-0-571-27394-2

FSC
www.fsc.org
MIX

A story for Susie Q

CHAPTER I

It started an hour into the trip. The fluttering in my chest. The weakening of my legs. The tightening of my throat that made each breath feel like it was filled with broken glass rather than clear, fresh air. These feelings were nothing new. For nearly a year, they'd been the messages my body sent whenever it was slowing down, tiring out . . . drying up.

The difference this time was that I wasn't thirsty. We'd visited enough rest stops along Interstate 95 to be sure of that.

I was scared.

'Crisps?'

An economy-size bag of Walker's appeared between the two front seats. Shook back and forth.

'They're your favourite,' Mom said. 'Salt and vinegar.'

'Heavy on the salt,' Dad added.

I watched him take a plastic shaker from his cup holder and tilt it over the top of the bag. As the white powder fell onto the crisps, I thought about how the mere idea of this road-trip snack should make my stomach turn. But it didn't.

'No, thanks,' I said. 'I'm not hungry.'

'You haven't eaten today,' Mom said. 'And you barely picked at your dinner last night.'

'I'm saving my appetite. For Harbor Homefries.'

Mom glanced at Dad. His head lowered and lifted so slightly, you wouldn't notice the nod if you didn't expect it.

'So,' he said, leaving the bag on the console and replacing the shaker in the cup holder. 'Several of my students were renting a house in Kennebunkport this summer. It's supposed to be a pretty hopping place.'

'Hopping?' I said.

'You know – happening. Grooving. Or, as one young wordsmith alleged, slamming.'

'Slammin',' Mom said.

Dad looked at her. 'How come it doesn't sound nearly as ridiculous when you say it?'

'Because I said it correctly.' She tried to catch my eye in the rear-view mirror. 'You leave off the *g*. Right, sweetie?'

I turned my head, faced the window. 'I think so.'

'Well,' Dad said, 'if our Dartmouth-bound daughter thinks it's so, then so it is.'

I pressed my forehead to the glass, blinking away images of green ivy-covered walls.

'In any case, the town gets fairly busy, but it's by the water and is supposed to be beautiful. Maybe we should check it out. Like, today.'

'That's a great idea,' Mom said. 'The exit will be coming up soon.'

I sat up. 'Don't we have an appointment?'

'We do,' Mom said. 'And it can be rescheduled.'

'But you've been planning this trip for weeks. Why the sudden detour?'

'Why not?' Mom asked. 'It never hurts to know all your options. Especially when it comes to real estate.'

'But where we're going is also by the water. It's the most beautiful place I've ever been.' I tried to smile. 'And after last summer it shouldn't be too crowded.'

This final point was an attempt at keeping things light. For better or worse, my poor delivery broke through my parents' happy façade.

'We don't have to go back.' Mom said, squeezing the steering wheel.

'We can go anywhere,' Dad said. 'Try someplace new.'

'I know,' I said. 'You told me that six months ago and every week since then. I appreciate the offer, but it's not necessary. I don't want to try someplace new.'

Mom glanced over her shoulder. Her lips were set in

3

a thin, straight line. Behind her sunglasses, I knew her brows were lowered, her eyes narrowed.

'Vanessa, are you sure? I mean, *really* sure? I know you've visited a few times since ... everything ... but this is different.' She paused. 'It's summer.'

Summer. The word hung above us, heavy, expanding. I looked at the empty seat to my left, then reached forward and grabbed a handful of crisps.

'Yes,' I said. 'I'm really sure.'

Despite my countless assurances over the past few months, I understood their concern. We'd made the same trip each June for as long as I could remember, and this was the first time we were doing so without my older sister Justine. Not only that, due to our realtor's schedule – and a supposedly amazing property that'd recently hit the market – we'd had to leave today. Which just happened to be the day after my graduation from Hawthorne Prep . . . and the one-year anniversary of Justine's death.

As my body continued to remind me, this was scary. But one thing would be downright terrifying.

Not returning to Winter Harbor at all.

I washed down several handfuls of crisps with two bottles of salt water. For fifteen minutes, I half-listened and nodded along as my parents debated the benefits of all-weather cladding.

When we passed the Kennebunkport exit, I waited another five minutes for good measure, then settled back and checked my cell phone for the hundredth time since waking up.

V! SO EXCITED TO SEE YOU. WHO KNEW 20 HOURS COULD FEEL LIKE 20 YEARS?? AT RESTAURANT ALL DAY. STOP BY WHEN YOU CAN. XO, P

Paige. My best friend, recent housemate – and one of the main reasons why vacationing anywhere else this summer was impossible. I smiled as I texted her back.

CAN'T WAIT TO SEE YOU, TOO. STILL A FEW HOURS AWAY. WILL WRITE AGAIN WHEN CLOSER. DON'T WORK TOO HARD! L, V

I sent the note and scrolled through older messages, hoping, like I always did, that I'd missed one. That maybe there'd been a glitch in my service and I hadn't been notified of every incoming text.

There wasn't. A quick call to my voicemail proved that it, too, was working fine.

I swapped my phone for the Dartmouth course descriptions I'd printed from the school website and curled up on the back seat. I already had a pretty good idea of what I wanted to take in the autumn, but my parents didn't know that. And more than anything else, looking like I was thinking about my future stopped them from bringing up the past. In fact, the course descriptions were such an effective shield, no one asked how I was or what I needed for the rest of the trip.

Of course, by the time we pulled off the highway, they didn't have to. Not out loud anyway. Mom looked in the rear-view mirror more than she did at the road, and Dad gave a bag of pretzels an extra coating of salt before propping it between the two front seats.

'I'm fine,' I said, as my pulse pounded in my ears. 'Promise.'

This seemed to appease them until we neared the sailing-boat-shaped WELCOME TO WINTER HARBOR sign. That's when Mom jerked the steering wheel to the left – and we took an unexpected detour bypassing Main Street and all the local businesses. I started to protest but then hesitated. Did I really want to sit in traffic and inch past Eddie's Ice Cream? Which had always been our first stop – and the official start of another wonderful family vacation?

Probably not. I let my parents have that one.

I took another water bottle from my backpack and focused on drinking. A few minutes later, the detour led to the same intersection we would've reached had we stayed on Main Street. Turning right would take us towards the mountains and down a long, winding road I knew so well I could drive it at night without headlights. I listened for the clicking signal, waited for the gentle pull west. Neither happened. We went straight instead.

As we drove, the straight, flat road began to incline. The houses grew further apart, the trees closer together. I'd never been in this part of Winter Harbor; before I could decide whether that was a good or bad thing, the road ended. The car stopped. We all stared straight ahead.

'Is this a joke?' I asked, peering between the front seats.

'I don't think so,' Mom said, after a pause. She handed the directions to Dad, rolled down her window, and pressed the button on a silver box next to her door. The tall gates, which featured iron mermaids with ornate tails rather than simple bars, swung open.

'Let's give it a chance,' Dad said, then busied himself with folding and refolding the directions.

I wanted to take the stack of course descriptions, hold them in front of my face, block out everything I didn't want to see. But I couldn't. My eyes were glued to the faceless heads, the flowing hair, the intricate fins. I told myself that these mermaids were decorative art, nothing more, but I still searched for something, anything familiar about them. As the gates closed behind us and we continued down the driveway, I even turned in my seat to watch them grow smaller. Or perhaps more accurately, to make *sure* they grew smaller.

The steep driveway curled through dense forest. About half a mile in, Mom, growing nervous, impatient, or a combination of both, hit the gas. The SUV shot up a small hill – and towards the edge of a cliff.

Dad and I reached for the grab handles above our doors. Mom gasped and slammed on the brake. The car skidded a few feet before rocking to a stop.

'A fence,' Mom said, exhaling. 'We'll just get a good, strong fence.'

She opened her door and hopped out. Dad slowly leaned forward, started to turn. Sensing a fresh wave of concern approaching, I opened my door and stepped down before it reached me.

'Jacqueline! So glad you could make it at such short notice.'

A woman strode down a wide stone path to our left. She wore white linen trousers, a white caftan, and leather sandals. Her hair was pulled back in a ponytail so tight the corners of her blue eyes lifted. I must've been even more shaken by the iron shield of swimmers we'd passed through than I thought, because for a split second, she looked just like another woman I'd met last summer.

But that was impossible.

Wasn't it?

'This must be your beautiful daughter.' The woman shook Mom's hand and beamed at me. 'The Ivy Leaguer. I've heard so much about you. Dartmouth, right?'

I forced a smile as I joined them. 'Right.'

'You're a parent's dream come true.'

I looked down. 'Vanessa,' Mom said quickly, 'this is Anne. Our realtor. And, Anne, yes, this is my beautiful daughter.'

'I'm the perfectly average-looking husband and father,' Dad said, shuffling up behind us. 'And this is quite a place.'

'I told you. Didn't I tell you?'

Anne took Mom by the elbow and led her down the path, rattling off details about bedrooms and bathrooms and energy-efficient construction. Dad followed close behind, hands in his pockets, eyes turned to the horizon on our right. I followed a few feet after him, keeping my cell phone in one hand in case someone turned around and I needed to look distracted. It wasn't that I wasn't curious; I just didn't want to influence the decision any more than I already had.

'The house has never been lived in,' Anne said, as we

9

neared the building. 'The owner, an architect from Boston, designed it for his wife. It was supposed to be a gift for their tenth wedding anniversary, but then, just last week, the missus decided to celebrate early with one of the mister's male co-workers. It's awful the way these things happen, isn't it?'

Under his red plaid shirt, Dad's back muscles tensed. Mom's head dropped as her hands shuffled through the papers she carried.

'Yes,' she said. 'But happen they do.'

'Is that a pool?' I asked.

Anne, instantly recovered from her disappointment in the state of modern-day relationships, shot me a quick grin. 'And hot tub. Wait till you see.'

She and Mom hurried inside the house. Dad paused by a tall, coral-shaped stone planter. I stood next to him.

'Thank you,' he said.

I nodded.

'It's not quite what we're used to, is it?' he asked, a moment later.

It took me a second to realise he was referring to the house, which looked like a cluster of glass boxes connected by wooden passages. There was no rickety front porch. Thanks to countless windows, I could see the back yard from the front yard, and there was no deck, either. Peeling paint, crumbling bricks and dangling gutters were also missing.

'No,' I said. 'But what is?'

I went inside. Mom's and Anne's voices echoed through the house from the right, so I headed left. I passed through the living room, dining room, and two bedrooms, all of which were decorated in various shades of taupe and still smelled like paint and sawdust. One particularly long corridor ended at a set of glass doors. I pushed through it into a third bedroom – and was nearly knocked over by a rush of wet, salty air. I automatically closed my eyes and inhaled, savouring the warmth as it travelled down my throat, soothed my aching body.

When I opened my eyes again, I saw water. As I stepped into the room, the slate-blue horizon seemed to curve, wrap around me. I kept my gaze level as I walked to a second set of glass doors and out onto a stone patio.

And there it was. The ocean. So close I could feel the spray each time it lunged against the rocks on which the patio rested.

'We won't do better than this.'

I jumped. Spun around. Mom stood in the open doorway, arms crossed over her chest, eyes aimed past me.

'The only way we'd get closer is on a houseboat . . . and no offence, sweetie, but my stomach simply can't handle that way of life.'

Personally, I thought she was a trooper for trying to handle this one. Not many women would.

'Do you like it?' she asked, joining me on the patio.

A wave slammed into the rocks below. I rubbed the spray into my bare arms. 'Yes. I don't know if it's really Dad's thing, though.'

'Your father will be fine with whatever we decide.'

I knew this. I also knew why. If it were possible to assign blame to such a thing, my parents agreed it was his fault we were here.

Mom tilted her chin towards the water and breathed deeply. 'I think someone else would've approved. The possibilities for unobstructed sunbathing are endless.'

I couldn't help but smile. 'Justine would've loved it.'

We stood quietly for a minute. Then Mom put one arm around my shoulders, pulled me close, and pressed her lips to the top of my head.

'I'll go work out the details. Stay here as long as you'd like.'

When she was gone, I walked to the patio's edge and surveyed the grounds. The pool and hot tub were off another patio about fifty feet south of this one. Bright green lawn filled the space in between. A stone stairway led from the garden down to a private beach.

Or, a nearly private beach. As I watched, a tall figure

dragged a red rowing boat across the sand. He had dark hair and wore jeans, a T-shirt . . . and glasses.

My heart thrust against my ribcage. My breath lodged in my throat. My feet moved, off the patio, down the rocks.

How did he know I was here? Did he find out from Paige? Had he stopped by the restaurant to ask? But how did he know *she'd* be there? Maybe he'd been checking in regularly, just in case?

It didn't matter. What mattered was that he was here. He'd found me. And we'd be together on my first day in Winter Harbor, the way we always were.

I scrambled across the last rock, jumped into the sand. 'Simon!'

He stood up straight, started to turn. I quickened my pace, wondering what he'd do if I threw my arms around him the way every inch of them ached to.

'Hey.'

My heels dug into the ground. My smile vanished as his widened.

'It's Colin, actually.' He released the boat, brushed his hands on his jeans, and held one towards me. 'Anne's son.'

I heard his words but they made no sense. Until I saw that he wore sunglasses, not eyeglasses. And that his hair was blond, not brown. And that the rowing boat was really a kayak.

'My mom's big on staging,' he said, noticing me notice the kayak. 'Not that this place needs it. Have you ever gone?'

My eyes rose to his. 'Gone?'

'Ocean kayaking?'

I shook my head, took a step back.

'Then you have to.' He stepped towards me. 'Maybe we can go together sometime. I'd be happy to give you a lesson.'

I stopped. My legs trembled. My chest tightened. I opened my mouth to thank him, to say I'd love nothing more than to be taught by such a skilled expert, to ask if we could make a date as soon as possible . . . and then I closed it.

When I was weak, only one thing made me feel better than salt water did, and that was enticing the interest of the opposite sex. But I hadn't resorted to such measures since doing so cost me the only relationship I ever had, the only one that had ever mattered, and I wasn't about to start now.

I didn't know if there was still a chance for Simon and me. But I did know I wasn't going to risk losing it if there was.

'Thanks anyway,' I said.

And turned around just as the tears started to fall.

CHAPTER 2

'Aubergine, boysenberry, blueberry pie.' Paige leaned the paint-cards against a napkin dispenser. 'What do you think?'

'I think they all look the same,' I said.

'Finally.' Louis, the restaurant's executive chef, came up the stairs and headed towards our table. 'A voice of reason.'

'What do you mean, finally? Reason is how I narrowed it down to these three. You try choosing one perfect colour from eight hundred pretty choices.'

Louis smirked as he placed plates before us. 'That's just one of the many differences between you and me, Miss Paige. I'd never choose from eight hundred pretty choices because the colour we have is already perfect.'

'Grey? Grey's not perfect. It's barely even a colour.'

'I disagree. In the right light, it can even look . . . purple.'

Paige opened her mouth to argue, then speared a strawberry with her fork instead. Louis topped up our coffee cups, winked at me, and headed back downstairs.

'A candy store,' she said when he was gone.

'Sorry?'

'That's what he thinks we'll look like if – when – we paint the place. He said if we change the colour, we should also change the name. To Marchand's Marshmallows and Other Gooey Goods.'

I smiled. 'It's not bad.'

'Except it's totally inaccurate. We're a chowder house. We've sold fish and clams and lobster for sixty years, and we always will. A new look won't change that.'

'You're right. Ambience matters, but food is most important. Like the regionally famous Sea Witch breakfast platter I've been dreaming about for weeks.' I cut into the pancake-wrapped lobster patty.

Paige was about to bite into a bagel but stopped. I held my full fork in front of my mouth.

'What?' I asked.

'That's not the Sea Witch,' she said, sounding sorry. 'I mean, it is – it's still eggs, lobster, seaweed, and pancake. But it's now called the Winter Harbor Sunrise.'

'That's going to be even harder to get used to than the colour change.'

'I know.' She put down her bagel and picked up the aubergine paint-card. 'But what can I do? Business is down. Like, ocean-floor down. Grandma B thinks the only way to stay afloat is to try to distance ourselves from last summer as much as possible. And since "Sea Witch" might suggest killer sirens to potential diners . . . let's just say it's a small change that can make a big difference.'

We weren't the only people on the employee break deck. In the far left corner, two waiters drank soda and fiddled with their cell phones. In the far right corner, a busboy and dishwasher sipped tea and watched the boats bob in the near-empty harbour. Maybe I imagined it, but at the mention of killer sirens, they all tensed, stilled. I waited for their conversations to resume before leaning towards Paige and lowering my voice.

'I thought people believed everything that happened last summer was because of the weird weather.'

It was a lot to expect of residents and visitors, since what happened had never occurred in Winter Harbor before. Like the sudden, isolated storms. The drownings. The icing over of the harbour itself, which up until last July had never frozen – not even in the middle of winter. But as Simon had said then, people believed what they wanted to. And without other logical explanations, they'd been willing to chalk up the strange events to moody Mother Nature.

Had they changed their minds?

'They did believe that,' Paige said, answering the question I was too scared to ask out loud. 'For a while anyway. But Grandma B and Oliver told me last night that people started to grow suspicious – and freak out – when similar things started happening in Boston last fall.'

Images flashed through my head. Colin Cooper, the Hawthorne Prep student, drifting down the Charles River. Matthew Harrison, the Bates College alumni interviewer, floating in the Hawthorne Prep pool.

Parker King, Hawthorne's water-polo superstar, standing by my locker, running across the Common, leaning towards me . . .

. . . kissing me.

I took the saltshaker from the table, unscrewed the top, and poured half its contents into my coffee. Then I held it up and motioned to Paige's cup. When she nodded, I dumped the rest in hers.

'But the weather was fine in Boston,' I said, after taking a big, long gulp. 'A little rainy every now and then, but nothing out of the ordinary.'

'Which was why people were extra concerned when the victims there resembled the ones here.'

I was glad she was vague. Chowder House employees didn't need to be reminded that the lifeless men had been found with their blue mouths lifted in permanent smiles.

'How did they know?' I asked. 'We both read the

Globe every day. There was never any mention of what the victims looked like when they were found.'

'Does it matter? Word spreads – and fast. Someone from Hawthorne probably told someone at another school and it went from there. The majority of Winter Harbor's summer visitors have always hailed from Boston, and once they put two and two together, or tried to, they probably decided to spend their vacations somewhere else this year. Because it's not just us. The whole town's hurting.'

My appetite now non-existent, I absently pushed my eggs around the plate as I thought about this. If what Paige said was true, this summer was off to a very different start from last summer, when business was booming and the tourist population multiplying. And even though my involvement had begun only after the sirens had made their first kill, I couldn't help but feel responsible.

'Ms Marchand!'

My head snapped up. A young waitress stood at the top of the stairs, wringing her hands and glancing down the stairs like someone was about to charge after her.

'Louis – he made this thing. With, like, special peppers? Only I didn't know? And so a customer ate it and practically choked – and now he's threatening to sue!'

Paige tilted her head. 'Louis is threatening to sue?'

'No, the customer –' The waitress gasped, peered down the stairwell. 'Oh no. He's in the kitchen. He's in the kitchen and yelling at Louis.' She looked at Paige, lips trembling and eyes watering. 'I can't be sued. I don't have any money. That's why I got this job. And it's my first day and I've only made two dollars in tips and –'

Paige raised one hand. The girl stopped.

'See that dock?' Paige motioned towards the harbour. The girl nodded.

'Why don't you take your break down there?'

'Now? But I've only been here an hour. And Louis said we –'

'Louis cooks,' Paige said. 'I manage. Take fifteen minutes to relax. When you come back, everything will be under control.'

I wouldn't have believed it if I wasn't there to witness it, but at Paige's assurance, the waitress bowed. She literally put her hands together, lowered her head, and tilted forward.

'Thank you, Ms Marchand. Thank you so much,' she said, and disappeared down the stairs.

I turned to Paige. 'Ms Marchand?'

'I told her to call me by my first name, I swear.' She took a grape from her plate, popped it in her mouth. 'But I guess I just command respect without even trying. The whole staff's actually been super-polite and attentive since I got here. With the exception of our infamous head chef, of course.'

'Is that because Betty put you in charge of day-to-day operations?'

'Probably.'

I leaned closer. 'Do you think it also has something to do with the fact that . . . I mean, could it be that they're acting differently because . . .'

'For the first summer ever, my evil sister isn't here to terrorise everyone? And their guilt for feeling relieved combined with genuine sympathy for me has them walking on eggshells?'

That wasn't exactly how I'd put it if I'd been able to find the words, but it was close enough. 'Yes?'

'Maybe.' Her blue eyes shifted towards the waiters ten feet away. When she spoke next, her voice was slightly louder. 'It's kind of cold up here. Wish I'd brought my jacket.'

The two waiters exchanged looks, then jumped up. Across the deck, the busboy stood so fast, the back of his chair smacked against the railing. The dishwasher, the only female employee present, frowned and sat forward, but stayed seated. In seconds, the busboy was by Paige's side, offering the sweatshirt off his back.

'Thank you.' She smiled, touched his arm. 'That's very sweet. But I'll be going inside any second.'

The busboy's face reddened. He nodded, backed away. The waiters were poised at the top of the stairs, ready to storm the kitchen in search of – I'm not sure what – chef coats? Thermal aprons? Now they straightened and returned to their table, casting curious glances in our direction. The female dishwasher sat back and pouted at the harbour.

Paige leaned close, whispered, 'It might have something to do with that, too.'

Before I could respond, she drained her coffee cup and got up.

'Time to restore order among the ranks.' She squeezed my shoulder as she passed behind me. 'If you ever want a job, just say the word. They might be respectful, but I could still use all the experienced help I can get.'

I smiled. My only restaurant experience had come last summer, when I'd spent a few days shadowing Paige and taking the occasional order. She'd offered me an impromptu job when we'd hit it off shortly after my return to Winter Harbor, and because her grandmother was the owner, no one had protested – much. Her older sister, Zara, hadn't exactly welcomed me with open arms. In fact, she'd been so cold, my head had pulsated with pain every time she was near; I didn't learn until much later that this wasn't simply because I'd grown severely anxious in her presence.

It was because we'd been linked. Even related, in a sense. Just like Paige and I were now.

Aware that the male employees' attention had shifted to me, I downed my eggs and coffee and started gathering dishes. The wind shifted as I stood, bringing with it a gust of moist, salty air. Instinctively, I closed my eyes, inhaled. When I opened them again, they locked on the car park below.

Unlike last year, when Betty's Chowder House was so busy an attendant was needed to check reservations and monitor the parking situation, the car park was nearly empty. It was almost noon, prime weekend brunch time, and there were only half a dozen cars.

Mom's black BMW SUV, which I'd borrowed after dropping her and Dad off at the lake house, was one of them.

A green Subaru was another.

'Excuse me, miss?'

I tore my gaze away. One of the waiters stood next to me.

'Are you all right?' he asked.

'Of course.' I forced a smile, wondered if he could hear the hammering of my heart.

'Can I take care of that for you?'

I followed his nod to the floor, where my feet were surrounded in shards of broken porcelain.

'Don't worry about it.' His voice was a combination of nervous and reassuring. 'I do that all the time.'

I looked at my hands. They were empty. I'd dropped my plate and coffee cup, they'd shattered . . . and I hadn't even noticed.

'Thank you,' I said, 'but that's okay. I'll go get a broom.'

I tried to focus as I grabbed the remaining dishes from the table and hurried downstairs. In the kitchen, I deposited the stack by the sink, flew by the cleaning supply closet, and headed for the swinging door. On the other side, I ducked behind the bar to check my appearance in the mirror behind the shelves of liquor, and then entered the main dining room.

But it was empty. Not completely – a few couples and families were scattered among the tables – but without the one person I'd hoped was there, it might as well have been.

The waitress Paige had sent to the dock came back inside. I waited for our eyes to meet, then smiled and waved her over.

'Hi.' Her eyes were dry but her voice still wavered. 'Does Ms Marchand want to see me?'

Visual fragments, like pieces of a jigsaw puzzle, spun

through my head. Silver eyes. Long, dark hair. Weak, emaciated figures. The most beautiful woman I'd ever seen, standing tall at the bottom of a darkened lake.

But the waitress wasn't talking about Paige's mother. She was talking about Paige.

'No.' I resisted shaking my head; the images slowly faded. 'Not yet anyway. I was just wondering if you waited on a guy earlier. Before you went outside.'

'Yes. The one who wants to sue.' She stepped towards me, scanned the dining room. 'Is he back?'

I was about to clarify when red brake lights shone through the windows facing the car park.

'Never mind,' I said, already running. 'And don't worry – Ms Marchand has everything under control!'

I burst through the front door as the Subaru turned around, revealing the Bates College sticker in the back window. For a split second, I was tempted to go back in: the familiar logo brought back the painful events of last fall and reminded me of all that I'd missed since then – and why. But then the car rumbled as it accelerated, and I lunged forwards.

I was halfway to the car-park entrance when the car stopped. The driver's door opened.

And Caleb got out.

'Vanessa. Are you okay?'

His eyebrows were lowered and forehead wrinkled as

he looked from me to the restaurant and harbour behind us, and back to me. It didn't take long to figure out why he was concerned.

My feet had frozen to the ground the second the door opened. I forced them to move now. Casually. Easily. Not like I was being chased the way I'd been – the way we'd *all* been – last summer.

'Hi.' I smiled and tried to peer past him to the passenger seat. 'I'm fine. I just saw your car and wanted to catch you before you left.'

His face relaxed. He started to return my smile, then stopped and tilted his head.

'You saw my car?' he asked.

'From inside Betty's. I was in the main dining room and just happened to glance out and –' I cut myself off, looked away from the empty Subaru. 'Oh.'

'Yeah. I don't have a car.'

'Right. I knew that.'

He nodded. I nodded. Neither of us spoke.

Nearly every day for the past eight months, I'd thought about what I'd say to Simon the next time I saw him. In all those months, I hadn't considered what I'd say to his younger brother – and the love of Justine's life – the next time I saw *him*. That was a mistake, because this was even more awkward than a chance meeting between two recently estranged friends should be.

Probably because the estrangement was due to the fact that one friend had lied to the other, along with everyone else she knew, about who – or what – she really was.

'So how are you?' I finally asked.

'Great.' He sounded relieved. 'Busy, but great.'

'Still at the marina?'

'More often than not. I did a lot of reading up on motors and outboards this year and Captain Monty's slowly but surely been letting me practise on the real deal.' He paused. 'Simon's been helping out, too. That's why I have the Subaru.'

My chest warmed. 'Is he . . . ? Does he . . . ? I mean –'

'He's okay,' Caleb said gently.

I exhaled.

'On any other day, you'd see that for yourself. Betty hooked us up with free lunch for life here, and Louis is under strict orders to cook us whatever we want whenever we want it. The only reason Simon sat this trip out was because Monty decided to go fishing and someone needed to stay behind and man the shop.'

If I'd given any thought to what I'd say to Caleb the first time I saw him in almost a year, I'd never have said the next thing I did.

'I miss him.'

He paused. 'He misses you, too.'

My heart lifted. 'He told you that?'

'He doesn't have to.'

A car approached, signalled to turn into the car park. Caleb and I stood together in the entrance and parted to give the car room. Unfortunately, the physical separation only added to our emotional distance.

'I should get going,' he said, checking his watch.

'Of course. Me too.' I held my breath, hoped he'd ask where – to my family's lake house, which was next door to his family's and wouldn't be ours for very much longer – but he didn't. He simply turned around and headed for the Subaru. Not wanting to watch it drive away without me yet again, I started to turn, too.

'Vanessa?'

I spun back.

Caleb looked down, fiddled with his frayed sweatshirt sleeve. 'You just got to town, right?'

'A few hours ago.'

He stopped fiddling. Our eyes met. 'Are you going back?'

He didn't have to specify where. I knew.

Chione Cliffs. That was where we'd gone our first day back last summer, and every summer before.

It was also where Justine had died.

'I don't think so,' I said.

He nodded. Then, 'See you around.'

This time, I watched him leave. For my sister. Because she should be here. And if only she were, the four of us would go driving together – just like we always had on our first full day in Winter Harbor, and almost every day after that.

When the Subaru reached the end of Main Street, turned right, and disappeared, I hurried inside the restaurant. I found Paige in the lobby, holding more paint samples up to the wall.

'Excuse me, Ms Marchand?' I asked. 'I was wondering if you were still hiring.'

CHAPTER 3

After a tumultuous, exhausting year, the summer before I started college was supposed to be dedicated to two things: spending time with my family and relaxing. Less than a week in, I saw my parents only at night and was having trouble finding the time to unwind. This was mostly because instead of not working at all over the next three months, I'd picked up two jobs. The first was hostessing at Betty's Chowder House. Paige let me make my own hours, but since the more I was at the restaurant, the better chance I had of seeing Simon, I often showed up before breakfast and stayed until after dinner. My long hours hadn't paid off yet; Caleb had probably mentioned seeing me there, because he was always alone when he came to pick up lunch. But I was going to make myself as available as possible, just in case.

The second job was helping Anne, our estate agent, show the lake house. I'd inherited this position by default. If Mom had her way, she'd have followed Anne's every move – and intervened as necessary – until the house sold. But she was determined to get us settled into our new vacation home, so was too busy shopping and decorating and organising to focus on the old one. And she didn't trust Dad to fill in for her; he'd bought the lake house before they'd even met and it had always been his more than anyone else's. He promised he was ready to say goodbye, but every now and then, regardless of whether we were by the beach, in town, or somewhere else in Winter Harbor, we'd catch him staring off in the direction of Lake Kantaka.

That left me. Mom assumed I was as anxious to move on as she was, and she was right. For the most part, anyway.

'Good Lord, what died in here?'

The front door slammed shut. I turned away from the living-room windows to find Anne standing in the small foyer. Her arms were filled with bakery bags and shiny blue folders. Her face was frozen in a scowl.

'What do you mean?' I asked.

'I mean, it smells like cute, little woodland creatures scurried into your walls and never made it out.'

'The house is old,' I said, a hot heat swelling in my chest. 'No one's lived in it for months. It always smells a little musty at the beginning of the summer.'

'Doesn't matter if it's must or a mouse. No one's going to reach for their chequebook if they're too scared to uncover their nose and mouth.' She came into the living

31

room, dumped the folders on the coffee table, and started for the kitchen. 'And given the price your mother's asking, this place had better smell like a florist's.'

I stood there, unsure of what to do. A second later, Anne's head appeared in the kitchen doorway.

'Windows?' she said.

'Sorry?'

'People will be showing up any minute. The best we can do now is open all the windows and pray for strong winds.'

Her head disappeared again. Cupboard doors squeaked open and slammed shut. Guessing she was looking for dishes for whatever she'd bought from the bakery, I debated telling her that Mom had left all kitchen staging items in the pantry . . . and then decided against it. Instead, I hurried around the living room, parting curtains and shoving open windows.

And then I went upstairs.

The door at the end of the hall was closed, just like it had been the last time I'd ventured to the second floor. There had been other showings and open houses over the past several months, while we were in Boston, but the air was so still and quiet now, it was hard to imagine anyone up here since then. It was also hard to imagine the events that had led me upstairs that afternoon, when I'd told Mom I'd be applying to Dartmouth as she packed the rest of Justine's belongings in boxes.

Hard, but not impossible. I was reminded of that every single day.

'Vanessa, how about candles? Do you know where . . . ?'

Anne's voice faded as I opened the door and closed it behind me. Inside the small room Justine and I had shared every summer for as long as I could remember, I lowered myself to the edge of one twin bed and let my eyes travel over the other. It looked different. The quilt was too white, the pillow too round. Mom didn't want to take any of the old furniture, but she'd saved a few smaller items, like the bedding. I guessed she hadn't wanted to risk strangers using – or even throwing out – the sheets and blankets her eldest daughter had curled up in during countless chilly summer nights.

The bed was so unfamiliar I couldn't picture Justine lying there. I couldn't see her propped up on one elbow as we talked about what to do the next day, or lying on her back and braiding her hair as we discussed movies and music and boys. Always boys. Eventually, one boy in particular: Caleb.

The thought made me want to lie down and close my eyes. Every day it became harder to see her, but it usually helped to block out other distracting images. I was just about to slide back on the mattress when the doorbell rang downstairs. Car doors slammed outside. I turned onto my knees and leaned across the bed, towards the window – and was happy it was still closed. Leaping out – and falling to the ground below – would be too easy otherwise.

Because there he was. Simon. My Simon, walking up the stone path leading to his family's house next door. His dark hair was longer, messier. His usual jeans and T-shirt were splattered with grease and paint. His tanned arms appeared bigger, stronger.

My legs trembled. My throat tightened. My knees gave. Suddenly, all my body wanted – all it *needed* – was to be in those arms.

'I'm here,' I whispered, bringing one hand to the glass. 'Right here. Look up . . . please look up.'

He didn't. He went inside without even glancing my way.

I sat back. Did seeing our house no longer remind him of me? Had it already come to that?

There was only one way to find out. Ignoring the small part of my brain warning the rest of me that he needed time and space, I jumped off the bed, lunged across the room, and threw open the door.

'Hi, there.'

34

A couple stood in the hallway. I resisted stepping back, closing the door again.

The man smiled. He had blond hair, brown eyes . . . and a pretty wife whose face hardened the second she saw me.

'Do you live here?' he asked.

'Yes,' I said. 'Sort of. This was – is – my family's house.'

'It's lovely,' he said.

'It's *old*,' his wife corrected him.

If he heard her tone, he ignored it. 'When was it built?'

I paused. This was one of dozens of facts that, up until ten seconds ago, I'd had memorised and could recite automatically.

'Nineteen-forty,' I finally guessed. It was definitely in that range.

'That makes it barely middle-aged.' He held out one hand. 'Brian Corwin.'

His wife looked from his open palm to me. Her lips lifted in a small, stiff smile, but her steady gaze suggested I'd better think carefully before accepting his offer.

'Vanessa Sands.' I waved instead of shaking and nodded past him, towards the stairs. 'And if you'll excuse me, I really –'

'Why are you selling?'

My eyes locked on his. 'Excuse me?'

'The house is in great condition. It's quaint. Charming. A stone's throw from the lake. It's everything this town was before it wasn't any more.' He shrugged. 'Your family must have a very good reason for leaving.'

Several, actually. Good memories. Bad memories. Its proximity to fresh – not salt – water. Our desperate need for a new start. But I couldn't share any of this with a possible buyer – at least not without inviting more questions. Plus, I'd been through enough to know that Brian wasn't asking the question because he truly wanted to know the answer; he was asking because he truly wanted to know *me*. Or at least the person his body was telling him I was.

'Maybe it's all the dark panelling,' his wife offered, when I didn't respond right away. Her voice was pleasant but strained. 'Or the peeling wallpaper. Or the faded carpet. Or the crumbling steps outside. Or *maybe –*'

'Did you or did you not say, all of three minutes ago, that it had amazing potential?' Brian's smile was gone. 'And that it could be the fixer-upper you've been dying to transform?'

My chest tightened. My fingers ached to scratch my skin as it dried across my face, neck and arms, but settled for taking the water bottle from my sweatshirt pocket. I drank as Brian and his wife argued and waited for my body to cool, relax. Stressful situations always accelerated my dehydration and zapped my energy and had been doing so even more lately. I'd increased my salt intake accordingly, but I wasn't sure it was enough.

As much as I loved this house and as sad as I'd be when it wasn't ours any more, I had to admit the oceanfront house had definite benefits. The main downside was that it was expensive – even though Anne insisted that before last summer, we would have paid double for it. Mom had said we'd be fine financially for a little while, but we'd need the money from the sale of the lake house sooner rather than later.

Given all that, wouldn't it be okay to make an exception to my very rigid rule of not using certain abilities for my own personal gain? At least this once? Especially since it could lead to not one but two positive outcomes – including the strength I'd need to walk up to Simon's front door and say everything I'd longed to for months?

I didn't know. But I drained the water bottle, swallowed, and took a deep breath anyway.

'Finished basement.'

Brian and his wife turned towards me. I continued before I lost my nerve.

'There's a finished basement. My mom renovated it five years ago. She used it as an office but it'd probably make a great gym.'

I was guessing this might be a selling point. The wife was thin and wore a sleeveless top that showed off defined arms. She carried a canvas satchel large enough to hold a yoga mat.

'Also,' I added, 'it's a mile's swim from one side of the lake to the other. That makes for a great morning workout.'

She gave me a slow once-over, clearly debating whether my motives were sincere. Fortunately, plenty of swimming over the past year had given my muscles definition, too. I didn't know how visible they were through my jeans and baggy tunic, but she must've seen something that satisfied her, because the slight wrinkles in her forehead smoothed as her face relaxed.

'I suppose it wouldn't hurt to check out the basement.' She slid one hand around Brian's arm and began leading him towards the stairs.

'Actually,' I said, 'there are a few other rooms up here. They need a lot of work, but –'

'I'll take a look.' Brian pulled his arm away. 'One of them might make a great walk-in wardrobe.'

He directed this at her – as some sort of reward, I assumed – but looked at me.

She hesitated, then sighed. 'Whatever. Keep your phone on.'

'Sorry,' he said, when she was gone. 'She has pretty particular taste.'

I forced a smile. 'No apologies necessary.'

I started down the corridor, casting what I hoped appeared to be the occasional coy, mysterious glance over my shoulder. I certainly wasn't coy, and if ever I was mysterious, the guy wasn't the only one in the dark. But between Paige's sister Zara, their mother, Raina, and my own biological mother, whom I'd met for the very first time last fall, I had learned a few things about what I could do – and how. I hadn't so much as smiled at a boy since the last time I smiled at Simon eight months ago, so I wasn't very good at any of it . . . but I also knew that didn't necessarily matter.

Because Brian was following me. Watching me. Grinning like his wife wasn't downstairs, like he wasn't even married. The worst part was he didn't even know what he was doing; he couldn't control his response. Only I could.

It was wrong. Uncomfortable. If my skin weren't so dry, it'd be crawling.

But it *was* dry – and getting worse. I brushed one arm with my hand and a flurry of translucent flakes fluttered to the floor. So I kept going. All the way to the guest bedroom at the other end of the hall.

'Wow.' For a split second, he focused on something besides me. 'That's some view.'

I joined him by the windows overlooking the lake. The big room was empty, except for an old sofa and desk, but we stood so close, our sleeves touched.

'You should see it at sunset.'

He turned to me. 'I'd like that.'

A warm surge of energy simmered low in my belly. Encouraged, I pictured Justine's beaming at Caleb and did my best to mimic the expression.

'So where are you from?' I asked.

'Providence. In Rhode Island.'

This time, my grin was sincere. 'I've heard of it.'

He shook his head, laughed lightly. 'Of course you have.' He looked up, tried again. 'I'm an adjunct econ professor at Brown. Marley's a yoga instructor.'

'And Marley, she's your . . . ?'

He inhaled sharply as I stepped towards him. The heat in my belly shot down my legs, up my torso, through my arms. In a matter of seconds, I went from wanting to collapse into a deep sleep to feeling like I could swim Lake Kantaka a dozen times. I pulled back to check my arms and saw that my skin was already smoother, softer.

And then I looked at Brian and felt a million times worse than I did before.

His eyebrows were furrowed, his smile uncertain. 'Marley . . . she's . . . that is, I think maybe she's . . .'

He couldn't even remember her. His wife. With whom he'd probably been having a perfectly delightful day looking at houses before they'd run into me.

'So I just wanted to show you the view from this room.' I took one step back. And another, and another. 'I'm glad you liked it. If you have any other questions or want to make an offer, our realtor, Anne, can help you.'

In the hallway, I ran. I flew downstairs, weaved through the small crowd exploring the house, and burst onto the back deck. There I paused briefly to catch my breath before hurdling the steps leading to the lawn. I still wanted to see Simon, to talk to him about where we were and where we could go . . . but after what I'd just done, I didn't trust myself to speak logically, rationally. Before I said anything else, I needed to calm down and sort out my thoughts.

I headed for the boathouse. Which was more like a run-down shed but still had a door that closed. The showing had just started, so chances were slim anyone would venture this far down the garden so soon.

'That makes no sense.'

'The whole thing was, like, boiling?'

I slowed down, listened to the hushed, unfamiliar

voices. They seemed to be coming from behind the shed.

'That's what I heard. The entire lake bubbled and swirled like some crazy whirlpool.'

The blood slowly drained from my face. I forced my feet to keep moving.

'But why? How?'

'No idea why. How is the reason we're here.'

Every ounce of energy I'd gained from my exchange with Brian slid towards my belly and slipped away. By the time I rounded the back of the shed and saw the cluster of people gathered around Justine's and my old red rowing boat, I was just lucid enough to make out the next thing one of the guys said.

'The stranger-than-fiction yet here-in-real-life ladies of the sea. Otherwise known as . . . sirens.'

Then I gave in.

And fell to the ground.

42

CHAPTER 4

The water was cold. Bitter. By comparison, Boston Harbor was a warm bath. Normal people wouldn't venture past their ankles in water like this. The more adventurous, like lifelong, headstrong surfers might – but with the protection of thick wetsuits and for short periods of time.

I was neither normal nor adventurous. Wearing just a swimming costume, I swam and dived, not caring how deep I went or for how long. I paid attention only to my lungs, expanding and releasing; my torso, freezing and warming; my muscles, tightening and lengthening. At first, I gulped water like runners do oxygen after a race, but breathing soon became easier as my body adjusted. It felt so good, so natural, I stayed under until the ocean's surface began to darken.

And then I paddled towards the beach, where Mom was waiting for me.

'Ninety-seven minutes,' she said. 'Not that I was keeping track.'

I smiled, took the towel she held out. 'Thanks.'

'So how was it?' she asked, as we headed for the steps.

'Great. A little cold, but great.'

We crossed the yard, stepped onto my bedroom patio.

'Do you feel better?' she asked.

It took me a second to respond. I was too distracted by the fire flickering in the iron pit Mom had bought that afternoon, the platters of food on the table, the fleece blankets folded on the new chaise lounge.

'I feel fine,' I said. 'What's all this?'

'Just a little welcome present. We've all been so busy, we haven't had a chance to really sit and enjoy everything together.' She motioned to the lounge chair and started fixing a plate.

'Should I get Dad?'

She peered across the yard towards the other side of the house. I followed her gaze. Through the glass kitchen walls, I could see him stirring something on the stove.

'I put him in charge of dessert,' she said. 'He'll join us when he's done.'

Her voice was firm so I sat down and pulled the blankets across my lap. I was still warm from my swim but the air was cold. It was only a matter of time before the heat faded and my body temperature lowered.

Mom handed me a plate, took one for herself, and sat in the chair next to mine.

'I talked to Anne this afternoon,' she said.

I dropped my hamburger bun. Reached forward for a new one. 'Oh?'

'She claimed the open house was a huge success.'

I looked at her. 'Did someone make an offer?' If so, maybe my terrible behaviour had been worth it.

'Not yet.' She bit into her burger, chewed. 'But she said there was a decent crowd. Especially considering that tourism's down and there are more sellers than buyers right now.'

'There was a guy.'

She tilted her head, raised her eyebrows

'I talked to him and his wife a while. They seemed really interested. I think his name was Brian?'

She nodded. 'Corwin. Yes, Anne mentioned him. Apparently he was ready to pay the asking price in cash right then and there, but his wife refused. They even got into a heated argument about it and Anne had to ask them to discuss matters outside. They left from there.'

My heart sank. I took a water glass from the table. 'That's too bad.'

'They may come around. Not everyone makes this kind of decision as quickly as we did.'

'Not everyone has to.'

She stopped chewing. Started again. Swallowed. 'Right.'

We ate quietly. Or, Mom ate. I drank. I'd been out of the water a matter of minutes and already my skin was tightening, my throat constricting.

'Was that where you were?' she asked a minute later.

The glass started to slip from my fingers. I squeezed it gently. 'When?'

'During the showing. Anne said you disappeared for a while. Were you busy talking up potential buyers? Showing them around?'

My fingertips, still gripping the glass, turned white. 'Yes. This one family wanted to know exactly where our property started and ended. I spent a lot of time with them outside.'

'Did you get their names?'

'Their what?'

'If you spent a lot of time with them, introductions must've been made, yes?'

I tried to think of random names, but my head was spinning.

'Vanessa.'

I looked down. Mom's hand was on my knee.

'I'm so sorry,' she said.

'What? Why?'

She sat back with a sigh. 'For asking you to be there. You *love* that house. Who could blame you for ducking out? What kind of mother am I to ask you to do something like that?'

I put down the glass. Faced her. 'The kind who'd turn her whole life upside down – more than once – for her daughter.' I shook my head. 'I do love the house and, yes, part of me will miss it. But that's not why I ducked out.'

I hoped this would put her at ease, but her frown only deepened.

'Mom, really, I promise –'

'Simon.'

My back hit the chair.

'You were with him, weren't you? Oh, sweetie. You know that's not a good idea. To try to rekindle things when they'll only have to end again in a few months? Long-distance never works, no matter how much you want it to, and –'

'I didn't feel well.'

Her mouth snapped shut.

I chose my words carefully. 'I didn't want to worry you, so I wasn't going to say anything . . . but I started to feel a little weird while I was there. So I hung out in the boathouse a while. And just rested.'

She nodded as she processed this. 'Weird, how?'

'The usual ways. Tired. Thirsty. Weak.'

'Headache?'

My eyes met hers. 'No. No headache.'

She looked down, pushed her food around her plate.

'Mom.' Now my hand was on her knee. 'They're gone. We don't have to worry about them any more.'

'That's what you say but how do you know? How do you *really* know? Because you also said you thought they were gone once, and then they weren't.' She trembled. 'Maybe this was a bad idea. Maybe we were better off at home. Or, I don't know, moving to Canada. Or somewhere else far, far away.'

My ancestors were actually from Canada. I didn't share this now, though. Unlike everything else I'd told Mom over the past several months, including the fact that I was stricken with blinding migraines anytime vengeful sirens were near, I didn't think that was information she needed to have.

'I saw the bodies,' I reminded her softly. 'I saw how fast they disintegrated in the lake. I had to for that very reason – to know there was no way they'd come back.'

She sniffed, brushed at her eyes. 'You've been through so much, Vanessa. More than any sweet young girl ever should. And I just want to do whatever I can to make you happy, to help you move forward.'

'Um, have you seen where we are?' I motioned to our surroundings when she looked up. 'Coffee-table books could be written about this place. Entire travel magazines could be devoted to its architectural marvels and natural splendour.'

She smiled. 'It's not bad.'

'It's amazing. And I'm the luckiest girl I know.'

She started to say something else just as my cell phone rang. I took it from the table.

'It's Paige. I'll call her back.'

'No, no. Take it.' Mom jumped up, patted down her windblown hair. 'I'll freshen up and check on your father. Say hello for us.'

She kissed the top of my head and hurried inside. I poured another glass of water and answered the phone.

'Aged grape.'

'Is this some sort of riddle?' I asked. 'Because it's been a long day and my brain's not exactly firing on all cylinders.'

'It's not a riddle,' Paige assured. 'It's the official new colour of Betty's Chowder House.'

'So you went with purple. Louis must be freaking out.'

'There's been some pot-banging and pan-slamming, but no total meltdowns. Besides, aged grape is a solid compromise. It's still in the blueberry pie family but more sophisticated than sweet. And it's going to be just the face-lift we need to attract new customers.'

'It sounds great. I can't wait to see it.'

'You and me both. Now, what's wrong?'

I forced the water I'd just sipped down my throat. 'What do you mean?'

'You said it's been a long day. Why? Did something happen at the open house?' She gasped. 'You saw him, didn't you? You saw Simon.'

I poured another glass of water and drained it before answering. 'Yes. Through a window about a hundred feet away.'

'You didn't talk to him?'

'Not a word.'

This was followed by silence. I knew she was pouting on my behalf.

'But it's okay,' I said. 'At least I know he's still around, right? He didn't flee town the second Caleb told him I was here.'

'That's the dullest silver lining I've ever heard.'

I couldn't help but smile. But then I remembered her other question and the expression faded.

'Something did happen at the open house, though. Besides that, I mean.'

'Hang on. I'm going to the dining room for privacy.'

On the other end of the phone, doors slammed and voices grew louder, then softer. While Paige moved, I did, too. I went to the furthest corner of the patio and faced the house to keep an eye on Mom and Dad. He was feeding her something from a pot on the stove, so I guessed I still had a few minutes before their return.

'We're good,' Paige said. 'Start talking.'

'Okay, so everything was fine for a while, but then – ' I stopped myself. 'Did you just say you went to the dining room for privacy?'

'Yes. It's totally empty right now.'

'But it's still dinnertime.'

'I guess people are eating at home tonight. Anyway, keep going. What happened?'

I took a deep breath and tried to ignore any reservation I had about sharing what I was about to. This was too big to keep to myself, and Paige was the only one I could tell. Plus, if it meant what I thought it did, she needed to hear it sooner rather than later.

'People know,' I said quietly.

There was another second of silence. 'Know what? Which people?'

'At the lake house today, I went outside for some air and found a few people behind the boathouse.' Through the wall of windows, I watched Dad kiss Mom's cheek. Mom put her arms around his neck. 'They were talking. About the lake boiling.'

The silence that followed was long. Heavy.

'Paige?'

'I'm here.' When she spoke again, her voice was quieter. 'What do you mean, boiling?'

'Bubbling. Swirling. Like it sat over an enormous pit of fire.'

'But how did they . . .? How could they possibly . . .?'

'Know about what happened last fall? When we were all so careful to make sure no one found out?'

'Yes. Charlotte sweet-talked the police who were there, right? So they wouldn't say anything. Were the other houses on the lake not totally empty, the way we'd thought?' As if to convince herself, she added, 'But that's okay. If someone saw, they probably blamed it on more weird weather. And whoever was there today was just curious.'

I paused. 'That's not all they were talking about.'

She swallowed. 'What else?'

I closed my eyes, remembered the hushed, excited voices. 'Ladies of the sea,' I practically whispered. 'Otherwise known –'

There was a loud *bang* at her end of the phone. She screamed. I jumped.

'Vanessa, I hate to ask, but can I call you back? Louis is granting us all the pleasure of another world-renowned temper tantrum.'

'Of course,' I said, slightly relieved. Just because we

needed to talk about what I'd heard didn't mean I wanted to. 'Good luck. Call me when you can.'

We said goodbye and hung up. I looked across the yard and saw my parents still in the kitchen; I quickly dialled our new home phone number and watched Mom take the cordless from the wall. I assured her I was fine but just a little tired, and asked if we could postpone our family sit-down till later tonight. When she agreed, I hung up and went inside my bedroom.

My brand-new bedroom. With its new four-poster bed. Its new dresser and desk made out of newly reclaimed wood. Its new quilt, pillows, paint and rug. Its new stone-and-tile bathroom.

It was unlike any bedroom I'd ever called my own. It should be the perfect place to start over, move forward. The way Mom wanted me to. The way *I* wanted to.

The question was – would it be enough?

Trying to answer the question was exhausting. So, still wearing my damp swimming costume, I climbed into bed, pulled the blankets over my head, and slid both hands underneath the pillow.

Where I'd put the Bates sweatshirt and water bottle. They were the first things I'd seen when I woke up, alone, after passing out at the lake house that afternoon. They didn't belong to me, but I'd taken them anyway.

Because they were Simon's.

CHAPTER 5

'Table for two, please.'

'Betty!' I closed the *Winter Harbor Herald* and hurried out from behind the hostess stand. 'Paige didn't tell me you were coming by.'

'That's because she didn't know.' Paige's grandmother opened her arms and gave me a squeeze. 'But it was so nice out, I decided to come see these amazing renovations she's been talking about.'

Our eyes met as we pulled apart. Hers were clear, bright – like a cloudless blue sky. They looked nothing like they had this time last summer, when Raina and Zara had locked Betty away and kept her severely dehydrated until her body weakened and her vision began to fail. They were also clearer than they'd been last fall, after she'd regained her strength but was still being manipulated by the resurrected sirens. Paige had said her vision was still compromised, but the sight made me so happy, I gave her another hug.

'Next time tell me the circus is in town, so I can bring

peanuts,' Oliver, Betty's boyfriend, joked as he scanned the paint cans and tarps spread throughout the lobby.

'It can't be that bad,' Betty said.

'Compared to a tornado's destruction? No. You're right.'

I leaned forward and kissed his cheek. 'It's nice to see you, Oliver.'

His face softened. 'Vanessa. Hello. Don't mind me, I'm just –'

'Looking out for his family's best interest.' Paige strode towards us through the dining room. 'As always.'

'Can you blame me?' Oliver asked.

'Not even a little – and I can't thank you enough.' Paige gave them quick hugs. 'How about a tour? I'll show you what we've been working on and fill you in on my other plans.'

Paige winked at me as she hooked one arm through Betty's and led her into the dining room. Oliver followed close behind. As they rounded the corner, out of sight, I heard one last exchange.

'Paige, dear, it's so quiet. Where is everyone? I thought we agreed to stay open during this process.'

'Grandma B . . . we *are* open.'

I checked my watch as I returned to my post behind the hostess stand. It was twelve-fifteen on a Tuesday. The restaurant should be packed with locals, part-timers, and tourists. It should be filled with the sounds of dishes clanking, knives and forks scraping, and the kitchen door swishing open and closed as harried employees flew through. But save for us and the staff, it was empty. The only sounds came from hammers and saws.

Paige had said Betty's Chowder House wasn't the only local business suffering, and according to the newspaper, she was right.

After Summer of Storms, Winter Harbor Braces for Drought

As 4 July – and the official start of the season – approaches, Winter Harbor retailers and restaurants are pulling out all the stops. In addition to the usual Maine-related merchandise and the freshest lobster to be had anywhere on the East Coast, businesses are offering discounts, coupons, and other incentives to jump-start visitors' vacations.

There's just one problem. The visitors, it seems, have gone elsewhere.

'Last summer, queues twenty people deep started at noon and lasted till midnight,' said Eddie Abernathy, owner of Eddie's Ice Cream. 'Now I'm giving away free cones every hour just to get people in the door . . . but the door's not opening.'

'It's strange,' added Nina Poole, manager of Waterside Beachwear. 'This time last year, the minute we displayed a swimming costume in the window, someone came in to buy it. Now we're lucky if someone glances our way as she passes by.'

Local real estate has also taken a hit. Last year's addition of the high-end Lighthouse Marina Resort and Spa prompted some out-of-towners to invest early in what seemed to be a burgeoning tourist boom. The resulting buzz led to a 100 per cent increase over the previous year's sales as well as a healthy jolt to the local economy. Business owners, simultaneously shell-shocked and giddy, scrambled to keep refrigerators and shelves stocked. For all intents and purposes, the summer was poised to be Winter Harbor's most profitable yet.

And then the rains came.

'Who can blame them?' said Captain Monty, owner of the town's namesake marina. 'Between the insane storms and bodies washing ashore every other day, it's amazing so many people lasted as long as they did. Heck, if this hadn't been my home since the day my momma shot me out and wished me luck, I'd have steered towards calmer waters, too.'

The economic downturn is unfortunate – especially since recorded rainfall has been consistently below average the past ten months, and the sun has shone every day since Memorial Day. It appears that those who were brave enough to weather the storms will likely be rewarded with ideal conditions this summer.

As for those who weren't?

'It's their loss,' said Paige Marchand, granddaughter of Betty, who founded Betty's Chowder House, a local institution, in 1965. 'Even covered in a foot of water, Winter Harbor's still the prettiest place on earth.'

'Where's your sign?'

I looked up; the quick motion made my head pulsate slightly. I slid a menu over the newspaper as a young woman crossed the lobby.

'I'm sorry?' I said.

'Your sign.' She held up a paper map, the kind with stick figures and cartoon drawings that the Chamber of Commerce hands out. 'According to this, this is where Betty's Chowder House should be. Not a construction site.'

'This is Betty's,' I said, with a smile. 'The sign's down

temporarily, for renovations. But we're open for business as usual.'

'All the more reason to make sure people know where you are, right?'

My face warmed. 'Of course.'

She held my gaze for a moment, then grinned. 'So is the soup really as good as they say?'

'It's better.' I took another menu from the rack on the wall and led her into the dining room.

'Is there a bar?'

I slowed and glanced over my shoulder. She looked about my age, maybe a year or two older. That would put her at twenty, tops.

'I hate eating at a regular table by myself,' she explained. 'And where there's a bar, there's usually a TV, which is the closest thing to company I'm going to get.'

I could relate. I'd come to Betty's alone last year to be among people without having to talk about myself – or what had just happened to Justine. I wondered if this girl were here for similar reasons, as I showed her to the bar and gave her the remote.

'Your waitress will be right with you.'

'Thanks.' She took the menu and I turned away. 'What's your name?'

I stopped. Turned back.

'The place isn't exactly crawling with employees. And

I'm not a demanding customer, but I might come across that way if I call out, "Hey, you!" to get your attention.'

She seemed friendly enough, but I still debated whether to dodge the question. It wasn't one most customers usually asked.

'Vanessa,' I finally said.

She held out one hand. 'Natalie. Thank you again for being so accommodating.'

'You're welcome.' I shook her hand. It was warm, firm.

She focused on the television perched on a shelf near the ceiling. I headed for the kitchen to find someone to wait on her. Because she was right. The place wasn't understaffed, considering the lack of customers, but service was definitely sporadic since it wasn't required on a regular basis.

'You need me.' Louis stood on the back steps, leaning against the door to keep it open and smoking a cigarette. '*Please* say you need me to do something.'

'I do,' I said. 'But for only one customer.'

'That's plenty.' He flicked the cigarette to the stone steps and put it out with the toe of his shoe. 'You, my dear friend, are a lifesaver.'

I was about to ask where our waitress was when footsteps ran down the staircase leading to the break area. Carla, the young waitress, flew past me in a blur of black and white and burst through the swinging door.

'I better keep an eye on her,' I said. 'Since Paige is busy with Betty and Oliver.'

Louis was already firing up the stove and didn't seem to hear me. The only other staff members on duty, a busboy and sous-chef, flipped through magazines on the other side of the room. No one was paying attention, but I still felt a little weird standing to one side of the swinging door and peering through the small square window.

The exchange lasted seconds. Carla greeted Natalie. Natalie asked about a few menu items and Carla stammered through answers before writing down the order. Carla started for the kitchen again, then seemed to think better of it and headed behind the bar, where she poured two glasses, one of water and the other of iced tea, and presented both to Natalie.

I kept watching, even after our single customer was alone again. I wasn't sure what I expected to see – Natalie looking around to see if anyone was paying attention to *her*?

She didn't, of course. She simply sat at the bar, drinking water and flipping channels.

I was being paranoid. I knew that even if I wasn't sure exactly why. Maybe it was because, with her super-short blonde hair, brown eyes, and long, tanned legs, she looked like the kind of girl most guys would be drawn to like magnets to metal – or men to sirens. Maybe it was because my head had throbbed – just once, and only slightly – when she'd walked through the door. The frequent, excruciating headaches I'd felt around Zara had always last much longer, but Betty had said that was because Zara was newly transformed and unable to control the signals her body naturally sent to other sirens. Maybe the reaction was less intense around more experienced sirens.

Or maybe it was because this was how it was going to be from now on. Because of everything that had happened, I was going to be instantly suspicious of any new, pretty girl I met, no matter how nice she was or how hard I tried to talk myself out of it.

I'd have to get over this soon. College was going to be challenging enough; I doubted I'd get through it without the support of a single new girlfriend.

'Heads-up, hostess with the mostest.'

I spun around just as Louis chucked two paper bags in my direction.

'The Carmichael-mobile's en route.' He nodded at the window over the sinks. 'I was so bored, I made them an hour ago so the fries are probably cold. But hungry men will eat anything, right?'

'So I hear.' I clutched the bags to my chest, where I'd

caught them. I could feel my heart beating through the sandwiches. 'Be right back.'

I gave Natalie a quick smile as I entered the dining room and passed the bar. She barely looked away from the TV. Then I practically ran the remaining distance to the lobby . . . where Caleb was waiting.

'Hey,' he said.

'Hi.' I tried to hide my disappointment as I held out the bags. 'Here you go. The usual, on the house.'

'Everything –'

'Okay,' I finished, guessing I hadn't succeeded. 'Yes, everything's fine.'

And it was. I had just been hoping, even more than I'd realised, that after he'd taken care of me at the lake house the other day, Simon might want to pick up their lunches. But Caleb didn't need to know that.

'Glad to hear it.' He nodded once, held up the bags. 'Thanks. See you tomorrow.'

'Right. Have a nice night.'

He left. I returned to the hostess stand, opened the newspaper, and stared at the words without reading them. Between the buzzing saws and my wandering mind, I didn't realise someone had come in until he stood right before me and spoke.

'Did Louis accidentally put the fries in the freezer instead of the oven?'

'Sorry, I – '

I stopped. *Everything* stopped. My voice. The saws. Time.

My heart.

'Simon.' I didn't feel my lips move, but somehow I said his name. 'I didn't . . . I thought . . . are you . . . ?'

The corners of his mouth lifted. It wasn't quite a smile, but it wasn't a frown, either.

'You have a beard.'

This was the first safe thing that came to mind. I started to cringe as soon as I said it . . . but stopped when he laughed.

'Yeah.' He rubbed one palm against the light brown scruff lining his jaw. 'I guess I kind of do. Must be the fishermen's influence.'

'They're not big groomers?'

'They can do amazing things with a knife and trout, but not so much a razor and their own skin.'

I offered a small smile and struggled to think of something to say. Something besides *I miss you. I love you. I'd give anything, anything at all, for just one chance to make things right again.*

For better or worse, he spoke first.

'Caleb's worried about you.'

Our eyes met. He looked down.

'He is?' I asked.

'He said you've seemed . . . on edge. Tense. A little tired.'

Caleb had got all that from a few brief exchanges? Thanks to this job, I'd now seen him several times, but our conversations never lasted longer than thirty seconds or ventured beyond polite pleasantries. And what about my spontaneous snooze by the lake? I could understand how that might be worrisome – for Simon, who'd found me. Not for Caleb, who hadn't.

'He knows that it's probably hard to be back here,' Simon continued, his eyes still lowered to his sneakers, 'especially this time of year, and with your parents selling the lake house. That'd stress anyone out.'

I watched him cross his arms over his abdomen, step from one foot to the other.

'But he wondered . . .' Simon's head lifted. His eyes found mine and stayed there. 'Is it anything else?'

Yes. I miss you. I love you. I'd give anything –

'I'm the ringmaster. Mistress. Whatever.' Paige led Betty and Oliver into the lobby. 'Vanessa will tell you.'

I looked from them to Simon, whom they hadn't noticed and who no longer looked at me, and back to them.

'Tell you what?' I asked.

'That although parts of the restaurant might seem

like they belong under a big top, I'm totally in charge. Everything's under control.'

'But we'd only discussed painting the exterior,' Betty said. 'Not the interior. And you didn't mention anything about a new porch or light fixtures or doors.'

'All of which are unnecessary,' Oliver added. 'The old ones worked perfectly fine.'

Paige turned to me. Waited for me to back her up.

'I'm sorry.' I stepped out from behind the hostess stand. 'I'd love to chat, I just need one minute to . . .'

Finish helping Simon with his lunch order. That's what I was going to say.

If Simon hadn't left.

CHAPTER 6

'Holy Bob Vila,' Paige said.

'Who?' I asked.

'Bob Vila. The old home-improvement guy. I've been watching clips of his show on YouTube to make sure my workers stay on track.'

We were in her car, approaching my driveway. I followed her gaze through the windscreen to the man standing before the opened iron gate, hammer in one hand, wrench in the other.

'He looks like my dad?'

'A little. But that's not what made me think of him.' She slowed to a stop as Dad squatted next to a shiny red toolbox. 'It seems Father Sands could use some tips from a professional handyman.'

She was right. Dad stared at the toolbox's contents like they were exotic fish in an aquarium.

'What's he trying to do?' Paige asked.

'No idea.' I unbuckled my seat belt. 'Do you want to come in? Maybe stay for dinner?'

'I'd love to but I'm kind of beat.' She rested her head

against the seat and gave me a small, tired smile. 'Plus, I need whatever energy I have left to convince Grandma B that change really can – and will – be good. Rain check?'

'Any time.' I got out and waved as she drove around the cul-de-sac.

'Vanessa!' Dad called out. 'Thank goodness. I could use a second opinion.'

I joined him by the toolbox. He held up a long black rod with a small silver knob on one end.

'What do you think this does?'

'Conducts a symphony?'

He chuckled. 'It does resemble an orchestra baton. That and a magic wand, which would be quite useful right now.'

I squatted next to him. 'Classical music is much more your speed. And what do you need magic for anyway?'

Sighing, he rolled back on his heels and then sat on the pavement. He pointed the black wand at the gate.

'The mermaids? You want to bring them to life?' I sat next to him. 'Hate to break it to you, Big Poppa, but that magic's already been made.'

He looked at me sideways, without moving his head. I shrugged.

'Quite the contrary,' he said. 'I want to take them down.'

I started to ask why but stopped. Because why *wouldn't* he want to remove such a reminder? As far as I knew, mermaids and sirens weren't one and the same, the main differences being sirens' lack of tails and their propensity for killing . . . but in popular culture, they were similar enough to be interchangeable.

'Your mother cringes every time we near this gate. It's reflexive – I don't think she even realises she does it. But I do.'

'Did she ask you to take it down?'

'Of course not. If she stopped to think of herself for even a second, she'd hire a professional to do the job. We all know I'm no Mr Fix-It.' He shook his head. 'But she hasn't thought of herself in a very long time. Which is why it's up to me.'

This was a lovely sentiment, but it made me sad. Dad loved Mom. They'd been married twenty years, and he adored her more every day. And she loved him, too, which was why she'd forgiven his transgression and taken me into their family of three when the time came. For seventeen years, she'd cared for me like I was her biological daughter, even though I must've been a constant reminder of what Dad had done. Still, she'd lived with it. She'd accepted it.

The past year, however, had tested her in ways no wife and mother ever should be. She'd lost Justine, her one biological daughter. She'd almost lost me. All because of a group of women who, up until last summer, we'd only read about in books. A group of which I was now an involuntary member.

That my parents were still together after these new, previously unimaginable realisations was a testament to their love for each other. But that didn't mean it was easy. Even though he knew that his involvement with Charlotte Bleu wasn't completely his fault, Dad's guilt hadn't gone away. It never would. And I knew he'd try to make it up to Mom every single day for the rest of his life.

'What did you say to her?' I asked a few silent moments later.

'When?'

I paused. 'When you apologised.'

He was quiet as he considered this. I was intentionally vague because I knew he'd said he was sorry more than once, and that he'd automatically think back to the time that had been the hardest for him. When that was didn't matter; I wasn't asking to find out at which point he'd felt worst. I just wanted to know what he'd said that helped them get through it.

'I guess . . . I said what you say. I told her I was sorry and that I never meant to hurt her. I told her that if only I could do it over, I'd do everything differently. I told her

I'd completely understand if she never wanted to see me again.'

'And that worked?' My voice was hopeful.

'No.'

'Oh.'

'She'd have left if I hadn't said one other thing.' He looked at me. 'Before I tell you what that was, you should know that I told her what happened before saying one word about you. She wouldn't have gone anywhere as soon as she knew you were in my life. But I had to give her the choice. I owed her at least that much.'

Now I knew which apology had been hardest, and this made sense. After all, he'd only recently learned the real reasons he couldn't resist the temptation that occurred nearly two decades earlier.

I nodded. 'Understood.'

He returned his gaze to the gate. When he spoke again, his voice was steady but soft. 'I told her I'd die without her. And that wasn't a line. I believed it then, and I believe it now.' His arm bumped lightly against mine. 'Not your old man's proudest moment. I wouldn't recommend it.'

'Except it was true. That's why it worked.'

'It was true, but that's not why Jacqueline stayed. She was too strong and proud to let something like her unfaithful husband's well-deserved end change her mind.'

'So then what did?'

'The other thing that *she* knew to be true.'

I waited. For a split second, his eyes welled; he brushed them with the back of his hand.

'Which was that for some strange, inexplicable reason, she . . . couldn't live without me.'

Now my eyes watered. I was thinking of my parents and all they'd been through, but I was also thinking of Simon.

If I said I'd die without him, would he say the same about me?

I leaned over, rested my head on Dad's shoulder. His arm trembled as he moved it around my back. We sat like that, in the middle of the driveway, not speaking, until his breathing slowed and my chest stopped burning.

'You know what we need?' I said.

'A glass of red wine?'

I jumped to my feet. 'A blowtorch.'

He sat up, peered into the toolbox. 'Can we make one appear with the magic wand?'

'The hardware store should have them. I'll make a quick trip.'

'That's okay.' He climbed to his feet. 'It's getting late. Your mother's already started dinner. It can wait until tomorrow.'

'And risk her cringing at these ridiculous mermaids who-knows-how-many times between now and then? I don't think so.' I nodded to the toolbox. 'Want help with that before I go?'

'No, thank you. I'll pack it up and leave it by the gate for now. It'll make a good doorstop until your return.'

I gave him a quick hug, then jogged down the driveway. I ran inside to say hello to Mom, grab the car keys and some water, and explain that I was running to town to pick up some ice cream for dessert. She'd find out the real reason soon enough and would probably argue and assure me it wasn't necessary if I told her now.

The sun was starting to set as I drove towards Main Street, casting the old cottages and newer colonials in a warm orange glow. It was a stark contrast to last summer, when every house, regardless of its paint colour, looked grey, morning, noon, and night. The town had barely had enough time to dry off before the next thunderstorm and downpour struck, soaking and darkening it once again.

This was the kind of night for which people came to Winter Harbor. Even when the sun disappeared behind the horizon, the air would be comfortable, but not cold. It'd be ideal for having a long, leisurely dinner, listening to a local band or two, and simply strolling through town with friends and family.

Given how quiet Betty's had been all day, I shouldn't have been surprised when I found only a dozen or so cars lining Main Street ten minutes later, but I still was. I found a parking spot right in front of the hardware store and hurried inside.

'That's a big toy for a little girl.'

I was in an aisle in the back of the store, trying to decide between two torch models that looked exactly alike. When the guy approached me, I put one back and turned away from him.

'What'd I say?' he called after me. He was tall and wore stained cargo pants, a ripped field jacket, boots, and a knitted hat. I didn't linger long enough to get a good look at his face, but I guessed he was in his mid-twenties. Given his attire, he probably worked on one of the commercial fishing boats that docked at the marina.

He's just a boy, I told myself as I headed for the register. *Flirting with someone he thinks is a normal girl.*

Maybe so. But that didn't stop my hands from shaking as I took cash from my wallet. It had been almost a year, and I still wasn't used to the attention. 'S'mores?'

'Excuse me?' The question was so unexpected, I couldn't help but respond.

A second guy in faded overalls, a thick cable-knit sweater, and a Winter Harbor High baseball hat stood

74

behind me. He nodded to the counter, where the (female) cashier tried to find a price on the blowtorch.

'Looks like you're getting ready for a little chocolate-marshmallow action. Tourists dig that kind of stuff . . . though they usually dig it with sticks and bonfires, not butane-fuelled flamethrowers.'

He grinned. I did my best to return the expression before turning back to the counter.

'There was a sign.' I leaned towards the cashier. 'I think it said $49.99.'

'I'll go check to make sure.'

'No, that's okay, I'll –'

But she was already gone. Behind me, the first guy joined the second. They smelled like salt, nicotine and raw salmon. They talked about hooks and bait in a way that suggested fish wasn't what they were looking to catch.

'You're not from around here, are you?' the first guy asked, raising his voice.

Given that we were the only people in the store besides the cashier, I assumed this question was directed at me.

'Not really,' I said, without turning around.

'Didn't think so. We couldn't forget that face, could we, Griff?'

'Definitely not.' Their stench grew stronger as they

75

stepped closer. 'We kind of pride ourselves on getting to know all the pretty girls in town. It's, like, our thing.'

'That's nice.' Now I wasn't sure whether to be scared or relieved. They were being rather aggressive, while most guys were stunned into shyness unless encouraged to interact. Maybe they really were like this with all girls. Maybe it had nothing to do with the fact that I was nothing like all girls.

'Know something?' the first guy said. 'It was a long day. I'm pretty hungry . . . and could go for something sweet.'

It didn't matter what their motivation was. The last word was spoken near my ear. Fear won.

'I changed my mind!' I backed up, towards the store entrance. 'Thanks anyway!'

Outside, I forced my feet to walk, not run, the short distance to the car. I glanced at the store as I climbed in and saw the two guys talking to the cashier, who'd returned to the register. She was older, so they probably weren't interested in her the same way they'd been in me. And if they still tried to stir up trouble, she was surrounded by pocketknives, screwdrivers and other tools. Certain she could ward off unwanted attention if necessary, I felt only a mild pang of guilt as I started the car and hit the gas.

Eddie's Ice Cream was nearby. Deciding I might as

well pick up dessert so that I had something to show for the trip to town, I drove there and bought three sundaes and as many tubs as I could carry. Though I hadn't directly caused last summer's storms I still felt partially responsible, which made me partially responsible for this summer's slow business. The least I could do was help Eddie move his inventory.

Back in the car, I took back roads to avoid passing the hardware store on my way home. I'd just turned down a narrow residential street when headlights appeared behind me, in the distance. My pulse quickened then slowed again as the car, an old orange pick-up, turned down another road and disappeared.

I put on the radio for distraction. Reached for my handbag in the passenger seat, found my cell phone, and placed it in the cup holder. Grabbed a handful of pretzels from the emergency bag in the middle console and washed it down with the bottle of salt water I'd brought for the ride.

I was about to check my phone for messages when the orange pick-up skidded to a stop at the next crossroads. My foot came off the gas and the SUV slowed. I waited for the truck to turn out ahead of me, but it stayed there, engine grumbling.

It's okay . . . they're just lost . . . they probably want to drive down this way but the street's so narrow, they need you to pass first . . .

I pressed the gas. The sun had set by now but as I neared the truck, it was still light enough to make out the fishing rods hanging out the back, the brim of a baseball hat inside the cab. I slid down in my seat, rested one elbow by the window, and tried to hide my face with my hand. I looked straight ahead as I passed.

The truck didn't move.

I held my breath as I continued driving, watched the rusty hood grow smaller in the rear-view mirror. By the time I reached the stop sign at the end of the street, I couldn't see it anymore.

Exhaling, I turned left, towards the ocean.

Behind me, headlights appeared.

They came closer, grew brighter. I sped up but that only made them do the same. I went faster. The speedometer needle inched towards forty. Forty-five. Fifty. The speed limit was twenty in town and strictly enforced, but I didn't care.

Neither, it seemed, did the young fishermen.

Reaching the next T intersection, I veered left without stopping. The SUV flew up and around curves that the old truck had a harder time manoeuvring. I relaxed slightly, confident that at this rate, I'd be home with the iron gate closed behind me before the truck caught up . . . but then I realised what that meant.

They'd know where I lived. Even if they were too far back to see which driveway I pulled into, they'd still have a pretty good idea. This road, though long, wasn't lined with many houses. It ended at our cul-de-sac. Which meant I'd be safe tonight . . . but what about tomorrow? The fishermen might simply be playing games right now, but what if they felt like tracking me down and doing something more serious later?

I slammed on the brake. The SUV swerved and I used the momentum to spin it around, change direction. I shot past the truck a quarter-mile down; it slowed instantly and began to turn.

The speedometer needle hit fifty-five. Sixty. Sixty-five. Keeping one hand clamped on the steering wheel, I reached for my phone. I started to punch in the number I could still dial in my sleep even though I hadn't called it in months . . . and then hung up before the last digit.

My instinct was to call Simon. To tell him I might not be okay, because once upon a time, he'd wanted to know. So he could help. He'd taken care of me at the lake house the other day, but that was only because he probably felt like he had no other choice – I was right there, next door. And if we had any chance together, the choice always had to be his. Just like it had been Mom's.

I tossed the phone on the passenger seat and sped back towards town. The truck caught up as soon as I was slowed by stop signs and the occasional car. I turned down random roads, hoping the lack of direction indicated I was trying to lose them, to throw them off, so that they wouldn't think to return to the winding road set high above the ocean.

This lasted minutes but felt like hours. I'd just blown past the Winter Harbor Library when red and blue lights flashed in my rear-view mirror. They were so bright, I couldn't see past them – or if the old truck was tailing the police cruiser – but I pulled over anyway.

'I'm sorry,' I said, when the officer reached my open window. 'I was speeding, I know, and I'm so sorry. But these guys in an old truck followed me from the hardware store and were chasing me all –'

I stopped. What was the point? The officer was male, young, and already smiling. He appeared to be listening, but I knew he didn't really hear what I was saying. On top of which, besides our cars, the road was empty.

The fishermen, at least for now, were gone.

CHAPTER 7

V! EMERGENCY STAFF MTG. THIS A.M. CAN YOU
BE AT RESTAURANT AT 9? XO, P

BTW, SUPERSHORT NOTICE, I KNOW. SO SORRY!

MISSED YOU AT MTG! HOPE EVERYTHING'S OK.
WILL FILL YOU IN WHEN YOU GET HERE. PS NO
RUSH. PLACE IS DEAD.

WOW, RIDICULOUS CHOICE OF WORDS. ME:
IDIOT! YOU: FORGIVING? :)

HAVE I TOLD YOU LATELY THAT YOU'RE MY
FAVOURITE PERSON? LIKE, EVER?

I finished reading Paige's texts, pushed the blankets aside, and sat up – or tried to anyway. My shoulders lifted but my chest wouldn't budge. My entire torso felt weighted down, like my lungs had been replaced with cinder blocks. I shifted my arms and pressed my elbows into the mattress for support, but my torso rose only an inch or two before falling back again. The effort made my head spin; I closed my eyes as I reached for the water bottle on my nightstand.

I always woke up weaker than when I went to sleep, and so thirsty, I could down a gallon of salt water in less than a minute, but this felt different. Like I might be coming down with flu or some other real illness. I hadn't been sick since my body's transformation last summer, and I wondered how it might affect my other physical challenges.

My cell phone message light blinked red. Still drinking, I opened the text folder.

LOUIS EXPLOSIONS REACHING RECORD-BREAKING DECIBELS. COME SOON??? XOXO

I wrote back with one hand.

ON MY WAY. —V

I finished the water bottle and waited a few seconds for the liquid to reach my limbs. My chest was still heavy when I tried sitting up again, but the rest of me was strong enough to pull it upright. I took two more water bottles from the small refrigerator Mom had placed in my bathroom and kept fully stocked, and guzzled both before putting on my swimming costume and venturing outside.

It was late morning but the sun hadn't yet burned the chill from the air. I rubbed my bare arms as I jogged across the patio and started down the stone steps. Halfway to the beach, my chest grew heavy again and my knees threatened to buckle. I debated going back inside but quickly decided against it. I felt bad now, but I'd feel a million times worse if I skipped my morning swim.

My energy started to return the second my feet hit ocean. I pushed through the break and then dived under, relishing my body's instant weightlessness. I breathed deeply and succumbed to the current, letting the waves carry me towards the horizon and bring me back towards shore. Eventually, I tested my arms and legs; when a single motion propelled me forward several feet, I changed direction and aimed for the beach.

'Are you okay?'

Seeing the boy standing there, wearing cargo shorts and nothing else, I stopped in the break. My body didn't move as water crashed into it.

'What are you doing here?' I demanded.

Colin looked at me and pointed at the kayaks behind him. 'I came to get this since the house is off the market.

My mom asked your mom, who said I could stop by any-time and –' He blinked, shook his head. 'Are you *okay*?'

I was tempted to retreat below the surface until he gave up and left. But there was a good chance he'd return with professional medical assistance, so I crossed my arms over my chest and hurried across the sand instead. As I passed him, I noted the T-shirt, fleece, and sneakers lying by his feet. The fact that he'd been about to come in after me prompted me to answer his question.

'I'm fine,' I said.

'But you were under, like, a really long time,' he called after me. 'Most people couldn't . . . I mean, how did you . . . without a tank or . . .'

I stopped again, this time by the rocks leading to my bedroom patio. Not because I wanted to keep talking but because as quickly as it'd returned, my energy was waning. A swim like the one I'd just taken usually kept me going until early evening. Was it the surprise? The stress of some stranger seeing me do what no one could? The terrifying thought that he'd tell others?

Whatever the reason, my body was shutting down. My knees sank towards the rock. My palms landed next to them.

'It's okay,' I said, fighting to keep my voice normal. 'I'm fine, I just need to –'

His hand pressed against my back – barely, like he was

afraid he'd hurt me – but the contact fired a bullet of strength that exploded through my chest. I gasped at the sensation, which made him pull away.

'I'm sorry,' I whispered. 'Can you just . . . would you mind . . . ?'

I didn't even know what I was asking. Fortunately, Colin did. He took me firmly by the arms, guided me to a seated position on the rock. He lowered himself next to me and then tensed. I did, too, but only briefly. The urge to close my eyes and lean against him was too powerful.

The second our bare flesh met, his arms were around my waist.

It's okay . . . it's just Simon . . . my Simon, taking care of me the way he always does. . . .

'Are your parents inside? Do you want me to –'

'No.' I wrapped my fingers around his forearms, squeezed gently. 'I just need a minute. Please don't go.'

He tightened his hold until I could feel his heart beat fast against my back. After a minute, he released one hand to brush my damp hair off my face. I felt stronger – and guiltier – with each passing second. As soon as I felt able, I wanted to pull away and run up the steps . . . but to be on the safe side, I knew I needed to do one thing first.

'Colin?'

His head lowered next to mine, giving my body another surge. I shifted in his arms until our eyes met, and then I struggled not to look away.

'Thank you for staying.'

'Are you kidding? There was no way I was leaving after you –'

I pressed my palm to his cheek. His mouth froze as he seemed to forget what he was saying.

'I didn't do anything.' I tried to smile as my thumb traced his jawline. 'Nothing worth mentioning to anyone else anyway. And I'd really, really appreciate it if you – if we – kept this morning to ourselves. Would that be okay?'

He swallowed. Nodded. His eyes lowered from my eyes to my lips. As his face neared mine, I turned my head and focused on the sun's glinting across the ocean's surface. His mouth landed near my temple and lingered there. I gave it a few seconds for good measure before sitting up and explaining I had to get ready for work.

Back in my bedroom, I watched him go. He wandered around the beach a minute, as if confused about why he was there, but then he focused on the kayaks and started dragging them across the sand. When he was out of sight, I dashed to the bathroom to shower and dress. My energy was holding, which helped lessen, though not eliminate, the sting of guilt.

86

Ten minutes later, I hurried through the house, looking for my parents. Despite the many glass walls, it was still possible to miss each other as you moved from one room to the next, so I tried calling both their cell phones once I reached the empty kitchen. When the calls went to voicemail, I headed for the garage to check for their car – and found a note and a separate envelope taped to the door.

Dear Vanessa,

Your father and I have been waiting for the perfect time to give you your graduation present. We knew you'd refuse it unless you really, really needed it . . . and that you'd have to get to work while we were at appointments today. So please do your best to enjoy it. If you absolutely must protest, we'll be available for dissuasion later this afternoon.

We're so proud of you and love you more than you know.

Below Mom's neat handwriting, Dad had added a separate message in his crooked chicken scratch.

Electric windows and a functioning defroster will take some getting used to, but I know you can adjust. Because you can do anything.

ALSO, PLEASE REMEMBER TO BUCKLE UP. YOUR MOTHER DIDN'T WANT TO CLOUD HER NOTE WITH OVERPROTECTIVE NOTIONS, SO I'LL CLOUD MINE ON HER BEHALF. SAFETY FIRST!

Electric windows? A functioning defroster? Buckle up?

I had to give them credit. Because if they'd been home

when I opened the door and found the brand-new, forest-green Jeep Wrangler in the garage, I wouldn't have climbed in. Or taken the key from the envelope and turned the ignition. But since they weren't and I had to get to work somehow, I did.

I grinned as the engine rumbled to life. I'd never had my own car before; the closest I'd come was Dad's ancient Volvo, which I used until it wheezed to a slow, final stop last spring. Because we were supposed to spend a lot of time together this summer, the plan had been to share the SUV – or so I'd thought. I realised now my parents had probably decided to do this months ago. Maybe even as soon as I'd been accepted to Dartmouth. After all, were they really going to drive me to and from New Hampshire for every break or new semester?

But new cars weren't cheap. Could they afford such a generous gift, especially with Mom taking such a long leave of absence from her job? And when they were concerned about selling the lake house so we could pay for the beach house?

Get over it. That's what Justine would say if she were here. She'd tell me it was their decision and they wouldn't do it if they couldn't. For further reassurance, I told myself that the gift wasn't extravagant; it was practical. Safe, reliable transportation would help my parents as much as it helped me. So after calling their cell phones and leaving long, grateful messages, I buckled up and backed out of the garage.

I'd found the Jeep with the top down and as I sped towards Betty's, the moist, salty air provided a fresh infusion of energy. I felt so good, I even managed not to dwell on everything that had happened prior to finding the note taped to the garage door. It had been a fluke, a one-time thing. Now that Colin had taken what he'd come for, I'd never again emerge from the water to find him waiting for me. Which meant I'd never again be shocked, instantly drained, and in desperate need of his attention.

'Vanessa!' Paige waved and jogged towards me as I pulled into the restaurant car park. 'Thank goodness you're here!'

I stopped near the entrance and hopped out.

'Nice ride.' Paige smiled as she checked out the Jeep. 'Beamer in the shop?'

'Beamer's with the parents. This is actually – '

I was cut off by a loud bang. Paige spun around. I looked past her to see one of the construction workers shrug sheepishly as he lifted the wooden plank he'd just dropped onto the new porch.

'They've made a lot of progress,' I said. The porch appeared to be complete except for missing railings, and the front of the restaurant had been given another coat of purple paint.

'Yeah.' Paige nodded. 'I think one of the new guys has a little thing for me. It's amazing what some old-fashioned flirting can do.'

I looked at her. She started towards the restaurant.

'So we had a minor catastrophe first thing this morning,' she called behind her as I hurried to catch up. 'Carla came in twenty minutes before her shift started and Louis went ballistic.'

'Because she was early? Isn't that a good thing?'

'Usually.' Reaching the porch, Paige gave the cute, young construction worker a quick smile. He dropped the wooden plank again and lunged across the porch to open the door. 'Unfortunately, it was pre-caffeine for our favourite chef – and he let everyone know it.'

The worker held the door open for me, too. I kept my eyes lowered as I thanked him and followed Paige inside.

'Anyway, Carla had a total meltdown. I tried to do damage control, but I was home when it happened and by the time I got here, it was too late.'

'Louis fired her?'

We stopped in the dining-room doorway. Paige turned to me and cocked one eyebrow.

'Right,' I said. 'That's your job.'

'And I didn't do it. She was a bit emotional, but I actually thought she had potential.'

'So what happened?'

'She quit. Leaving us with zero waiters right before the breakfast rush.'

'There was a rush?' I asked.

'Well, no. But I was hoping for one.' She held up her phone. 'That's why the emergency meeting and countless texts. I had to rearrange schedules and keep the remaining waiting staff calm. The tips haven't exactly been rolling in, so they were already on edge. I was afraid they'd all jump ship – some of them did – and that you and I'd have to do double duty.'

'You know I'd be happy to help however you needed me to.'

'I do, thank you. But fortunately, that won't be necessary.'

She tilted her head back. I leaned to the left and looked past her to the bar . . . where a pretty blonde was polishing glasses.

'Natalie?' I said.

Paige's eyes lit up. 'You know her?'

'I met her. She came in for lunch the other day.'

'Well, she came in for breakfast today – just as Carla was tearing off her apron and storming out. There was a family here who'd been seated but hadn't ordered and a couple still waiting to be seated, and no one was helping them. So Natalie did.'

'What about Louis?' I asked. 'And the other staff? They couldn't have filled in?'

'Sure they could've. And if Louis hadn't been so busy howling about how no one quits on him, and if the rest of the staff hadn't been cowering in the corner of the kitchen, maybe they would've.'

I watched Natalie rearrange wine goblets and shuffle shot glasses. She moved quickly, confidently, like she'd spent quite a bit of time behind a bar counter.

'She worked at the same restaurant back home in Vermont for five years,' Paige said, as if reading my mind. 'She's here for the summer because her dad insisted they have one last father–daughter adventure before she leaves for college in the fall.'

'Then why has she come here alone both times?'

Paige looked at me. 'Because he was swimming? Napping? Reading the newspaper? And she had time to kill?' She studied my face, which reddened under her gaze. 'Vanessa . . . is something wrong?'

I started to say no but stopped. I'd heard the suspicion in my voice, too, and denying something was up would only invite more questions that I didn't know how to answer. Paige knew me too well to let it slide.

'Sorry,' I said. 'Weird morning, that's all.'

She stood up straight. Her eyes widened. 'Was it the orange truck? Did it follow you here?'

'No, thankfully. I haven't seen it again since that night.' I'd told Paige about the chase because I had to tell someone and didn't want to worry my parents. Also, with the exception of last year, she'd been a full-time Winter Harbor resident her whole life; I thought she might have some idea who the truck belonged to. She didn't, but said she'd keep her eyes and ears open. 'I just didn't feel great and it took longer than usual to get going.'

'Thank goodness. About the truck, not about – '

'Got it.' I smiled. 'How've you been, by the way?'

'What do you mean?'

I waited for a busboy to pass before lowering my voice and continuing. 'Physically, since we've been back. Do you feel any differently here than you did in Boston?'

She considered this. 'Not really. Maybe a bit more tired, but only because thinking about this restaurant stuff keeps me awake at night. Everything else feels pretty normal.' She paused. 'Why? Do you?'

I didn't want to give her something else to worry about unnecessarily, so I shook my head. 'Just tired, too. But I guess it's to be expected, considering the new house and moving and everything.'

'Absolutely.' She took my hand. 'Come on. I know what'll help.'

She led me through the dining room. As we passed the bar, Natalie's head was hidden behind an open cabinet door. Paige, apparently deciding formal introductions could wait, breezed by without slowing down.

In the kitchen, she instructed me to sit on a stool by the meat freezer while she dodged Louis, who was quiet but still cranky, and gathered food. Two minutes later, she handed me a plastic tray and sat on the stool next to mine.

'Bagel with seaweed-infused cream cheese, fries, iced water, and an extra-large coffee. All coated, dipped, or filled with salt.'

I followed her finger as it pointed at different dishes. 'This should be the most unappetising, inedible meal I've ever been served.'

'But?' Paige asked.

'It's perfect.'

She stayed with me while I ate and kept an eye on Louis to make sure he didn't terrify anyone else into leaving. We kept the conversation light, talking about my Jeep and her plans to paint the lobby and build flower boxes. It had been days and we still hadn't returned to the topic of what I'd overheard at the open house, but that was fine with me. I was hoping it was a fluke – and one we could eventually forget.

I'd felt fine when I'd arrived, but after eating and visiting my best friend, I felt even better. In fact, Colin could burst into the kitchen and declare his love for me right then . . . and my heart wouldn't even skip a beat.

As it happened, Colin didn't burst into the kitchen. Natalie did.

'Someone's here about a takeout order?' she said. 'Cute guy with glasses?'

I lowered my coffee cup. Louis tossed Natalie two brown paper bags. She disappeared back through the swinging door.

'Cute guy,' Paige said, after a pause. 'With glasses.'

I nodded, sipped.

'Don't you want to say hi?'

I did. So much so, it was taking every calorie of energy I'd just consumed to keep from leaping off the stool and flying from the kitchen. But I couldn't help thinking about what Dad had said about Mom, and I didn't know if I should.

'The ball's in his court,' I explained. 'I can't jump the net.'

'But he knows you're here. If he didn't want to see you, he wouldn't have come inside.' Paige shrugged. 'I'm no athlete . . . but that sounds like a serve to me.'

I put down the cup and handed her the tray. 'Be right back.'

I dashed into the dining room. As I passed the

mirrored wall behind the bar, I made the mistake of checking my appearance. Driving with the top down had dried my shoulder-length brown hair into a network of knots and tangles. And I'd been in such a hurry to get here, I hadn't stopped to put on mascara and lip gloss, the two basic touch-ups every girl needed to make before going out in public – or so Justine had always said. Both my brush and make-up were home, so the best I could do was pinch my cheeks and force my fingers through my hair as I headed for the lobby.

I needn't have made the effort. By the time the front door came into view, Caleb – not Simon – was already passing through it. Through the window, I watched him lower sunglasses – not spectacles – from the top of his head to in front of his eyes as he walked to the Subaru.

'I know that look.'

I turned to Natalie. In my disappointment, I'd forgotten she was there.

'Actually, I *own* that look.'

I tried to smile. 'I don't know what you mean.'

She leaned against the hostess stand, pulled on a thin chain around her neck. A small silver circle with a single diamond slid out from beneath her tank top.

'My boyfriend proposed to me two months ago,' she said.

'Wow.' I couldn't tell if I was more surprised, since she was my age, or envious. 'Congratulations.'

She hooked the ring on the tip of her thumb, twirled it with her pointer finger. 'We'd been together three years but I still thought we should wait. He didn't, and I loved him too much to put up a fight. His point was that we knew we were always going to be together, so what difference did it make when we made it official?'

I nodded, wondering why she was telling me this, but too curious to ask and potentially prevent her from continuing.

'Anyway, we decided to get married at the end of the summer. A big thing – two hundred people, ice sculptures, a reception at his family's house on Lake Champlain.'

'Sounds nice,' I said.

She looked up from the ring. 'It does, doesn't it? And it would've been . . . if he hadn't called it off three weeks ago.'

'Why?' I asked. I couldn't help it.

'All the reasons I'd given for waiting – we were too young, there was no rush, dating was fine for now – plus one more.'

I waited. She gently flicked the ring from her thumb; it fell to her chest.

'He was in love with someone else.'

I pictured a red rowing boat. A beautiful girl with silver eyes and short black hair. Simon, leaning forward, closing his eyes . . . kissing her.

'Maybe he's not,' I offered quickly. 'Maybe he only thinks he's in love with someone else – because he got cold feet with you.'

She gave me a sad smile. 'Thanks. But believe me, I know him and I'd know if that were true. If there were any chance it was, I wouldn't have let my dad talk me into this extended vayscape.'

'Sorry?'

'Vacation slash escape. We've consolidated syllables in the interest of time and painful reminders.'

As Natalie started to walk away, I thought her story explained why she was here in Winter Harbor. It might also explain why she was here at Betty's Chowder House; last summer, I, too, had jumped in and accepted an impromptu job for distraction. What it didn't explain was why she'd shared it with me.

'My boyfriend . . . my ex-boyfriend . . . he never proposed,' I offered.

She turned back. 'But you still want to be with him?'

The answer was easy, automatic, but I couldn't say it out loud. Fortunately, Natalie filled in the blanks.

'Then you better make it crystal clear. Because if you don't . . . someone else will.'

CHAPTER 8

Later that night, I stood in the lake-house kitchen, staring at my cell-phone screen. No matter how much I wanted them to, the words wouldn't write themselves, but everything I'd tried in the past hour had sounded wrong. I needed to be casual yet serious. Charming yet sincere. Undemanding yet irresistible. And the longer I took trying to be all those things, the less time I'd have to enjoy the fruits of my labour. Assuming my labour paid off, which it might not. That possibility only made it even harder to figure out what to say.

You're a siren, I chastised myself. *Like it or not, this should be easy.*

I stared at the phone another minute, then put it down. Picked it up again. Opened the refrigerator. Closed it. Turned on the radio. Spun the dial.

I was trying to decide between jazz and oldies, the only two stations that didn't sound like they were broadcasting from the centre of a funnel cloud, when there was a knock on the kitchen door.

My eyes locked on the shadowy outline behind the

shade I'd lowered earlier for privacy. I reached reflexively for the ceramic jar of knives and wooden spoons, and when it wasn't there, reminded myself that the surprise visitor was probably Anne, the realtor, or people who'd seen the FOR SALE sign by the road and wanted a closer look.

As I headed for the door, I squeezed my phone in one hand and made a mental note to talk to Mom about this. After all, it was eight o'clock. The house was still ours. Just because we no longer lived in it didn't mean anyone could swing by at all hours of the night.

'Vanessa. Hi.'

Unless, of course, anyone was Simon.

'She drives an Audi,' he said.

I leaned against the door for support. 'Who?'

'Sorry.' He shook his head, motioned towards the driveway. 'Your realtor. She drives an Audi. Black, with a roof rack. When I saw the Jeep, I didn't know . . . I mean, I wasn't sure . . . I just thought I should check and . . .'

'The Jeep's mine,' I explained quickly. 'It was a graduation gift from my parents.'

'Oh. Nice.' One side of his mouth lifted. 'And in forest green. I'm pretty sure I know whose pick that was.'

I grinned, too. 'The Dartmouth bumper sticker and antenna flag will be arriving any day. And the backseat is just big enough to hold my new Dartmouth duffel bag when it's stuffed with my new Dartmouth sweatpants, sweatshirts, towels, and pillowcases.'

'Pillowcases?'

'Those were actually my pick. They're flannel and surprisingly comfortable.'

His smile relaxed, then faded. 'Congratulations, by the way. On graduating. And Dartmouth, and everything else. Those are some major accomplishments.'

His words were happy but he sounded sad as he said them. I knew why. It was the same reason I'd accepted my diploma with tears in my eyes, and why I'd automatically dialled the Maine area code, then hung up, when I got the letter from Dartmouth.

He should've been there. And if last fall hadn't happened, he would've been.

'Do you want to come in?' I asked.

He inhaled. 'Do I *want* to?' His eyes met mine, stayed there. I held my breath, scared that if I moved even an inch, he'd talk himself into leaving. 'Yes. But should I?'

And just like that, my words were failing me again. How could I convince him to come in without actually convincing him? What could I say to help him make the decision all on his own? Since talking to Natalie, I'd had to do something to make sure Simon knew how I felt, but after my conversation with Dad a few days ago, I still wanted him to have as many choices as possible. Which was why the plan for the night had been to simply let him know I was there. If he wanted to see me, he could. If he didn't, he wouldn't. Whatever happened after that would be totally up to him.

'There's a new shower curtain,' I finally said. 'In the downstairs bathroom.'

'You mean the vinyl one with the pastel world map ... ?'

'Gone. Fifteen years was an impressive run, but our realtor said it'd make potential buyers put their wallets away, and Mom wasn't about to let it into the fancy new house. So we threw it out. The replacement has stripes, not countries.'

He nodded slowly. 'Now, this ... I think I have to see.'

My heart lifted. Mentioning bathroom décor wasn't exactly twisting his arm ... so this was totally his call, wasn't it?

I moved aside, opened the door wider. He took one step and stopped.

'Oh. You're expecting company.'

His gaze was fixed on the table set for two. I'd brought dishes from the other house and had arranged them while procrastinating over my perfect text.

'I should go.'

'No.' My hand was on his arm, my heart in my throat. 'Don't. Please.'

'Vanessa,' he said, his voice strained, 'I know it's been a while . . . but I can't. I still can't see you with . . .'

As he struggled to finish what neither of us wanted to hear, I realised three things. The first was that he assumed I'd arranged a romantic date – without him. The second was that he couldn't have moved on, at least not completely, if he didn't want to see me with anyone else, nine months after watching me make out with Parker King, Hawthorne Prep's water-polo star.

The third was that I was going to blow this chance, if I didn't do something – and fast.

'It's for you,' I said. 'Or at least I was hoping it'd be.'

His eyes moved from the table to me. I opened my cell phone and held it up so he could see the screen, which still showed the blank text I'd been writing. His cell number was displayed at the top of the white box.

'I was trying to figure out how to invite you over without actually inviting you over. Because I thought if I came out and said it, you wouldn't come.' I closed the phone, looked down. 'And I just . . . really wanted to see you.'

He didn't say anything but he didn't leave, either. Encouraged, I continued.

'Our new house overlooks the ocean. My bedroom's so close, when the wind's right, the spray reaches the windows.' I paused, fiddled with the phone. 'I can hear the waves and tell when the tide's coming in or going out. It's slow. Consistent. Nothing like last summer.'

He was perfectly still. My eyes lifted to his chest; it didn't move.

'Every night, I lie in bed listening to the water, and I think about how nice it would be to sit there, on the beach ... with you. When the sun's shining and the tide's moving exactly as it should. We could just be together the way we used to be, before everything got so complicated.'

I stopped, waited. This was as much as I could say. Anything else would be like grabbing him by the arm and pulling him inside.

'We can't go back,' he said quietly, a moment later. 'Too much has happened.'

'I know.' I was only slightly aware of my pulse hammering in my ears. 'But that still leaves forward.'

He looked at me. I leaned against the door to keep from launching towards him.

'As friends?' he said.

My pulse fell silent. 'Yes. Of course as friends.'

His lips pressed together as he gave me a small smile.

'Do I smell garlic bread?' he asked.

I stepped into the kitchen and opened the door as wide as it would go. Happy tears sprang to my eyes as he came all the way inside, and I blinked them away before he noticed.

I'd got a takeaway from the Italian place in town and kept the food warm in the oven. We used paper plates I found on the top shelf of the pantry instead of the ceramic dishes I'd brought, and filled paper cups with water instead of the wine I'd taken from the beach house. Rather than sitting at the kitchen table, we wandered out back and ate on the deck steps.

One of my favourite things about being with Simon was the way we could be together and talk about nothing. It didn't matter what we did; we could go hiking or watch a movie or hang out on the lake, and literally not speak for hours. The silence was always easy, always comfortable.

Tonight, however, we talked. About my last semester of high school. His classes at Bates. Dartmouth. His parents. My parents. Caleb. Paige. Music. Movies. The benefits of manual gears versus automatic, and other car-related issues. The only topics we avoided were those that would've reminded us why we had so much to catch up on, and that was fine by me. I'd spent enough time mentally replaying the exact moment at which I'd stopped kissing Parker and seen Simon's Subaru speed away, and the second he'd said he needed space to figure out how he felt after learning who I really was, and the various other points at which everything went wrong. Right now all I wanted was to stick to normal conversation and hope that maybe, someday, everything could be right again.

And it seemed like I might not be the only one. Because two hours later, when I finally confessed to being cold and asked if he'd like to go back inside, which I'd been putting off for fear he'd realise how long he'd been there and decide to go home, he said yes without hesitating.

Moving indoors did interrupt the flow of conversation, but not uncomfortably. We were quiet as we cleaned up the kitchen together, making sure it shone until it looked like we were never there, and as we returned to the living room. The silence didn't make me nervous until I sat on one end of the couch and he sat on the other. Then it felt awkward, unnatural – just like the physical distance between us.

'Is this better?' he asked, a long moment later.

'Better?'

'Warmer?'

'Oh. Yes, much. Thank you.'

He nodded, then looked around the living room. I took advantage of the opportunity to watch him in a way I'd longed to for months. He wore dark jeans, a grey track jacket, and worn-in Nikes. His dark hair was longer than usual, curling slightly over the tops of his ears and against his zipped-up collar. Light scruff still lined his upper lip and jaw, but it was cut close to his skin. He'd got new frameless glasses that showed off his eyes.

He looked different. Older.

Even better than I'd remembered.

'It's so strange,' he said.

My heart thrust against my chest. 'What is?'

'Your family selling this place.'

My heart settled back down.

'I mean, no one else has ever lived here.' He crossed his arms loosely over his chest and rested his head against the back of the couch. 'I didn't think anyone else ever would.'

I looked around the living room. At the plaid curtains, the stone fireplace, the wooden ducks lining the mantel. Things we'd left so potential buyers could get a feel for real lakeside living.

'Me neither,' I said. 'But I guess my parents thought things would be easier this way. To be back here while still moving on.'

We were quiet for another moment. Then Simon said, so softly I almost missed it, 'Just because you don't see something every day . . . doesn't mean you let it go.'

His head, still resting on the couch, turned towards

me. I lowered my eyes, afraid of what I'd say or do if they connected with his. I told myself it didn't matter what I said or did, since, according to Charlotte, my abilities didn't work on Simon; he'd fallen in love with me before I was fully transformed, so any feelings he had for me, good and bad, were genuine.

Which meant the choice was still his.

He stood up. Assuming he wanted to leave before we entered even more dangerous territory, I did, too. Keeping my gaze lowered, I started for the kitchen to show him out – and immediately stopped short to avoid running into him.

'Sorry,' I said.

I waited for him to continue. Stepped to the side when he didn't. Nearly fell over when his fingers grazed my wrist.

'Simon –'

'I know.' His fingers slid across my skin, his thumb lingered lightly over my pulse. 'I know what I said. But if it's okay with you . . . I'd just like to see something.'

I had no idea what this meant, but his voice, though quiet, was steady. Certain. So much so that I resisted the automatic urge to dissuade him from whatever he was about to do in hopes that he wouldn't regret it later.

I stayed perfectly still as he stepped towards me and kept my eyes focused straight ahead, on the zipper of his jacket. My breathing quickened as it neared. Soon it was so close, I could make out each tiny, silver tooth, every stitch of the white seam running along each side.

I could smell him, too – his soap, the saltiness on his clothes, left over from working outside all day. I could feel his warmth. His breath soft against my forehead.

His arms circling my waist.

I closed my eyes and braced for the sudden jolt of energy . . . but it didn't come. Instead of strengthening, the entire length of my body seemed to weaken, melt.

His arms tightened around me. I lifted mine and rested my palms against his chest. Feeling his heart beat faster, I slid my hands up, over his shoulders, around his neck. Sensing the slightest pressure against my back, I came forward until our torsos touched. When he trembled, I started to pull away, but he wouldn't let me.

We settled against each other, his chin on top of my head, my cheek against his chest. I thought this was it, the thing he'd wanted to see – although I still wasn't sure what exactly he was checking for – but then he moved again. His chin lifted. I raised my head as his breath travelled slowly down my ear, across my face.

You haven't done anything wrong . . . this is happening because he wants it to. . . .

'Vanessa,' he whispered, his mouth nearing mine. 'I –'

He stopped, pushed me away, and kept both hands

on my shoulders, like I might lunge against him. Which, given the way every inch of my body ached the instant we separated, wasn't out of the question.

'What is it?' I asked. 'What's wrong?'

He shook his head, looked towards the living-room window. With the lights on inside but not outside, I couldn't see past our reflections.

'I thought I heard something,' he said, a moment later. 'Sorry.'

'It's okay.' We stayed like that, his hands on my shoulders and mine on his arms, a few seconds more. When there was nothing to hear but crickets and leaves rustling, I asked gently, 'Maybe you imagined it? To keep from doing something you weren't sure you wanted to do?'

He looked at me, then offered a small smile. His hands were on my hips and I was reaching around his neck when a bright white light flashed through the room.

I froze. 'Was that –? That looked like –'

Lightning. That's what I was about to say – but then it happened again. And twice more after that. The blinding bursts were so fast, I couldn't see for several seconds after they were done. By the time my vision cleared, I was alone, and the back door was wide open.

'Simon?' I hit the light switch as I ran outside. The

deck and part of the back yard illuminated in a dull yellow glow. Both were empty. I looked out at the lake, then up. The water was flat, calm. It glittered in the light of a half-moon, which shone down from a clear sky.

Whatever we'd just seen, lightning wasn't it. I told myself to calm down as I found myself doing something I hadn't done since Simon and I had been trapped at the bottom of this very lake nine months earlier.

I was listening. For Raina. Zara. The other sirens who'd served them in near death just as they had in life. I pictured them swimming, swarming around us, their limbs frail, their silver eyes blank.

But my mind fell silent. There was nothing to hear.

And then – footsteps. Hushed, urgent voices. Coming from the western side of the house. I bolted in that direction, aware that they could belong to anyone – trespassers, burglars, the fishermen from the other night – and that I had nothing to defend myself with, if necessary.

But I didn't care. All I could think about was finding Simon.

I charged across the grass, careful to stay in the shadows. I crept along the far side of the deck and peered around the corner of the house. Seeing two figures running for the driveway, I started to go after them . . . but the side yard sloped up. And my body had

III

to be running dry, because my muscles were tiring. I was still several feet from where the grass levelled off when I had to lower to a squat to catch my breath.

A car started. Headlights appeared overhead.

A hand clamped over my mouth, an arm across my abdomen.

I tore at both as I was yanked back, towards the deck, but fighting made me only weaker.

'Vanessa,' a familiar voice whispered. 'It's me.'

My body relented. Simon held me close as the head-lights swooped across the yard. An engine roared and tyres spun through gravel. The car, which we couldn't see, flew up the driveway, out onto the road, and towards town.

'Who were they?' I asked, when he finally released me.

'I don't know. But they dropped this.'

A small square brightened the darkness. In its centre was an image of a couple. They held onto each other like they needed the kiss they were about to share like other people needed oxygen.

The square was a digital camera screen.

The couple was Simon and me.

CHAPTER 9

'You're so getting back together.'

I handed Paige a stack of purple paper. 'Did you hear anything else I said?'

'About the people spying on you? And the psycho stalker pictures? And the car tearing out of your driveway like there was a jet engine under its hood?' She took a leather menu from the tower in front of her and opened it. 'Yes. How could I not, when all of that led up to the most important moment of the entire night?'

'When Simon followed me home?'

She shook her head. 'That was nice, but I meant when he invited you to spend the night. With him.'

'It wasn't an invitation,' I corrected her. 'Not like that. It was late. I was a little freaked out. He offered up his family's guest room so I didn't have to drive home by myself.'

'He might've *said* guest room, but he *meant* his room. That's totally where you would've ended up after talking for hours and being so comfortable, you would have fallen asleep – or done whatever – together.' She shrugged. 'You know it, I know it, and Simon definitely knew it.'

She sounded certain and I'd even omitted some key details about what had happened before the camera flashes lit up the living room – including how close Simon and I had been to kissing. Given the interruption, I hadn't had enough time or mental clarity to figure out what it meant, so I wasn't ready to share. It didn't help that Simon hadn't offered any explanation; his brain had automatically switched to analytic mode after the car sped away, and he made no mention of what had almost happened, before following me back to the beach house.

The only indication he gave that he hadn't completely forgotten was when we reached the gate and he got out of his car to say goodbye. As he came towards the Jeep, I looked away to turn off the radio. It was only a split second, but it was enough time for him to lean through the open window, lift my hair away from my ear, and whisper six words.

'*I saw what I needed to.*'

And then he left.

'Can we just focus for a second on the psycho stalker part?' I asked Paige now. 'Please?'

She closed the menu and looked around the dining room to make sure the restaurant's three brunch guests weren't listening. When she turned back, the playful glint in her blue eyes was gone.

'Sorry,' she said quietly. 'I want nothing more than for you to be reunited with the love of your life . . . but I also like to think that, compared to last summer, this summer could actually be normal. Talking about psycho stalkers makes that difficult.'

'I understand. Believe me.'

She folded her arms on top of the stack of purple paper and leaned towards me. 'Were there other pictures? Besides the ones they took last night?'

'Yes. We weren't in them, thankfully, but neither was anyone else. They were just a bunch of ordinary nature shots – the beach, hiking trails, rocks. Without last night's pictures, the camera could belong to anyone visiting Winter Harbor.'

'Do you think it belongs to the people you saw a few weeks ago? At the open house?'

'Maybe. That makes the most sense. But if so, why were they there so late last night? When the house is usually empty?'

Paige opened her mouth to respond. Before she could, a coffeepot appeared on the table between us.

'You guys look hard at work,' Natalie said, setting down two cups and a sugar bowl. 'Thought you might need some extra fuel for that fire.'

'Thank you!' Paige beamed and sat up straight, clearly grateful for the distraction. 'You're the best. Isn't she the best?'

Considering how long we'd known Natalie, I thought this was a generous assessment. But then, deciding I was still feeling lingering paranoia from our first meeting as well as new, likely unnecessary concern that she'd just been listening to Paige's and my conversation, I tried to push all doubt aside.

'She definitely has good timing.' I smiled as Natalie filled my cup. 'Thanks.'

'No problem. So what are we tackling today? Backsplash tiles? Crown moulding? Copper tap fixtures?'

Paige's head tilted to one side. 'Copper. Huh. I hadn't thought about that.'

I held up a leather folder. 'New menus.'

'What's wrong with the old ones?' Natalie asked.

'Exactly that,' Paige said. 'They're old. Ancient, actually. And made of laminated construction paper that used to be red but faded to grey, like, fifty years ago.'

'Has the menu changed at all?' Natalie asked.

'Not the dishes,' Paige said, 'but their names.'

Natalie glanced at the paper Paige held up. 'Why?'

'For the same reason the paint changed. To breathe new life into Betty's and attract new business.'

Natalie nodded. Slowly.

'What?' Paige asked.

'Nothing. New life is always good.'

I watched Paige's eyes lower to the menu, her lips turn out.

'It's just . . .' Natalie continued, 'I don't know if purple paper will make a difference.'

'Would pink be better?' Paige asked.

'It wouldn't matter if you used every colour of the rainbow. People don't care what the menu looks like.'

I kind of agreed, but Paige's face fell so fast, I had to interject. 'If they don't, they will as soon as they see how nice these are.'

'Maybe,' Natalie said. 'But I doubt it.'

'What would you suggest?' I asked. 'You worked at another restaurant, right? How was business there?'

'So good, people showed up at three o'clock to wait for us to open for dinner at five.' She looked at Paige, who stared at the stream of sugar she was pouring from the bowl into her coffee. 'But it was a very different type of place.'

I waited for Paige to respond, or at the very least, look up. 'A few tips wouldn't hurt, would they?' I asked when she did neither. Paige sipped her coffee, forced a smile. 'Sure.'

'You know what? I'm so sorry. Forget I said anything.'

Natalie started to back up. 'Not only is this none of my business, I'm just a waitress. What do I know?'

The apology and excuse seemed to soften Paige, who finally looked away from her drink. 'Probably as much as us. If you have any secrets to restaurant success, I'd love to hear them.'

Natalie glanced behind her. When her customers appeared to be content, she hurried back and dropped into the empty chair.

'The place was called Mountaineers, and it was a dive,' she said, her voice quiet but excited. 'A run-down shack that most people would normally cross the street to avoid walking past.'

'Was the rest of the area nice?' Paige asked. 'Local business owners have always said we have the best location – in town and right on the water.'

'Worst neighbourhood in the city. Nowhere near the water, the university, or any other place people had regular reason to visit. The best nearby attraction was a laundromat that turned into an undercover gambling house at night.'

'Sounds lovely.' Paige shot me a look.

'It was awful. My parents never would've let me work there if they didn't know the owner – and if the tips weren't amazing. Which they were. Every single night.'

She reached into her shorts pocket and pulled out a worn cardboard square. 'This was the menu.'

'That looks like a coaster,' Paige said.

'It is a coaster, complete with beer and hot sauce stains.' Natalie turned it over, held it up. 'I carry it everywhere. I'm a little sentimental.'

'Monday, ribs,' I said, squinting to read the messy script. 'Tuesday, wings. Wednesday, chicken fingers.'

'Bar food?' Paige asked. 'And only one kind a day?'

'That's all they needed. The owner switched the days around every few months, but the dishes themselves didn't change once in the five years I was there.'

'That must've been really good bar food,' I said.

'It wasn't bad . . . but you could get as good, if not better, at a dozen other nicer places in town.'

'So, then, why was it so successful?' Paige took the coaster when Natalie handed it to her, examined it like the stains contained clues. 'What made people wait two hours to get in?'

Natalie paused. 'The entertainment.'

'Like a band?' Paige asked.

'Not exactly.'

Paige's eyebrows lowered, then lifted. 'Oh. No way. We're definitely not that kind of place. Grandma B might not be as involved as she once was, but this is still her restaurant. That kind of thing would give her a heart attack.'

It took Natalie a second to figure out exactly what kind of thing Paige was referring to. When she did, she laughed. 'If they'd had adult entertainment, my dad would've died of embarrassment a long time ago. And Will was so sweet, he'd –'

She stopped. Her hand lifted, her fingers brushed across the circular bump underneath her T-shirt.

'There's this popular café back home,' I offered quickly, 'where you can do karaoke twenty-four-seven. Does Mountaineers have something like that?'

Natalie's hand lowered as she continued. 'Not officially, though regulars do often break into song if they hang around long enough.'

'So the entertainment has nothing to do with music,' Paige said. 'What does that leave?'

Natalie grinned. 'Ice fishing.'

Paige looked at her. 'I don't get it.'

'There's this small community of serious ice fishermen in northern Vermont. As soon as the lakes freeze over each year, they're on them every day, carving holes, dropping poles, and seeing what comes up. It's a pretty isolated sport, so after spending countless hours alone, they head to Burlington to warm up and hang out.'

'Yeah . . .' Paige shook her head. 'Still not computing.'

'Eight years ago, when Mountaineers was lucky to get a dozen customers a day, this guy named Tuck Hallerton stopped by for a drink after a long day's fishing. It was so cold out, he didn't bother storing his catch in coolers; he simply filled his truck bed with snow and threw in the fish. When he went to the restaurant, he parked the truck on the side of the road, and what was inside got the attention of the few other patrons.'

'Because they'd never seen fish packed that way?' I asked.

'Because they'd never seen such *big* fish – especially not in the middle of winter.' Natalie looked behind her. Noting that her tables were still occupied, she turned back. 'The things were supposedly enormous – the size of sharks. That night, people asked Tuck where he'd caught them, and he said that was between him and the fish. Those dozen locals – mostly men – were so impressed, they told their friends, who told their friends. No one had ever heard of Tuck before, but they were so curious about this mysterious ice fisherman who caught things no one else could, they started coming every night to see if he'd be there with more monstrous creatures of the deep. And he did return every now and then, so they did, too.'

I caught Paige's eye. At the mention of monstrous

creatures of the deep, this conversation had to be venturing into dangerous waters for her, too.

'Fast-forward to today,' Paige said casually. 'How'd Tuck's truck of fish lead to so much business?'

'It got people talking. Soon, other ice fishermen started stopping by to see how their catches compared. Then more curious patrons came to check out the new guys' stock and do some comparing themselves. Now there are contests every night to see who's caught the biggest, strangest fish that day.' Natalie patted the stack of purple paper. 'Word of mouth is the best promotion any business can get . . . and I'm sorry to say that no one's going to be talking about Betty's pretty new menus.'

'Okay,' Paige said, 'but they *will* be talking about the food. They always have, and what we serve hasn't changed.'

'How about your clientele?' Natalie asked.

'It's smaller. Hence the menus and renovations and everything else.'

'Numbers aside.' Natalie nodded to an elderly couple at a nearby table. 'Are the people who come for brunch once the kind who'll come back again and again – with friends?'

Paige considered this as she watched the couple. 'Maybe.'

'What about the summer?' I asked. 'When the lakes

weren't frozen? What kept people coming back to Mountaineers then?'

'Its reputation.' Natalie stood. 'Because after a single winter, it had a good one. Even if people couldn't see how the place earned it, they still wanted to see where the crazy things they heard about happened. To be part of the experience in some small way.'

As she left to check on the couple, I looked at Paige. 'It sounds like the Bull and Finch Pub.'

'Where everyone knows your name?'

'Where everyone *knew* your name – until word got out that it inspired the bar in *Cheers*, that old TV show. Now it's a Boston tourist hot spot.'

'Without crazy fish.'

'But with the kind of reputation Natalie's talking about. The actors are never there, but people line up on the sidewalk anyway.'

Paige sighed. 'Betty's has a reputation. It's been here more than fifty years. It's been featured in countless travel magazines. People should already know about it and be coming to Winter Harbor just to try our famous soup.'

'But they're not,' I said gently.

'Maybe it's a slump. If we ride it out, maybe everything will eventually go back to normal.' Her voice was bright, but her frown deepened.

123

'You don't think it will?' I asked.

'It might. Crazier things have happened, as we know.' She tried to laugh. 'It's just . . . remember that hospitality-management training programme I was looking into? In San Francisco?'

I nodded. Before deciding to stick closer to home, she'd spent hours every night last semester poring over the website and course offerings.

'Well, I've been thinking about it and I'd really like to go –'

I gasped. 'That's great!'

'Yeah, it is. Thanks. But it's also really expensive. And between paying for Hawthorne last year, fixing up the house after Oliver wrecked it last fall, and pouring a boatload of money into these renovations, Grandma B's change purse is getting a little light. She keeps saying we can afford it, but if the rest of the summer is as slow as the past few weeks have been . . . we're in trouble.'

For a moment, my mind lingered on an image of Oliver in the basement of Betty and Paige's house, cutting out pictures and newspaper articles as a dozen sirens – myself included – lay submerged underwater in make-shift holding tanks. Under Raina's command, Oliver had chopped up furniture and torn up carpet to build the tanks. I hadn't been there since returning to Winter

Harbor, and according to Paige, I wouldn't recognise it the next time I went.

I blinked the image away. Then, anticipating a stress-induced energy zap, I reached for my coffee.

'So what do we do?' I asked, as I added a spoonful of sugar.

Paige swapped the coaster for a notebook. 'I guess we figure out how to entertain Winter Harbor.'

As she began brainstorming, I sipped the coffee – and made a note to compliment Natalie on her brewing skills. It was the perfect blend of bitter and salty, and tasted so good, I poured myself a second cup after finishing the first.

I was halfway through that cup before realising something wasn't right. I took another sip just to make sure, then picked up my spoon, dipped it in the glass bowl, and brought it to my lips.

The white powder wasn't sugar.

It was salt.

Heart racing and mouth drying, I leaned across the table. 'Paige, you didn't happen to mention anything to Natalie about –'

I stopped. Sat back.

'Mention anything to me about what?' Natalie asked, standing next to us.

I thought quickly. 'The ice maker. In the bar. The

lever sticks so you have to jiggle it to keep the bin from overflowing.'

'Good to know.' Natalie nodded towards the lobby. 'Vanessa, there's someone here for you.'

I looked past her. Not seeing anyone, I stood. 'Thanks. Be right back.'

As I started across the dining room, I checked my watch. It wasn't even eleven, which meant Simon and Caleb weren't on break yet. Had Simon left early? Because he couldn't wait to see me?

The thought made me so happy, I quickened my pace. When the hostess stand came into view, it occurred to me that Simon wasn't the only one who might want to make a surprise visit. There were the fishermen from last week. The trespassers from last night. They'd all followed me at some point, so could've followed me here.

It's the middle of the day, I told myself. *This is a public place. If they were going to make trouble, they wouldn't do it here, now.*

It was a logical argument. Still, my legs trembled so much by the time I reached the doorway I started to lean towards the wall for support –

– and was caught before my shoulder hit the wall.

Not by Simon. Or by one the fishermen or trespassers.

By my mother. Charlotte Bleu.

126

CHAPTER 10

'What are you doing here?'

She held my arm until I was upright and steady, then released me. 'I'm sorry for startling you. I actually wasn't sure you'd be working.'

But she knew I worked there sometimes. We hadn't spoken in months, so that meant someone else had filled her in . . . or that she'd been listening without my knowledge. This in mind, I struggled to silence my thoughts.

'Do you have a minute to talk?' she asked.

I turned and checked the dining room. Natalie had taken my seat, and she and Paige were deep in conversation.

'Yes,' I said. 'But not in here.'

She stepped aside to let me lead the way. Eager to get a real answer to the question I'd just asked, I hurried through the lobby, down the porch steps, and around the building. I assumed she was following close behind, but when I walked onto the dock and it didn't wobble a second time under her weight, I turned and saw that she was still several yards away.

My head was a shield and my thoughts an onslaught of arrows as I watched her approach. I hadn't seen her since the day after she'd saved Simon and me from Raina, Zara and the other sirens at the bottom of Lake Kantaka last fall. That was when she'd said that while she'd love to see me every single day and make up for seventeen years of lost time, the nature of our relationship was up to me. If I wanted to see her that often, I could. If I wanted some time apart to process and accept all that had just happened, that was fine. Or if I thought it was best that things went back to the way they were before I knew she existed and had accidentally found her working at a coffee shop in Boston, that was okay, too. She understood her presence would be another major adjustment for my family and me, and that I might want nothing more than to try to forget the other changes the past six months had brought. She'd be available if I needed her in the meantime, but otherwise, I could continue to live my life without her in it.

I went with the last option that day. Part of me had wanted to know everything about her, and in turn, me, but a bigger part had wanted to pretend we'd never met. I didn't know if I could handle any other truths. Plus, I could always change my mind. I'd come close a few times, too, like when I wasn't feeling well or didn't understand a particular reaction from a guy at school, but then I'd watch Mom, the woman who raised me, hug Dad. Or Dad kiss the tip of her nose. Or the two of them dance around the kitchen together. And I'd resist.

If I hadn't, Charlotte's appearance now might not be such a shock. I'd been too taken aback to get a good look in the restaurant lobby, but as she made her way towards the dock, there was no mistaking a change. Six months ago, she'd been tall, thin. Her blue-green eyes had shone. Her dark hair had been long and thick. Her fair skin had been smooth, without a single blemish or hint of a wrinkle. Not only had she looked great, she'd also moved that way; in the lake, she'd dived and swum effortlessly, like a young athlete in her prime.

The woman nearing me now walked with a slight limp, her upper back rounded. Her eyes were still bright, but her lids hung lower. Her skin was soft and fell against itself in gentle folds. Her hair was short, and the white strands far outnumbered the brown ones. She wore dark jeans, a long cashmere sweater, and silver leather sandals, so she was still more stylish than almost every woman in Winter Harbor . . . but given what the clothes couldn't hide, she also looked like she'd raided her daughter's wardrobe.

Her daughter. I didn't know if I'd ever get used to the fact that was me.

'I know what you're thinking,' she said.

I held out one hand when she started to step onto the dock. Hers shook as she took it.

'Of course you do,' I said.

She smiled, and for a second, her entire face lifted. 'Not like that. I promised I wouldn't listen and I haven't.'

I tried to return her smile but couldn't help wondering if that were true.

Now on the dock next to me, she squeezed my hand and released it. 'You're thinking you didn't call. You didn't reach out to me, yet here I am, going back on our agreement. I don't have to hear it – I see it. On every inch of your face.'

'I'm just surprised,' I said, grateful that was all she suspected. 'But I'm still happy to see you. It's been a long time.'

She looked away, started walking down the dock. 'Indeed it has.'

I looked back at the restaurant as I followed her. The car park was still nearly empty. Two employees sat out on the break-area deck, but they talked to each other and paid no attention to us.

'How are you?' she asked.

I considered my response. If she hadn't been listening, she wasn't fishing for a particular answer. 'Fine. Good. Busy, but good.'

'It must've been quite a year. Last semester of high school, graduation, applying to colleges.'

'College,' I corrected. 'Just one. Dartmouth.'

'Where Justine was going to go.'

I paused. She didn't know the truth – that Justine had only pretended to apply and feigned acceptance in anticipation of running away with Caleb. Apparently, Dad had left out some details in his recent e-mails.

'Right,' I said, since that was easier than clarifying. 'And I got in. I leave at the end of August.'

She started to put one arm around me, then seemed to think better of it and clasped her hands behind her back instead.

'That's wonderful,' she said. 'Congratulations.'

'Thank you.'

We reached the end of the dock and looked out across the harbour. Like the car park, it was nearly empty. Last summer, it had been filled with powerboats, sailing boats, jet skis, kayaks, canoes – basically, anything that floated. This summer, it was mainly a fishing-boat thoroughfare, and that traffic wouldn't resume until the fishermen returned late this afternoon.

'How are you feeling?' she asked quietly.

Tired. Weak. Thirsty. Even more than usual, for longer periods of time.

'Great. Our new house practically sits in the ocean,

which helps.' I shifted my eyes towards her without moving my head. 'I'm sure Dad told you we moved.'

'I'm sure he would've, if we were still in touch. But since we're not, no, he didn't.'

Her eyes met mine. I looked away. Their communication had also been part of our deal. They'd been in regular contact since she'd asked him to care for me, but had stopped writing after our official introduction. And since I could offer her updates myself, we'd agreed there was no longer reason for them to be in touch. Especially since it must've killed Mom to learn that Dad had been harbouring a secret pen pal – and not any secret pen pal – for so many years.

'How are *you* feeling?' I asked, a moment later. I wasn't simply trying to deflect; I genuinely wanted to know.

A cool breeze blew across the water. As she tightened her sweater around her torso, I could make out the outline of her ribs.

'Vanessa,' she said, her voice soft yet serious, 'I don't plan to stay long.'

I turned towards her. 'But you just got here.'

She probably heard the disappointment in my voice, too, because her head tilted to one side as she looked at me. 'I only stopped in Winter Harbor on my way to Montreal. There are some people there I need to see –'

'Nenuphar people?' According to Charlotte, the Nenuphars were a group of very successful sirens who'd grown so powerful over the years they'd developed abilities other sirens lacked. We were their descendants, which was the main reason Dad had been unable to resist her draw, despite being completely in love with Mom.

'Yes,' Charlotte said. 'I have some matters to attend to with several relatives.'

'I thought you stopped talking to them years ago. When you left there and moved here.'

'I did. But just like it was time to see you, it's time to see them.'

'Even though they've killed more men than any other group of sirens in the world? Which was why you left in the first place?' Realising immediately how I sounded – judgemental – I looked away.

'Yes,' she said. 'Even though.'

I nodded, unsure of how to feel about this. Despite being related, we were practically strangers, so it really wasn't any of my business. On the other hand, Charlotte had taken a life herself last fall; it was the first time she'd participated in the type of behaviour she'd left home to escape, decades earlier, and she did so only to gain the energy needed to help defeat Raina and the other Winter Harbor sirens. She'd said afterward that she'd felt even worse than she imagined she would and vowed never to take another victim.

So what business could she possibly have now with the most dangerous sirens in the world?

'Anyway,' she continued, 'I wasn't certain I'd stop here until I was about to pass your exit on the highway, which was why I didn't contact you ahead of time. But I don't know . . .' Her gaze fell to the dock as her voice trailed off. A second later, she raised her head and tried again. 'I don't know how long I'll be gone. So I wanted to at least say hello and see if you needed anything before you couldn't reach me any more.'

'What about your cell phone?' I asked. That was the only number I had for her. 'Won't you have it with you?'

'I'm only meeting my cousin in Montreal. After that, I'll be travelling through some very remote regions of the country. Cell service will be unpredictable at best.'

'But –'

'Vanessa!'

I spun around, bringing one hand to my forehead to shield my eyes from the sun.

'Is that Simon?' Charlotte asked.

My heart leapt to my throat as I realised it was. He stood at the edge of the car park, facing the water. The Subaru, with Caleb inside, was behind him.

'You're still together. I had a feeling you would be.'

'Actually, we're not.' I waved, held up one finger to let him know I needed a minute. 'He broke up with me in October, after . . .'

This time, my voice trailed off. I didn't have to explain.

'Trust me,' she said, sounding a combination of pleased and disappointed, 'you might be broken up . . . but you're still very much together.'

I turned back. She gave me a small smile.

'Go. Say hello.'

'It's okay, I can – '

'Vanessa.' She touched my arm. 'I'll be here when you're done.'

I didn't move as she lowered herself to the edge of the dock, rolled up her jeans, and removed her sandals. I waited until she dipped her bare legs into the water, as if the salt would lock them in place until my return, and then finally started down the dock. While I hurried towards Simon, I tried to sort out my feelings. Charlotte lived in Boston. Back home I could see her every day if I wanted to, but I hadn't. And now that she wouldn't be so accessible, I suddenly wished I'd taken advantage of the opportunity.

For better or worse, those mixed emotions gave way to only one as I neared Simon.

Happiness.

'Hey,' he said.

'Hi.' I stopped two feet away, wanting to hug him, but not sure I should.

'I'm sorry, I hope I didn't interrupt . . . ?'

'You didn't,' I said quickly. 'But for future reference, please feel free to anytime, anyplace.'

'Noted.' He nodded towards the dock. 'Is that Betty?'

I glanced behind me. I couldn't say it was, because Simon knew Betty and might want to say hello. I was tempted to say she was a friend of my parents, or even a potential Chowder House hire, because I didn't want to remind him of everything I wished we could both forget . . . but I couldn't do this, either. If Simon and I had any chance of moving forward, we had to do so the right way. And that meant being honest, no matter how uncomfortable it might be.

'It's Charlotte,' I said, turning back. 'She's on her way to Canada and stopped by to say hello.'

'Oh.' His face tensed for a moment, then relaxed. 'I won't keep you, I promise . . . I just wanted to make sure you'd made it here okay.'

My chest warmed. 'I did.'

'Anything out of the ordinary?'

'No, not that I could tell.'

'Good.' He stepped towards me, lowered his voice. 'There's something else.'

My eyes fell to his lips, only inches away from mine.

'Would you like to have dinner tonight?'

I looked up. Smiled. 'I'd love to.'

'Great. What about Paige?'

I paused. 'What about her?'

'Do you think she can come, too? Because, based on last night, these people are obviously willing to take some risks to find out what they want. The more brainpower we have to figure out who they are and why they're here, the better.'

Three thoughts immediately came to mind. The first was that, based on what I'd overheard at the open house, I had a pretty good idea why trespassers were watching us last night. The second was that I didn't want Simon to know that, because I didn't want him to worry. They were probably curious thrill seekers who'd picked up on an Internet rumour and meant no harm, but I knew that was enough to call Simon to action.

The third was that he was already worried. Just like always.

'I'll ask,' I said.

'Great.' He exhaled, stepped away. 'We have to get back to the marina, but how's seven? Murph's Grill?'

I nodded. He gave me a small smile before turning and jogging to the car.

As I headed for the dock, I thought about how this

wasn't the way the summer was supposed to go. I knew there was no denying who I was, regardless of how much I often wanted to . . . but if it continued to be the focus of any time Simon and I spent together, would we ever really be able to move forward? And at the very least, have a normal friendship – or the closest thing to normal we could get?

The thought was so upsetting, by the time my feet hit the dock, I could barely feel them. My mouth was dry and my throat burned. When my torso started to sway to one side, I quickened my pace and half-ran, half-stumbled the remaining distance.

At the edge of the dock, I sat down, yanked up my pant legs, and dropped my legs into the harbour. Relief didn't come fast enough, so I leaned forward and splashed water on my arms and face. It was a solid minute before I felt strong enough to sit upright without instantly falling forward again.

At which point, Charlotte, who was still there as promised, finally spoke. Her voice was soft, serious.

'So, Vanessa . . . is there anything you need from me?'

'Yes.' I took a deep breath and slowly released it. 'I need you to stay a little longer. Please.'

CHAPTER II

'I've been single two hundred and forty-two days, nine hours, and three minutes,' Paige said.

'And?' I asked.

'And I don't know if that's enough time. To heal and be ready to date again.'

I parked the Jeep and turned to her. 'First of all, you broke up with Riley, not the other way around, so I'm pretty sure you've fully recovered from that heartbreak.'

'That was a lot harder than you'd think. I'd never broken up with anyone before and I didn't even really want to break up with him. I only did it because I felt like I had to.'

'I understand.' And I did. After Paige transformed into a siren to help stop Raina for good last fall, she'd wanted to become familiar with her new abilities without influencing someone she genuinely cared about, so she'd ended her relationship with Riley, Simon's friend and roommate at Bates. 'But before tonight, you hadn't so much as mentioned his name in about two hundred and forty days.'

'Maybe that's because it was too upsetting.'

'Or maybe it was because you were too distracted by the dozens of cute preppies suddenly vying for your attention.'

'Well.' She shrugged. 'Warding them off *was* pretty time-consuming.'

'And second of all,' I continued, giving her a quick grin, 'this isn't a date.'

'Right. It's a double date.'

'It's a meeting.'

'With food, drinks . . . and a pretty new outfit I've never seen before.'

I glanced down at the turquoise skirt I'd bought on my break that afternoon. 'I was just doing my part. To support local business.'

She patted my knee. 'How very civic-minded of you.'

I looked at her. 'Is it too much? Maybe I should run home and change. Because this really isn't a date and I don't want Simon to think I'm trying to turn it into one. That's the last thing I need.'

'Are you kidding? You love this guy. You need to take advantage of every opportunity you have to remind him that he feels the same way about you. Trust me, we could be meeting at a gas station and that –' she motioned to my ruffled tank, my denim jacket, my beaded necklace – 'still wouldn't be too much.'

Her hand was still on my knee; I squeezed it. 'Thanks.'

'Anytime. Now let's go do our part for Winter Harbor's favourite grease pit.'

As we hopped out of the Jeep and crossed the street, I wondered, not for the first time that day, why Simon had chosen it for our meeting place. If we were going to be talking about things we didn't want anyone else to hear, wouldn't somewhere a bit more private, like one of our houses, have made more sense?

The reason didn't become any clearer as we entered the restaurant. Because it was packed. Every table and bar stool was taken.

'I don't get it!' Paige declared, over the din of classic rock, conversation, and laughter. 'Do their burgers come with cash instead of fries?'

'Evening!' A heavyset man holding a half-empty beer stein turned away from the pool game he was watching, and towards us. 'Buy you ladies a drink?'

'No, thanks!' I hooked one arm through Paige's and tugged her through the crowd.

'Need a seat?' another guy shouted from the bar. 'I've got two!'

Paige cringed. 'He just patted his legs!'

I pulled harder.

'Wrong way!' a third called out from a group of

twenty-somethings gathered around a bar-footy table. 'We're over here!'

A dozen similar comments fired at us like bullets as we made our way to the back of the restaurant. The guys who were either too drunk or not drunk enough to speak up as we passed gave us slow, appreciative once-overs as they sipped their drinks. Even the ones wearing wedding rings stopped talking to check us out. This kind of attention wasn't unfamiliar – but receiving so much of it at once was. As I did my best to avoid eye contact, I found myself wishing I'd gone with jeans and a fleece instead of my pretty new outfit.

'Vanessa!'

That voice was familiar. Slowing slightly, I spotted Colin across the crowd. He was sitting in a booth with three girls – the only other girls present besides Paige and me.

'Come join us! We'll make room!'

As he waved and slid down the bench seat, the crowd shifted, giving me a better view of his company. I'd never seen two of the girls, but I definitely recognised the third.

'Natalie!' Paige called out, tugging my arm. 'Let's say hi!'

As she started to head towards them, my chest tightened slightly. Paige had seemed eager to embrace

Natalie's new friendship, but I wasn't totally sold yet. Between the strange feeling I got when we'd first met, the salty coffee she'd served, and something else I couldn't quite put my finger on, I thought it best to be cautious.

That was one reason why I didn't want to say hi right then. The other was that I didn't want to keep *our* company waiting – or have to explain later if Colin seemed even more excited to see me than might be expected. So when Paige tugged harder, I stood my ground. She glanced back at me and I nodded to the pub's second room.

It was smaller but equally packed. And Simon and Caleb sat at a tiny table in the corner.

Paige gave me a thumbs-up, then turned towards Natalie and held one hand to her ear like a phone receiver, telling her she'd call later. I waved to Colin as Natalie leaned towards him and spoke by his ear. Something crossed his face, but the crowd pushed us along before I could decide what it was.

'Is that a laptop?' Paige asked, as we neared Simon and Caleb.

Reaching the room, which was a designated eating area and noticeably quieter than the bar section, I saw that it was indeed a laptop. It sat on the table between Simon and Caleb and was surrounded by notebooks, pens, and index cards, like we were meeting at the library.

'My mistake,' she said, near my ear. 'A computer does not a date make.'

Maybe not, but that didn't make me any less happy to see Simon. He stood, pulled out the chair next to his, and waited until I was wedged in the narrow space between it and the table before sitting. Caleb did the same for Paige.

'Thank you.' She smiled. 'It's nice to know some mothers are still teaching their sons manners.'

'I'm so sorry,' Simon said. 'We had no idea it'd be this crowded.'

'We had no idea there were even this many people still in town,' Caleb added.

'Which is why no apology's necessary,' Paige said. 'It's actually nice to see. How have things been at the marina?'

I couldn't tell whether she intentionally directed this question at Caleb (knowing her, she probably did), but he launched into a lengthy update about his boss, Captain Monty, and the marina's current state of affairs. Too aware of Simon sitting inches away, I was only half-listening to the exchange, when he leaned even closer and apologised again.

'It's really okay,' I assured. 'But why didn't we meet at one of our houses?'

'I thought it'd be best to avoid the parents. My mom would've been so happy to see you she wouldn't have let you leave the kitchen without sharing a pot of tea with her first. And I wasn't sure, but I thought your parents might've been just as happy to see Caleb and me.'

'Absolutely. And even if we managed to somehow escape the endless questions about school and family, they would've found a million reasons to interrupt us – hot chocolate, snacks, more hot chocolate.' Feeling strangely shy, I gave him a small smile. 'You made the right call.'

His lips turned up as his eyes lowered briefly to my necklace, then rose back to mine. 'You look really nice, by the way.'

My cheeks warmed. 'Thanks. So do you.'

I'd decided to try not to overanalyse every word and gesture in hopes of figuring out what Simon was really thinking and feeling, but I couldn't help noticing that he'd shaved off his scruff and gotten a haircut. And that he wore khakis instead of jeans and a brown cotton sweater instead of his usual T-shirt. Unlike our impromptu visit at the lake house, he'd known about this one in advance . . . so maybe he'd put extra effort into his appearance? The way I had for him?

'Hi, there.' A waitress stood behind us. 'What can I get you?'

I picked up the menu as Paige elbowed me in the side. When I looked at her, her chin lifted towards the waitress. I didn't know what she wanted me to see – that the waitress wore a mask of make-up? And a shirt so tight, it rose up her abdomen? Or that even though she seemed to be the only employee assigned to the back room, she was completely at ease, like she'd been so a million times before?

'*Carla*,' Paige hissed, after we'd ordered.

'Who?' I asked.

'The newbie waitress I hired, who quit after Louis made her cry.' The words flew from Paige's mouth. 'That was her.'

'No way.' I swivelled in my seat for another look.

'I'm sure of it. She's wearing a silver bangle bracelet engraved with her initials and flowers, the same one Carla wore every day when she worked at Betty's.' Paige shook her head. 'Did you see how she took our order without writing it down? That's the mark of a seasoned professional, yet a few weeks ago, she couldn't hold a pencil and pad at the same time without dropping one of them.'

'You taught her well.'

'I'm good,' Paige said, 'but I'm no miracle worker.'

Carla disappeared into the crowd in the other room. I turned back to find Simon's laptop open and facing Paige and me.

'My digital-camera cord was compatible with the camera you guys found,' Caleb said. 'We downloaded the pictures to see if we were missing anything.'

He clicked slowly through the shots, each of which took up the entire computer screen. I searched for clues as to whom the camera belonged to, but the bigger images didn't reveal anything the smaller ones on the camera screen hadn't.

'They still look like ordinary tourist shots to me,' I said.

'Me, too,' Simon said, with a sigh.

'Not quite,' Paige said.

We looked at her, then back at the screen.

'What do you mean?' Simon asked.

She pointed to the track pad. 'May I?'

He slid the computer across the table. She scrolled back to the beginning of the slide show.

'A few of these could pass as tourist pictures – the lighthouse, the wide shot of the ocean, even the rickety dock jutting out into the harbour. But if this camera really belonged to a random visitor, it'd also have pictures of the sailing-boat-shaped "Welcome to Winter Harbor" sign, the ten-foot-tall inflated lobster waving

147

outside Harbor Sports Rentals, the bronze fishing captain at the end of the wharf. I've spent enough time talking to tourists at Betty's to know what they're always most excited to see.'

'That lobster does get a lot of attention,' Caleb admitted.

'Plus, where are all the people?' Paige asked. 'Tourists love taking pictures of whoever they're travelling with. Mostly so they can laugh at each other when they relive the memories later on.'

I thought of the old, fat photo albums lining one of the glass shelves in the beach-house living room. My family and I hadn't been tourists in a long time, and we still had countless pictures of one another standing and smiling by the exact spots Paige had just listed.

'But this is what really makes me think something else is up.' She stopped on an image of boulder. 'It's a gigantic rock. On the beach. A lifelong landlubber might want to document such a sight, but if he did, he'd try to get as much of it as possible so everyone back home could see how big it really was. A nature photographer might be into it, too, but he'd probably balance it better against the surroundings. This shot's of the top of the rock with a sliver of sand and water behind it. What's the point?'

She was right. And the boulder was the first of several similar shots. Some were of smaller, rounded rocks, like the kind that blanket the local shoreline. Others were of granite slabs. Still others were of red and grey pebbles that could've filled a driveway. And then there were the other close-ups, of logs and driftwood and beach grass.

'Wait.' I put one hand on Paige's to keep her from clicking forward. 'That looks familiar.'

'Really?' she asked, studying the image. 'It looks like more random cropped rocks to me.'

I pulled the computer close, squinted. 'I think I've been there.' I glanced at Paige. 'That doesn't look like anywhere you've visited before?'

'It looks like everywhere I've visited. That's the problem.'

I shifted the computer so Simon and Caleb had a better view. 'What do you think?'

Caleb shook his head. 'I'm with Paige.'

I watched Simon examine the image, hoping for a flash of recognition to cross his face. It didn't, but something else did: a mixture of excitement and seriousness. I'd seen the look before, like last summer, when, with the help of an old science teacher, he'd figured out how to freeze Winter Harbor for the very first time. Seeing it now made me hopeful – and nervous.

Simon slid his thumb across the track pad. The cursor flew across the rocks and landed at the top of the screen.

The next series of clicks happened so quickly, I couldn't keep track of which files and folders it opened.

Seconds later, the image of the rocks was replaced by a map.

Of Camp Heroine.

'Isn't that where . . . ?' Paige's voice faded. 'Didn't you guys . . . ?'

'Yes.' I swallowed as Simon zoomed in closer. 'We did.'

'Tom Connelly,' Simon said quietly. 'That's where we found his body the day of that sudden storm, when we were looking for Caleb.'

'Are you sure?' Paige asked.

'The camera's equipped with GPS,' Simon explained. 'It records the longitude and latitude of every picture. The scenery looked familiar, but using those numbers, I was able to pinpoint exactly where this one was taken.'

'And that's why it looks familiar to you?' Paige asked me.

I nodded, unable to take my eyes off the red dot on the digital park map. It had been nearly a year, and I could still see every part of him as clearly as if he'd washed ashore yesterday. His bloated torso, the Rolex tight around his swollen wrist . . . the smile frozen across his face.

'I don't get it,' Caleb said, a moment later. 'Whoever

was at your house last night was there to see *you*, Vanessa. We all know your involvement with everything that happened last summer, but the general public doesn't. Even when you and Simon found that body at Camp Heroine, you stayed in the car while Simon talked to the police on the beach. They never knew you were there.' He stopped, took a deep breath. 'Besides Justine, there's no way to connect you to the rest.'

'And since all the other victims were men, most people no longer associate her with them,' Simon added gently.

I looked at Paige. She nodded.

'They know.' I hated the words as soon as I said them and chose my next ones carefully. 'About who was responsible. I don't know how, but I overheard people talking about them . . . us . . . at the lake house's last showing. Based on this picture, I assume those people are the same ones who showed up last night.'

This was met with a long pause.

'They actually said the word?' Caleb asked. 'The one that, until last summer, we'd only read in books?'

We all knew the word he referred to but couldn't say aloud. The one I still had a hard time saying aloud, even when I wasn't surrounded by an entire restaurant of potential eavesdroppers.

Siren.

'Yes,' I said.

'Did you see who said it?' Caleb asked.

I shook my head, then sneaked a peek at Simon, who was staring at the computer screen. 'I didn't have a chance.'

This was followed by more silence. I wasn't sure if they were processing, waiting for me to offer more information, or both. I was beginning to wish I hadn't said anything when Caleb spoke again.

'We should check the other pictures.'

Simon focused on the rock image for another second, then nodded and began entering numbers and mapping co-ordinates. The rest of us watched without speaking as each familiar location appeared. Three pictures in, Caleb opened a notebook and started writing.

Finally, just when I'd finished off the table's water pitcher and felt my throat start to close again, Simon reached the slide show's last photo.

'Wow,' Paige said.

I agreed, though I couldn't speak. Not only did my mouth feel like it was stuffed with cotton, I was instantly paralysed by the image of Simon and me. It was the picture that had interrupted us last night, and though I'd seen it on the small camera screen, it looked completely different now. Because it was blown up, I could see just how tightly Simon's arms held my waist. And how deeply my fingertips dug into his neck. And the way our bodies pressed together, like we were strapped together and about to jump out of a plane twenty thousand feet in the air.

'I'm surprised you even noticed the flash,' Paige joked.

I reached across the table and closed the laptop.

'So what does this mean?' I managed.

'It means', Simon said quietly, 'that these people are serious. They've done their research.'

'But they could still be anyone, right?' Paige asked. 'The *Herald* covered the drownings pretty thoroughly last year. They probably just read the back issues online.'

'The *Herald* gave general locations,' Caleb said. 'The lighthouse, the pier. It never said anything about second rock to the left, or rotting piece of driftwood closest to the lifeguard stand.'

'But that's impossible. Besides the police and other emergency responders, the only people who knew exactly where the bodies were found were . . .' Paige shook her head, stopped herself. A second later, she shoved back her chair and jumped up. 'I'm going to check on our order.'

As she disappeared into the crowd, Caleb stood, too.

'I'm going to check on our Paige,' he said.

And then it was just Simon and me, alone the way I'd

hoped we would be when he'd first asked me to dinner. Only instead of talking and laughing and reconnecting, I was gripping my empty water glass with both hands and he was slowly shredding his paper napkin.

'Why didn't you say anything?' he finally asked.

'I didn't want you to worry.'

'I was already worried.'

'I know, but . . .' I exhaled, looked at him. 'I didn't want to do this.'

His eyes lifted to mine. 'What?'

'Focus on who – what – I am. And let it get in the way again.'

'Vanessa, even without these pictures and what you overheard . . . you'd still be you. We'd still have to deal with it.'

It. Like who I was was a problem. A disease. Something irritating and bothersome for which there was no known solution or cure.

'You're right,' I said. 'Of course you're right, but –'

I was stopped by a sudden, familiar sound coming from the next room. Simon looked up, his face tense, and I knew he heard it, too. One by one, nearby diners stopped talking and listened.

To Paige.

Who was in the next room . . . singing.

CHAPTER 12

WHAT WAS THAT??

WHAT WAS WHAT?

PAIGE. COME ON.

IT WAS REO SPEEDWAGON. HOW COULD I
RESIST?

BY TAKING ONE LOOK AT ANY OF THE FACES
STARING BACK AT YOU. THAT'S HOW.

I leaned against the Jeep and waited. When the cell
phone screen remained dark, I sent another text.

YOU KNOW WHAT OUR VOICES DO TO THEM.
WHY MESS AROUND?

Still nothing. I wanted to call and ask her these questions directly, since I was certain she knew better. If

nothing else, she knew that Raina, Zara and the other sirens had sung in order to lure their male targets to the harbour floor during the Northern Lights Festival last year. So why be so careless with her power?

Unfortunately, the call would have to wait. She was with Simon and Caleb, who were driving her home, since she lived closer to them than she did to me. And they'd only just left after following me all the way to my driveway to make sure no one else did, so she wouldn't be able to talk for at least another twenty minutes.

CALL ME WHEN YOU CAN. XO, V

I hit send and headed for the house. Fortunately, Murph's Grill didn't skimp on the salt when it came to their food; if they did, I wouldn't have made it through dinner without falling face-first into my fries. We'd even changed the subject from murders and stalkers after Paige returned to the table, since that was presumably why she'd left in the first place, and I'd still felt my throat closing and my skin tightening like I was lying on the beach, baking in the sun. If Simon hadn't been driving ten feet behind me, I would've broken speed limits and blown past stop signs all the way through town to get home as fast as possible.

Because I wanted to swim. I *needed* to swim.

'I'm home!' I closed the front door, dropped my bag on the floor, kicked off my sandals. 'I'll come say hi in a second. Just need to take a quick dip first!'

I started for the hallway leading to my room – and stopped when my eyes caught the reflection in the windows to my left.

It was the kitchen doorway. Through which I could see the table . . . and who was sitting at it. The view didn't change when I turned around and looked at the actual doorway.

I crossed the room, noting various items as they came closer. Three coffee cups. A half-eaten cheesecake. An overnight bag. Slippers.

'I didn't know we were having a pyjama party,' I said, entering the kitchen.

Mom's spoon, with which she'd been stirring her drink, froze. Dad choked on the coffee he'd sipped.

Charlotte smiled.

'Hello, Vanessa.'

'Hi.' I looked from her to my parents, who were doing their best to recover. 'What's going on?'

'We were just having some dessert.' Mom jumped up, squeezed my arm as she passed me to get to the cabinets. 'Sit. I'll get you a plate.'

'That's okay. I'm not hungry.' I stood next to the counter. Waited.

'How was the fabulous foursome?' Dad asked finally, then turned to Charlotte and spoke like I wasn't there. 'Vanessa met up with some friends for dinner. Paige, the sweet girl she met last summer, actually spent the school year with us in Boston. And the Carmichael boys –'

'She knows who they are.'

Dad's mouth snapped closed. Behind me, Mom dropped a fork. The utensil clattered against the tile floor.

'What's going on?' I asked.

'Charlotte was just passing through town.' Mom's voice was pleasant, like my biological mother was a distant cousin she didn't know well but was still happy to see.

'I know. But what is she doing here? In our house?'

I looked at Charlotte as I asked this. She opened her mouth to explain, but Mom beat her to it.

'We bumped into each other at the market. When Charlotte mentioned she was staying at the Lighthouse for a few days, I invited her to stay here instead.'

'And she accepted?' This, too, I aimed at Charlotte.

'Yes.' Mom's voice was soft near my ear. 'It's okay, sweetie. Really.'

I wanted to believe her, but it was difficult. They'd only met once, the day the sirens had dragged Simon and me to the bottom of the lake. Given what had happened between Charlotte and Dad, how could Mom play hostess like nothing was weird or wrong? Was it because she thought I'd want Charlotte as close as possible? Even though she thought I hadn't seen her since the day at the lake?

'Your father was just telling me about your private beach,' Charlotte said. 'I'd love to see it.'

'I'm sure Vanessa would love to show it to you,' Mom said.

The dull ache that had lingered in my chest since dinner suddenly sharpened. I hadn't lied earlier – I really had been happy to see Charlotte. That was one of the reasons I'd asked her to extend her stay. But between the two, my allegiance to the woman who raised me trumped my allegiance to the one who'd caused her so much pain. It always would.

Which was why I said, 'Sure. How about right now?'

'I don't know.' Dad glanced at the windows facing the water. 'It's late, and dark. Why not wait till morning?'

'Because', Charlotte said, sliding back her chair, 'I think Vanessa and I have both waited long enough.'

I wasn't sure what she meant by this, but it stopped Dad from protesting further. He looked down and poked at his cheesecake as she stood. Her legs quivered briefly and she gripped the side of the table for balance. I almost expected him to leap up and throw one arm around her for support, and was relieved when he offered to help Mom clean up the kitchen instead.

And Charlotte was fine. She still moved with the speed of an arthritic woman twice her age, but she was more than physically able to walk from the kitchen to the back door without assistance.

The stone staircase leading to the beach, however, was another story.

'Go ahead,' she said, stopping on the top step.

I stood on the step below hers and held out one hand. 'They look steeper than they are. We'll just go slowly.'

She shook her head. 'You need to swim – I can smell the salt evaporating from your skin. I'll be down there by the time you're done.'

'Don't you want to swim, too? Won't you feel better? Less tired?'

'I might wade a bit and if I do, I'll be fine. I promise.' She tilted her head. 'Please, Vanessa. Go.'

The longer we stood there, the heavier my body seemed to weigh. I was torn between listening to her and insisting on helping her down the steps, but if I stayed a few seconds more, we'd probably both be stuck.

'Okay,' I relented. 'I won't be long.'

I jogged down the steps, looking back twice to make sure she was okay. She hadn't moved the first time, but by the second, she'd made it to the next step. Reassured,

I ran the rest of the way to the beach. I considered running up the other side of the lawn by my bedroom so I could change into my swimming costume, but then decided I didn't have the strength. Instead, I waited until I was hidden from view by rocks before shedding my skirt, jacket and sweater. Then, wearing only my underwear and tank top, I dived into the ocean.

I had to be more stressed than I realised because it took longer than usual to feel the familiar rush of energy flow from my fingers to my toes. Thinking about that only made me worry even more, which made it take longer. Hoping to quicken the process by infusing my body from the inside as well as the outside, I opened my mouth and drank while I swam.

Several minutes later, my feet hit sand and my head broke the water's surface. Moonlight shimmered against my bare legs as I pushed through the surf, and without meaning to, I thought of Simon. Feeling instantly guilty, like an uncontrollable part of me wanted to convince him to be with me by any means necessary, I focused on the beach – and Charlotte.

She'd made it down as promised and sat in the sand, letting the foamy runoff curl around her outstretched legs. She looked away as I crossed the beach, allowing me time to pull on my skirt and jacket, and waited until I sat beside her before speaking.

'I'm very sorry for startling you again. I had no intention of showing up unannounced, but when Jacqueline … your mother … and I got to talking, she insisted I stay here.'

Her voice was uncertain as she said my mother's name and corrected herself, and for a second, I was compelled to try to explain the difference between them and ease her worries. But then a cool rush of water flowed across my feet and the urge passed.

'I know,' I said. 'She's been on a mission to be as accommodating of my condition as possible. That apparently includes giving me round-the-clock access to you.'

'This all must be very difficult for her.'

'Probably a million times more than she lets on.'

'I'd be happy to invent a reason to leave and stay at the inn, if you think she'd be more comfortable.'

I considered this. 'Thank you for offering … but now that you're here, she'd probably feel even worse if you left.'

'Because she'd feel she was depriving you?'

'Exactly.'

She nodded thoughtfully. A moment later, my cell phone rang. I pulled it from the pocket of my skirt to see Paige's name flashing across the screen.

'I'll call her back,' I said, before Charlotte could say it

was okay to answer. Now wasn't the time to talk about what had happened at Murph's. I started to replace the phone as it beeped with a new text message.

V, JUST TRIED CALLING. TOTALLY BEAT, GOING TO BED. TALK TOMORROW??

In the next instant, another text popped up.

BTW, S? 100% SMITTEN. YOU GUYS ARE SO GET-TING BACK TOGETHER!!

My heart raced as I typed.

APPRECIATE THE CONFIDENCE, AS ALWAYS. TALK ABOUT EVERYTHING TOMORROW. SLEEP WELL.

'That must be nice,' Charlotte said. 'To have a friend you want to talk to ten minutes after seeing her.'
I smiled. 'It is.'
'Were you and Justine that close?'
The question caught me off guard, but I managed to answer. 'Closer.' Which was hard to imagine, since Paige and I, in many ways, had more in common now than my

sister and I ever had . . . but still true. 'Can I ask you a question?'

'Of course.' She sounded pleased.

I looked at her. 'It's personal.'

'I don't mind.'

I formed the question carefully. 'Were you ever in a relationship? Like, a real relationship? With someone you didn't . . .'

'Use my powers on?'

I exhaled. 'Yes.'

'No.'

My heart sank. 'Oh.'

She slowly brought her knees to her chest and folded her arms on top of them. 'I was only thirteen when I transformed. That was too young, unfortunately, to have loved and be loved – genuinely – in return.'

'But what about after? You never had a boyfriend?' The word sounded so silly, especially when compared to what Simon and I had had, but it was the only one I could think of.

'Not in the ordinary sense, no. A siren's life – particularly a non-practising siren's life – can be quite lonely.'

I glanced up at the house. Seeing the kitchen dark and TV light flickering in the living room, I continued. 'But what about Dad? Didn't you have feelings for him?'

'I did. Strong ones. Your father was and still is a wonderful man.'

'So if circumstances had been different, if you'd met him while he was still single . . . do you think you would've had something more together?'

Her eyes shifted from the horizon and locked on mine. 'I think I would've tried my hardest to make that happen.'

'By doing what?'

She didn't answer right away and I was worried she wouldn't – that despite her claim that she wanted to answer whatever questions I had, there was still a line. And I'd just crossed it. But then she faced the water and said:

'By convincing him I was someone else.'

My head spun with a dozen new questions. Like *how*? Why? Who would she have been instead? Would it have worked? But she spoke again before I could decide which to ask.

'I'm assuming what you're really asking is how you and Simon can move past what happened last summer and have the kind of relationship other young adults get to have. Is that correct?'

It was only one word, but it was hard to get out. 'Yes.'

A large wave crashed onshore. The runoff was so strong, Charlotte tilted back as it wrapped around her. She waited for the water to retreat, and then continued.

'Vanessa, if we weren't so closely linked, my answer would be simple: you can't.'

'But –'

'You love him. And he still loves you despite everything.'

'The first part, yes. I'm not sure about the second.'

She reached one arm to the side without turning towards me, and placed her hand on my knee. 'I am.'

That made two people. She and Paige seemed so certain they'd probably start booking florists and DJs soon.

'It should be enough, right? That real, intense, undying feeling for one another? Because your love is stronger than anything else, it should be able to overcome every obstacle.'

It was exactly what I was hoping for, but I was aware of how naïve it sounded as she said it.

'But it's not enough,' Charlotte said.

'How do you know? If you've never experienced it yourself?' I inhaled, clamped one hand over my mouth. 'I'm sorry. That was a terrible thing to say.'

'Don't apologise. It's a good question.' She brought her knees closer to her chest. 'Unfortunately, I know because I've seen it happen with countless others. Just as an ordinary woman thinks true love can conquer all, a siren thinks the same thing – until she learns otherwise.

Though a relationship might start out well, it simply can't survive the challenges she eventually faces.'

'You mean the thirst? The weakness? The constant need to swim?' I shook my head. 'Simon would be okay with all of that. He'd even want to protect me, to take care of me.' I was surer of this than I was that he still wanted to be with me.

Her eyes found mine. 'That's wonderful . . . but it's not enough, either.'

'But –'

'That's not all, Vanessa.' Her voice was sharper. 'The thirst, the weakness, your body's other needs . . . this is only the beginning. Especially as a Nenuphar. We're capable of much more than others like us, and we also require much more.'

'What do you mean?'

'Compared to normal sirens,' she said, her voice softening slightly, 'our bodies adjust very quickly after transformation. They're like sponges, not just with salt water, but with signals both given and received. They know what we can do, with men and one another, long before we're consciously aware. It might not feel like it, but we're always ten steps ahead of other sirens – even when we haven't been actively practising or honing our talent.'

I considered this. 'So right now I have power I don't know of? Or how to control?'

'Absolutely. And yours may be greater and different than mine or that of other Nenuphars. It varies greatly from one siren to the next. I can offer some guidance, but for better or worse, you must learn on your own, through personal experience and discovery. And often the lessons will come when you least expect them.'

Images of Raina and Zara flashed through my head. To them, the idea of unplanned power trips would be exciting. To me, it was reason to crawl into bed and hide under the covers for ever.

'In certain circumstances,' Charlotte continued, 'this power can be an enormous benefit. In others, especially those in which advanced capabilities aren't needed or desired, it's an exhausting detriment. Because our bodies are constantly working, they require constant fuel. More often and in much larger amounts than sirens not of our lineage.'

My head whirled as I tried to process this. 'But . . . what if we can't keep up?'

She forced a small smile. 'Why don't we focus on one thing at a time?'

I held her gaze, then looked away. As the tightness in my chest extended to my legs and arms, I pressed my palms into the wet sand, letting my skin absorb the moisture.

'If you were just a young siren coming to an experienced elder for advice,' she continued, 'I'd tell you as kindly as possible that having a normal romantic relationship is impossible. I'd suggest you end the situation before it gets even more complicated. And I'd reassure you that as difficult as ending it will be, doing so sooner rather than later would save you and your significant other pain you simply can't imagine – and that you'd likely never recover from.'

I asked my next question five times silently. When she didn't offer a response, I took a deep breath and said it out loud.

'But because I'm your daughter . . . ?'

We were surrounded by sound – the wind, rolling waves, rushing water. I could hear her quick intake of breath over it all.

'But because you're my daughter,' she said quietly, hesitantly, as if testing whether she'd misheard, 'I'll suggest you do what I would've done. Convince Simon you're someone else.'

I looked at her. 'Who?'

Her eyes glistened. 'The person you were before you changed into the one you are.'

'How do I do that? My abilities don't work on Simon. You said so yourself.'

'You don't need them. Just be together. Have fun. Talk about whatever you used to talk about. Do all the things you did that made you fall in love in the first place.'

'But he's so questioning, so sceptical . . . I don't know if he'd be able to just have fun. Especially without talking through everything else – all the transformation and siren-related stuff – first. Not only would he want to know so he could understand, he'd want to know because he cares. And that could take a really long time.'

'Vanessa, trust me . . . there will come a point when you'll both wish you hadn't wasted a single second.'

I tried to process this as waves pounded the shore and water rushed towards us. My skirt was completely soaked and my denim jacket clung to my arms, but I barely noticed. After several minutes, I asked two final questions.

'If the relationship has to end the way you say all relationships have to . . . won't it still hurt?'

Her lips pressed together like they wanted to lock up her answer. 'Yes,' she finally said. 'It will.'

'So then why shouldn't I let it go now?'

Her fingers quivered as she pressed one cool, damp palm to my cheek.

'Because Simon makes you happy, and you deserve every bit of happiness this life gives you.' She slowly lowered her palm. 'And because I know you can't.'

CHAPTER 13

I decided to take Charlotte's advice. It was what part of me had wanted to do anyway, but more importantly, it was what Justine would've suggested I do. Just as my sister had once told me to pretend the dark was really light as I lay awake at night, too scared to sleep, I knew she'd tell me now to pretend that the situation wasn't as serious as it seemed. She'd be certain that was the only way to keep my fear from leading to paralysis – and lost opportunity.

She'd be right.

Still, making Simon forget – or at least not fixate on – the events of the past twelve months would be difficult. He was Mr Science Guy, after all, and always questioned more than he accepted. But based on our lengthy catch-up session at the lake house, I was hopeful some small part of him wanted the same thing I did, and that with the right encouragement, he'd relax enough that we could talk or not talk, laugh or not laugh, the way we always had.

All I had to do was figure out what that

encouragement was. I'd never planned a real date before (Simon and I hadn't been an official couple long enough for that to happen), but when choosing a place, I started with two essential criteria.

The first: it should be somewhere we'd never been together.

And the second: it should be nowhere near the ocean.

Which is how a week after Charlotte's and my conversation on the beach, we ended up driving to Crawford, a tiny town two hours west of Winter Harbor. According to my extensive online research, it was quaint, quiet and surrounded by mountains, making it the perfect spot for a romantic reconnection.

And, it turned out, breakfast.

'You didn't mention today's adventure would include the world's best pancakes.' Simon shoved a heaping forkful in his mouth.

'No? How about the sweetest, richest maple syrup in Maine?'

'Made on the premises,' our waitress said, refilling our water glasses. 'From the trees you're sitting under.'

I looked up at the leafy boughs overhead. The sun filtered through, warming my face. There had been plenty of empty tables inside the restaurant, which, at first glance, looked more like a run-down red shack, but there had also been a few farmers enjoying their early-morning coffee. Most barely glanced our way when we walked in, but one dropped his knife and had trouble picking it up, since he looked at me instead of the floor. That was enough attention to request a table outside, where it was apparently still too chilly for other diners.

I lowered my eyes. Simon held the saltshaker towards me.

'The syrup's not that sweet,' I said.

'Don't you want to put some in your water?'

I took a piece of toast from my plate, focused on eating. 'Nope. I'm fine.'

'But doesn't it help keep you hydrated?'

'Sure.' I shrugged. 'Sometimes.'

My heart thumped as I waited for him to question further. When he still hadn't, a moment later, I looked up to see him chewing and the salt in its rightful place next to the pepper.

'So how'd you find this place?' Simon asked. 'It's kind-of off the beaten path.'

'I overheard some people talking about it at Betty's.' This was the response I'd rehearsed so he wouldn't know how many hours I'd spent scouting for the perfect date location. 'They said it was a great day trip – and that the drive was spectacular.'

'They definitely got that right. After travelling them one way or another for twenty years, all pretty country roads look alike. But that one, with the sun coming up over the hills? And all those flowers? That, with the top down, you could smell like they were right in front of you?'

'Not bad,' I said.

He grinned. 'Not at all.'

I returned his smile as my body relaxed. So far, this was going even better than I'd hoped. When Simon came to Betty's yesterday to pick up lunch and I asked if he'd like to hang out today, he said yes without hesitating. He didn't even question where or why; he simply agreed and told me to text him details later. When I did that, suggesting an early mini-road trip, he texted back seconds later and said that sounded like a nice way to spend a morning. Then, when I picked him up so early the sky was just brightening from grey to pink, he was waiting for me on the porch of his family's house and jogged towards the Jeep before I'd put it in park. We talked some during the drive, mostly about our jobs or songs on the radio, but were otherwise quiet as we took in the brisk air and scenery.

It was all so comfortable, I was beginning to think this just might work after all.

'I meant to tell you,' he said, 'Caleb and I put an ad on the *Herald* website. In the lost-and-found listings. We're hoping whoever dropped the camera will want it back badly enough to follow up.'

Or it might not.

'Good thinking.' I leaned across the table and lowered my voice. 'Do you think that truck's serious?'

He leaned to the side and peered past me to the pickup idling in the dirt car park. A tall white sandwich board stood in the truck's bed; Simon read its message out loud. 'Follow the horse's you-know-what to Maine's one hundred magical acres.' He sat back. 'Well, it is pulling a trailer. And the trailer appears to be moving, even though the truck's still. So, yes, I suppose it could be serious.'

I waited for his eyes to find mine again. 'Do you want to go?' I asked.

'To the hundred acres?'

I nodded and held my breath. There were countless reasons why he could say no – we didn't know where exactly they were or how far away; it could just be some cheesy tourist trap; we should probably get back to Winter Harbor sooner rather than later so he could check in with Caleb and do some more sleuthing. And he took long enough to answer that any of these responses were real possibilities.

But instead, he popped another piece of pancake in his mouth, chewed, swallowed, and said, 'We better hurry. If the land's magical, who knows what that truck can do?'

I laughed. We jumped up, then stalled briefly when we took our wallets out at the same time.

'You get the next one,' he said.

My smile widened. 'Deal.'

We waved and thanked our waitress, who did the same through one of the restaurant's open windows, and ran to the Jeep. The driver had returned to the truck and was already pulling out onto the road. The pick-up was no flying carpet; once we caught up, I had to brake repeatedly to avoid colliding with the trailer – and the horses' you-know-whats, of which there were two. Simon and I spent the next twenty minutes joking and laughing, and I decided wherever we were going was indeed magical long before we got there.

It was beautiful, too, which we learned as we turned down a long gravel driveway and drove through rolling farmland. About half a mile down, the pick-up pulled up to a large white barn. We went a little further, joining a dozen or so parked cars in a dirt lot, and hopped out.

'Hi, there,' the driver said as we approached. 'Welcome to Langden Farm. I'm Jack one-third driver, two-thirds marketer.'

'Hi.' Simon shook Jack's outstretched hand and looked around. 'This is some place.'

'Indeed it is. Which is why I'm sorry to tell you that I'm late.'

I glanced at Simon. 'For what?'

'For announcing the morning ride.' Jack shuffled along the side of the truck, wedged one boot between the top of the rear tyre and its well, and stepped up. 'There was a situation with the hitch and by the time it was fixed, the first one was already gone. I left the sign up in case folks wanted to join the afternoon ride, but that won't leave for another six hours.' He took the sandwich board in both hands and lowered it till it lay flat in the truck bed. 'Where are you from?'

'Winter Harbor,' Simon said. 'It's a small town on –'

'I know where it is.' He hopped down and faced us. 'That was some summer you had last year.'

Simon nodded. I looked down.

'Yes, sir,' he said. 'It was.'

'The wife and I took the grandkids skating on the water after it froze. It was twenty-four degrees when we left here and dropped to about four by the time we got to your neck of the woods. Never seen anything like it.'

'And hopefully you won't again,' Simon said.

'Got that right.' Jack nodded to me. 'You bring a change of clothes?'

Their conversation had turned my face the same colour as my new linen skirt: bright red. Besides the skirt, I wore a white tank top, my denim jacket, and leather flip-flops. 'No,' I said.

'Okay.' He opened the trailer and patted the horses' haunches until the animals started backing up. 'Rest here a minute. I'll see if we can't work something out.'

He led the horses into the barn. Simon leaned against the truck. I leaned next to Simon.

'It's still strange to hear other people refer to it,' he said quietly. 'I know most of the country knows at least some of what happened . . . but it still feels like this thing that only we experienced, you know?'

I did. But I didn't want to talk about it. Fortunately, Jack wasn't gone long enough for Simon to question my silence.

'How much riding time have you clocked?' he called out as he shuffled towards us.

'None,' I called back.

'About ten minutes around the pony pole at the 1998 Country Fair,' Simon said.

Jack chuckled. 'All right. Then you have two options.' He stopped in front of us and pointed back at the barn. 'We've got two horses ready to go, but with no experience, you can't wander far without a guide – and the three we have are all out. I'd take you myself, but I have meetings all morning. That said, you're more than welcome to ride through the main meadow. It's flat, safe and in full view of the house, so if you have any trouble, someone's bound to see and come running.'

I peered past Jack to the meadow, which was more of a large front garden. It was pretty enough, but it was also completely exposed to anyone coming, going or passing through.

'What's the other option?' Simon asked.

'Come back in six hours,' Jack said. 'We'll have two horses with your names on them.'

Simon looked at me. I shrugged. 'The first might be nice,' I said.

'Okay.' Simon nodded. 'We're in.'

'Fantastic.' Jack chucked a cloth ball at me. 'From the gift shop. On the house, if you want them.'

'Thank you.' I caught and unravelled the ball, which was actually a pair of khaki shorts with the Langden Farm logo – a herd of black horse silhouettes galloping under a starry sky – stamped on one pocket. 'That's so nice.'

'Least we can do for our neighbours.' He turned and started shuffling away. 'Someone will bring you your rides shortly, and we'll handle payment later. Enjoy!'

When he disappeared inside the barn, I faced Simon and held up the shorts.

'Be right back.'

I could've easily pulled on the shorts and slid off my

skirt right there and not shown any extra skin, but changing was a good excuse to steal a few minutes alone. I grabbed my bag from the Jeep as I headed for the side of the barn. After making sure Simon was still by the truck and not paying attention, I swapped clothes and gulped the two bottles of salt water I'd stowed in my bag. I'd swum for two hours and drunk so much that morning, tiny droplets of water in my pores had made my skin glitter, and so far, I felt fine. But there was no telling how my body would react to being so close to Simon for an extended period of time, and some pre-emptive salt consumption was better than running dry in front of him.

'That's some tank.'

I spun around. A young guy in jeans and a Langden Farm fleece came towards me with a shovel.

'Sorry?' I said.

He nodded to the empty water bottle I held. 'You downed that whole thing without coming up for air once. I'm impressed.'

'Thanks.' I tried to smile as I walked backward. 'Guess I was thirstier than I realised.'

'Are you lost? Can I help you with something?'

He was quickening his pace. I did the same – and stumbled back when my heel hit rock. I cried out when two hands grabbed my arms from behind and pulled me firmly to my feet.

'She's good,' Simon said. 'We're good.'

I struggled to breathe normally. The guy stopped walking, his shovel slightly raised. A second later, he lowered the tool and began to retreat.

'No worries, man. I was just doing my job.'

We didn't move until he disappeared around the back of the barn.

'Maybe we should leave,' Simon said.

I shoved the empty bottles in my bag and turned towards him. 'No way. I'm fine – and I really do want to go riding.'

'That guy could've –'

'That guy was harmless. He wouldn't have tried anything and even if he had, I could've handled him.'

I was less certain of this than I sounded, but Simon seemed somewhat reassured. He didn't protest when I squeezed his hand and said, 'Come on. Let's go saddle up our unicorn or Pegasus or whichever mythical creature they call a horse around here.'

As it turned out, our transportation around the outskirts of Maine's one hundred magical acres really were ordinary horses. Mine was a deep chestnut mare with a slight limp and a white stripe running down her face. Simon's was an older, grey stallion. Our trainer was a married, grandfatherly gentleman, who gave us a few pointers for stopping, starting and steering, and demonstrated how to climb into the saddle.

I went first, stepping my left foot in the stirrup and gripping the saddle to pull myself up. I was about to swing my right leg over when Simon gently took my hips in both hands. He tried to give me a boost, but his unexpected touch made me lose my breath – and my balance. I threw my other arm across the saddle, and used all my upper-body strength to pull the rest of me into position.

'Piece of cake.' I smiled and brushed the hair out of my eyes.

Simon patted my horse, as if asking her to be gentle with me, then went to his. It took him a few tries to get in the saddle, but it was hard to tell if that was because the horse was skittish ... or because Simon was.

Once we were both steady on our steeds, we walked them up and down the driveway. The trainer, apparently satisfied with our newfound skills, permitted us in the main meadow and instructed us to stay within the fenced perimeter and keep the farmhouse in sight. We did as we were told ... until I spotted a trail entrance in the far corner of the lawn.

'Where do you think it goes?' I whispered, like someone might be listening. 'Cinderella's castle? A mad tea party? Oz?'

'All of the above?' Simon guessed.

Seeing only the roof of the farmhouse, I turned my horse around and guided her back up the small hill. The farmhouse's second storey had just come into view when I tugged on the reins. The horse stopped.

'Something wrong?'

I turned back. Simon's eyebrows were lowered, his hands tight on the reins. I smiled to reassure him, then gave the sides of my horse a quick dig with my heels. She started with a jolt towards the trail.

'Vanessa, where are you . . . ? Jack said to . . .'

I held my breath as we passed him and entered the trail. Initially, I couldn't hear anything but my horse's hooves clomping against the packed dirt, but soon, a second, faster set sounded behind us.

I exhaled and gave the mare another gentle jab. She sped up, trotting between lush green hills that seemed to stretch on for miles. At first I bounced awkwardly – and painfully – in the saddle, but with some experimentation, I soon figured out how to lift and move to the horse's rhythm. My heart raced as I listened for more hooves, maybe even a car, coming up behind us, surrounding us, ordering us to hand over our steeds and leave the premises, but none did.

Ten minutes later, the trail entered a dense patch of trees. I pulled lightly on the reins, listened for Simon's suggestion to turn back, head out. But like a disapproving Langden Farm staff member, it didn't come. So we continued on.

It didn't take long to learn how the hundred acres earned their magical status. The path narrowed as trees grew wider, taller. Thin rays of sunlight filtered through shifting branches, making the air glow and ground glitter. Flowers in shades of purple, red and yellow flourished beneath the protective canopy. Butterflies flitted between petals. Birds called out, their songs soft, sweet. As we meandered, it felt like we were enveloped by this place rather than simply cutting through it.

Simon and I were quiet the entire time. When we came to an old, covered bridge, neither of us asked the other if we'd like to stop for a while. We just did, sliding off our horses, looping their reins around a tree trunk, and heading for the red wooden structure. We walked silently to the middle of the bridge, then leaned against one low wall. As we watched the stream flicker ten feet below, I was aware of only two things: the natural beauty all around us . . . and Simon's arm brushing against mine.

Sometime later, he spoke.

'When'd you get so brave?'

My eyes raised from the water, locked on a tall, distant evergreen.

'You never would've done that before.' His voice was quiet, thoughtful.

'Done what?'

'Defied authority. Broken rules. I know Jack wasn't exactly intimidating, but still. He told us where to stay . . . and yet here we are, a world away. The old Vanessa would've been too scared – not necessarily of getting in trouble, but of disappointing an adult – to come this far.'

The old Vanessa. Did that mean my attempts to convince him I was someone else, someone new and improved, were working?

As if to answer my question, Simon continued.

'There have been other things, too. Like the way you shrugged off that guy behind the barn. And the way you insisted on driving home alone the other night –'

'Which you didn't allow,' I reminded him. 'You followed me all the way to my driveway.'

'I know, and I would again. But that doesn't mean you weren't convincing. Before, you might not have come out and asked me to make sure you got home okay, but you wouldn't have protested when I offered.'

I didn't say anything. He was right.

'Even this,' he said, his voice softer. 'You inviting me to hang out, especially when things between us are so . . . undefined. It's new. Different.'

'The old Vanessa would've waited for you to come to her.'

'Yes. I think so.'

'Would you have?'

He laughed once, lightly. 'See? That, too. You never would've asked that question.'

This was followed by a long pause as I waited for his answer.

'Um . . .' He stood straighter, rested his hands on the top of the wall. 'Would I have come to you? As something other than a friend?'

His elbow bumped mine. My breath caught.

'I don't think I would've had a choice.'

At which point the old – as in, week-ago – Vanessa would've immediately talked herself out of doing what the new Vanessa did next.

She kissed him. *I* kissed him. Without turning and waiting for him to turn to me, or stepping closer and hoping he did the same. I put one hand on his arm, pulled him just enough that I could fit in the small space between him and the bridge wall, reached up . . . and kissed him.

Maybe this was what Charlotte had meant on the beach a week ago. My body was acting on its own when my head would normally slow it down. Was this my power at work?

Either way, if I'd known what would follow this single act, I would've done it much sooner. Because everything, all of the hesitancy, questions and reservations, disappeared. Nervousness was replaced with excitement, shyness with boldness. Our kisses, especially the first ones shared after not seeing one another for a few days, had always started softly. Delicately. Tenderly. Now we skipped ahead, our mouths moving and lips parting the way they had only in the midst of our most heated make-out sessions. His hands were firm as they moved down my back and took my hips. I pressed the length of my body against his like I knew, without a hint of doubt, that's what he wanted, that he wouldn't pull away.

And the surprising thing was I did.

He leaned forward, pushing me against the bridge. I released his sweater just long enough to put both hands on the wall and lift myself up. My legs squeezed his waist, his hands gripped my thighs. His mouth moved down my neck, across the bare skin above my tank top. I wound my fingers through his hair, bringing his face even closer. He slid one hand across my waist and up my back, took the collar of my jacket and tugged until the denim slid down my arm. As his lips brushed my shoulder, his fingers travelled back up my arm, pulled the thin tank-top strap aside. His other hand inched up my right thigh, under the cuff of my shorts. I tightened my legs around him and kissed wherever I could reach – his neck, his jaw, the soft space beneath his ear.

I'm okay, I thought, preparing to answer the question I knew was coming. *I'm amazing, actually. This . . . you . . . it's exactly what I want. It's all that I want.*

Only, the question, the one Simon always asked, no matter how many times we were together, never came.

Either I was even more convincing than I realised, or someone else had become braver, too.

'You two aware your rides left without you?'

Simon leapt back. I covered my mouth, as if to erase evidence of what we'd just been doing, and then hopped down from the wall.

Jack sat on a tall horse at the end of the bridge. He nodded up the trail, where our horses were strolling back the way we came.

'Might want to catch up,' he said. 'We got half a dozen employees looking for you, and a couple of empty horses won't do much to ease their worries.'

With that, he turned and galloped away – but not without giving us a quick wink first.

The air was still for a second, and then Simon and I cracked up. The release felt so good, so energising, I didn't even worry about what kind of trouble we'd likely get into when we returned to the farm.

'Come here,' Simon said, when we calmed down. He held out one hand, which I took, and pulled me into a loose hug. 'Vanessa . . .'

When he didn't say anything else, I nodded against his chest. 'I know. Me, too.'

He kissed the top of my head, the tip of my nose, my lips. Softly. Delicately. Tenderly.

And then we retrieved our horses and headed for the farm, where we didn't get into trouble – or a warm invitation to return.

We took our time returning to Winter Harbour. We drove around a while, grabbed some lunch, wandered through a few antique shops, and stopped for a leisurely dinner. We kept the conversation light and never referred to last summer, fall, or even week. For my part, those topics barely crossed my mind.

I didn't think either of us wanted the day to end, but we agreed not worrying our parents was essential if we were going to have another like it. So when the sun started to set, we headed east.

The fact that Simon wanted to spend more time together was so reassuring that when he offered to drive back, I gave him the keys. It had been twelve hours since my swim, and though I'd continued to sneak sips of salt water, my energy was steadily waning. Plus, it had been such a full day, I thought my fatigue could be easily attributed to everything we'd done.

I must've dozed off at some point, because in one instant, I was watching the sky turn purple over a field of flowers, and in the next, I was wide awake, staring at flashing red lights.

'What is it?' I asked, sitting up straight. 'Where are we?'

'It looks like an accident.' Simon's voice was tense. He inched the Jeep forward in the slow-moving line of traffic. 'And we just crossed the Winter Harbor border.'

Accidents happened all the time. I *knew* they happened all the time, to ordinary people for ordinary reasons. Which was why I managed to stay calm as we passed two police cars and an ambulance, and neared the circle of paramedics administering CPR.

But then one of the paramedics moved. The plastic mask came off the girl's mouth and her head dropped to one side.

And Carla's lifeless eyes met mine.

CHAPTER 14

**Breaking News: Winter Harbor High Track Star
Dead At 18**

Little more than a year after Justine Sands, the
first victim of last summer's string of fatalities, was
found at the base of Chione Cliffs, the body of Carla
Marciano, a recent Winter Harbor High graduate
and 400-metre record holder for the school's track
team, was discovered at the intersection of Maple
Lane and Washington Avenue.

Investigations are under way and police are actively seeking witnesses. If you or someone you
know has any information about the events leading
up to Miss Marciano's death, please call the WHPD
at 207-555-3900.

Story developing, check back for updates.

'That made it to the *Herald* website in less than twelve
hours,' Paige said, scrolling to the top of the page. 'First-
time visitors would never guess that until last summer,

the only thing on this page was a cartoon crab telling you to pick up the paper in town.'

'That's it?' I asked. 'That's all you have to say?'

She closed her laptop and sat back. 'Of course not. It's awful. Tragic. And it totally freaks me out. But if I talk about how much it freaks me out, that'll just make me freak out even more. And it's too early in the summer to completely lose it.'

I glanced around to make sure we were still alone on the employee break deck. 'But you knew her. Did she ever, I don't know, say anything to suggest –'

'That she was being chased by evil sirens? No. And she only worked here a few days and spent half the time frantically running around and the other half crying. The most I learned was that she has an expensive addiction to Kleenex.' Paige looked down at her lap, then towards the harbour. 'She *had* an expensive addiction to Kleenex.'

I followed her gaze. The water was calm, flat. The cloudless sky was a brilliant blue. Like yesterday, and the day before, and the day before that, the weather in Winter Harbor was perfect. This should be reassuring, since last summer's victims, Justine included, had always been found after severe thunderstorms . . . but it also made the situation even more puzzling.

'What about you?' Paige turned back. 'I mean, it's

bad enough that you actually saw her lying there, in the middle of the road, but then to read that online . . . with your sister's name . . .' She pushed her sunglasses on top of her head and leaned towards me. 'Are you okay? Do you want to take the day off? Spend some time with your parents?'

'Thank you, but, no. I'm fine. I feel a little guilty, but otherwise I'm fine.'

'Guilty? What for?'

'For the very first thought that ran through my head when I got a good look at the victim last night.'

Paige put one hand over mine on the table.

'It's a terrible, tragic thing no matter what, just like you said, and –'

'It's okay, Vanessa.'

'I was relieved it was a girl.' The words flew from my mouth. 'It's awful, I know, but –'

'It's not awful. It's understandable. I'd think the exact same thing.'

I sighed. 'Thank you.'

'You're welcome, although I'm not saying it because I think it's what you want to hear.' She paused. 'But you know other people will probably make similar connections. That piece on the *Herald* website is just the beginning. The bigger news channels might not pick it up right away, but at least around here, people will be talking, comparing . . .'

'Like, Carla to Justine? Since she was the first victim and the only girl?'

Paige's face scrunched in apology.

'I know. But there are some major differences, the biggest of which being that Carla wasn't found near water. Also, there's a sharp turn by that intersection, so it's very possible it was only a terrible hit-and-run. And it's okay anyway, because despite what I thought last night, you and I know that there's no chance anything like last summer can happen again.' I shrugged. 'So let them talk.'

She squeezed my hand. 'Fearless. Just like handsome, perceptive Mr Science Guy said.'

I drained my iced coffee, like it would stop the heat from spreading across my face. 'Speaking of, I should probably get downstairs. He texted this morning to say he and Caleb were coming for breakfast today in addition to lunch. And don't worry – they'll pay for this meal. I'm sure he wanted to see for himself that I made it here in one piece.'

'Please. If Simon wants filet mignon instead of bacon on his egg sandwich, he can have it – and free of charge. Anyone who makes my Vanessa as happy as he makes you is entitled to whatever he wants.' A smile played on her lips as she stood up and gathered her laptop and folders. 'And Caleb's okay. By association, of course.'

'Of course.'

Her smile grew. I was about to ask if I'd missed something when her smile disappeared and she looked at me, instantly serious.

'I'm sorry, by the way. For the other night at Murph's. I never apologised and I really wanted you to know how bad I felt afterwards. I don't know what got into me . . . I guess it was just too much, you know? Seeing all those pictures and thinking about all that stuff again?'

I stood, too. 'It's okay. I understand.'

She opened her arms. We hugged across the table.

'See?' She sniffed. 'I'm about one tragedy shy of a total meltdown.'

'Then it's a good thing this most recent tragedy will also be the last.'

We went downstairs and parted ways in the kitchen. Paige headed for Louis, who appeared to be having his own mini meltdown by the fryer, and I veered towards the dining room.

'Vanessa! Thank goodness!'

I froze by the bar. The swinging door swung back, bumping me forward. Natalie took my movement as some kind of offer and thrust a coffeepot at me as she breezed past.

'Table eight needs to be topped off, ten needs another place setting, and four's out of sugar.'

'Okay, but I'm not –'

'Oh, and do you know how to work the air-conditioning? It's kind of hot with all those bodies in there! Thanks!'

Still holding the coffeepot, I scanned the room and counted.

Eight tables. There were twenty tables in the dining room . . . and only eight were empty. This was easily the busiest Betty's had been all summer.

Dishes clattered in the kitchen behind me. Voices grew louder. I bolted, starting with the topping off of table eight.

'About time,' one man grunted, as I filled his cup.

'Sorry for the wait,' I said. 'We're a little understaffed this morning.'

'Don't mind him,' said the man's friend. 'He usually takes his coffee one way: burned and from the gas-station snack store.'

My eyes fell to their hands as I smiled. The first man wore a wedding ring. The second didn't.

'Can I get you anything else?' I asked.

'A phone number would be nice.' The single guy drained the coffee I'd just poured. Grinning, he held out his cup. I refilled it.

'Your waiter will be with you shortly.'

'No rush. His grin widened. 'When the view's this nice, I like to enjoy it as long as I can.' I forced a smile and turned around. Aware of his eyes on my back as I left, I dashed to the bar and grabbed a silverware bundle and sugar bowl. I delivered both to their respective tables, too quickly to receive potential attention, and continued to the lobby where several customers waited to be seated. I snatched menus from the hostess stand and showed the customers – three parties, all male – to their tables. Glimpsing my reflection in the mirror over the darkened fireplace, I saw perspiration already lining my forehead and remembered Natalie's comment about the air-conditioning. The thermostat was on the other side of the room, next to the kitchen door; I ran there next, sticking to the room's perimeter to keep a safe distance from my admirer.

I'd just lowered the temperature from seventy-five, which Paige had said was as low as we could go for money-saving purposes, to seventy-two, when my cell phone buzzed in my shorts pocket.

CALEB OVERSLEPT. BE THERE SOON. —S

I texted back.

'Bottomless beverages.'

I looked up. Paige stood next to me, hands on her hips, eyes on the crowd, apron around her waist.

'What?' I'd heard her; I just didn't know what she meant.

'Natalie's dad promised some sort of deal to anyone who got here before eight. So let's give them free drinks and unlimited refills of whatever they want – coffee, tea, OJ, soda. And if they ask to fill up their thermoses before they head out on the water, let's do that, too.'

Something – suspicion, wariness, envy – simmered low in my belly. 'What do you mean, Natalie's dad? What does he have to do with this?'

She took an elastic band from her wrist, gathered her dark hair in a ponytail. 'She and I brainstormed a few ideas to boost business the other day, some of which she shared with her dad, who apparently shared them with the entire marina. I'd be mad . . . but *look* at this place.' She turned to me, blue eyes bright. 'Maybe we'll be okay after all.'

I opened my mouth to ask more questions, but stopped when she took a pen and pad of paper from her apron and held them towards me.

'You don't mind, do you? Taking a few orders in

between seating people? It's just for today, I promise. As soon as I have a free second, I'll call some of the waiting staff that quit a few weeks ago.' She leaned forward and kissed my cheek. 'Thank you. You're the best.'

I watched her take another pad and pen from her apron and dive into the sea of tables. Before she was a manager, Paige had been a waitress, and now she smiled and laughed, chatted and joked, instantly charming the customers. It wasn't until she passed my admirer and he gave her an appraising look that I realised how many more customers were male than female. Of roughly thirty diners, only four had handbags slung across the backs of their chairs. The rest were scruffy, weathered, hungry men. And not just any men: fishermen. Who were fuelling up before heading out.

Betty's had been around for ever, but in recent history, had been more of a tourist spot than one for locals. This crowd was definitely new – and needed. So despite my reservations, most of which had to do with Natalie offering giveaways without Paige's official consent, I headed for one of the tables I'd just seated.

For the next twenty minutes, I didn't stop. I barely breathed. Along with Paige and Natalie, I took orders, filled glasses, served dishes, cleared and wiped tables, and played hostess, over and over again. I also ignored compliments and dodged flirtation, which was even more challenging – and exhausting – than meeting my diners' needs before they could realise they had any. Soon I was so hot, thirsty and tired, I started ducking behind the bar between tasks for quick sips of salt water.

I'd just sneaked a drink and stood quickly when my cell buzzed with a new text from Simon.

ON OUR WAY. CAN'T WAIT TO SEE YOU.

The words were fuzzy. I blinked to clear my vision and brought one hand to my head, which spun. I closed the phone, squatted to drink more from the glass I kept beneath the counter, and stood again. This time, my body swayed to the left. I grabbed the cash register to steady myself.

'Ladies' room's out of TP,' Paige announced as she flew by en route to the kitchen. 'Toss in a few rolls? Please? Thanks!'

Grateful for the excuse to leave the dining room, I took a spare saltshaker from under the bar and hurried towards the lobby, where both lavatories were located. My legs seemed to grow softer with every step; when the restaurant's main entrance came into view, I lunged the remaining distance and burst through the ladies' room door.

Inside, I made sure both stalls were empty before

locking the door and turning on the water. As one of the handbasins filled, I unscrewed the shaker's metal top and dumped in the salt. Stirring the water with one hand, I checked my appearance in the mirror – and was glad I was alone so no one heard me gasp.

I'd looked fine, normal, after my regular routine of swimming and bathing earlier that morning. But now my skin was as white as the porcelain basin, even though I was so hot sweat trickled down my face and neck, darkening the collar of my T-shirt. I'd blown my hair dry but now it was as wet as when I'd stepped out of the ocean. The clear gloss I always wore had evaporated from my lips, which were light purple and chapped.

But the worst part was my eyes. They were usually hazel with the occasional blue tint. Every now and then, depending on the light, they appeared to be grey – silver, even. I'd been noticing the metallic sheen more frequently lately, which made my stomach turn, since silver eyes was a physical trait most sirens shared.

This, however, was worse.

It wasn't just the colour, which seemed to shift from slate blue to steel grey to blackish green, and reminded me of the ocean's murky depths. It wasn't even the mottled haze they seemed to hide behind. It was that they looked so much smaller . . . because my skin was softer, hanging lower. My eyebrows sunk, pushing down my lids. The inside and outside corners drooped. Beneath my bottom lashes, the normally smooth surface was creased.

I stepped back and stared.

What's wrong with me?

Without meaning to, I directed this silent question at Charlotte and listened for her response. When none come, I dropped my head and began splashing water on my face, neck and arms. I cupped both hands, dipped them into the basin, and drank. I did this until I could no longer taste salt and my face felt cooler. And then I looked up again.

Better. Not great – my eyes, though back to normal size, were still too dark – but my skin was firmer and slowly turning pink.

Was this what Charlotte meant when she said Nenuphars required more energy more often than ordinary sirens? Would I look like I aged ten years every day if I didn't constantly give it what it needed? And if I was capable of more than ordinary sirens, did that at least make it easier to acquire this energy?

The door rattled, making me jump. When she couldn't get in, the person on the other side knocked.

'One second!' I yanked paper towels from the bin on the wall. After drying my face, I took the keyring from my shorts pocket and went to the small supply closet.

I unlocked the closet door and reached for the extra toilet-paper rolls – which weren't there. The shelf was empty.

I left the Ladies, explained the situation to the woman waiting to get in, and said I'd be right back. I found Paige and asked where the extra supplies were, and she directed me to the main storage closet in the basement. On my way there, I caught another glimpse of my reflection in the mirror over the dining-room fireplace and saw that as quickly as it'd tightened, my skin was beginning to soften again. I also saw that my original admirer hadn't left yet . . . and that he was watching me.

I checked my watch. According to his last text, Simon should be here any minute. What we saw driving back to Winter Harbor last night had been a huge reminder of everything I wanted him to forget, and if I had any chance of making up for lost time, he couldn't see me looking like this. It wouldn't matter what I said after that – he'd be instantly, maybe even permanently, worried. The quickest, easiest solution would be jumping into the harbour, which was in Betty's backyard, but there was no way to do that without someone noticing.

There was, however, one other option.

'Hi, there.' I stood inches from my middle-aged admirer, smiled. 'How's everything here?'

'Slow,' the other man grumbled. 'But all right.'

Heart hammering, I rested one hip against the table and faced the younger man. 'How are *you*?'

He sat back in his chair, gave me an appreciate once-over. 'Still hungry.'

'I'm sorry to hear that. What else can I get you? Pancakes? French toast?'

His eyes narrowed slightly. We both knew he wasn't talking about food. Which was why I leaned forward, put one hand on his arm, and brought my mouth close to his ear.

'What's your name?'

Beneath my fingers, his muscles tensed. The release of energy shot from his skin directly into mine.

'Alex.'

I swallowed and tried again. 'Where're you from?'

He inhaled sharply. My legs strengthened.

'Portland.'

'Great town.' I brought my lips closer. 'Or so they say anyway.'

His head tilted in invitation. The surge in my legs lengthened, reaching through my chest and up my neck.

'You should come down. I'll make sure you have a good time.'

His voice wavered. I stood slightly and checked the results of this exchange in the mirror over the fireplace.

'Perfect,' I said.

I gave his arm a squeeze for good measure and crossed the room without looking back. In the kitchen, I was careful to avoid Louis's verbal and physical firing range, which took up most of the room, thanks to the unexpected breakfast rush, and stayed close to the wall as I made my way to the rear stairwell.

The basement, I quickly learned, was perhaps the only part of the restaurant Paige had decided didn't need a single paint stroke or light-bulb change during renovations. It was dark and damp, and smelled like mildew and French fries. Discarded furniture, linens, and appliances sat in tall, haphazard piles. The storage closet was at the back of the room, and it took several minutes to navigate the crooked narrow path that led there. I felt some small relief when the door opened easily and the overhead light worked, but that feeling faded when I spotted the extra toilet paper still in boxes on a shelf near the ceiling.

'Perfect,' I said again, less enthusiastically than I had moments before.

I picked my way back through the basement until I came to an old metal folding chair that didn't break in two when I opened it. I brought it back to the closet, placed it before the wall of shelves, and stepped up. With the extra height, my fingertips could just reach the bottom of the box. I inched it out slowly, until it was more than halfway out and beginning to tilt down. Then I grabbed it with both hands – and dropped it when the chair buckled beneath me.

I fell to the floor, landing hard on one knee. The box missed me as it tumbled down but it took out the ceiling light. As the fixture shattered and glass shards rained down, I covered my face and tried to duck under the lowest shelf.

'Vanessa?'

I barely heard the male voice over the sound of breaking glass, but knew it had to be Simon. Thank goodness. Paige must've told him I was down here.

'Hi!' I pulled out from under the shelf, tried to feel my way through the darkness. 'I'll be right there!'

Using my cell phone as a flashlight, I found the box and turned it right side up. It was still sealed shut, so I held the phone between my teeth as I took my keys from my pocket. I put one hand on the box, ready to slice the tape, and reeled back when a stray piece of glass dug into my palm.

I cried out. The phone fell to the floor, and its dim light went out.

'Hey. What happened?'

I spun towards Simon. He sounded different. Concerned, but something else too. Unfortunately, I couldn't check his face for clues. The closet was so dark

I could only feel, and not see, the blood dripping down my hand. 'Nothing.' I said. 'I just cut my hand. But it's fine. I'm fine.'

I was actually in a good amount of pain, but I didn't want him to know that. I closed my eyes when they watered and didn't protest when he took my hand gently in his. I waited for the automatic concern, the insistence that my wound wasn't nothing.

But he didn't say anything. He cradled my hand for a moment, then slid his fingers up, around my wrist. He stepped towards me and reached one arm around my waist.

I froze, not sure what he was doing or how to respond. Was I so convincing yesterday that he believed me easily today? If so, should I go with it to keep him from questioning?

He pulled me towards him. I pressed my good hand to his chest.

'Hey,' I said gently. 'I'm sure it's fine, but I should probably get something on it, just in case.'

His face neared mine. I felt him nod.

'In a second,' he whispered.

My cell phone, still on the floor, buzzed. The tiny red light did nothing to illuminate the room, but it was bright enough to see the stained, brown work boots pressed against the toes of my sandals.

Simon didn't wear work boots. He didn't even own a pair. But Alex, the guy I'd just flirted with, did. I noticed them when I leaned forward to talk near his ear.

I opened my mouth to yell, pulled my arm back to thrust it forward again, as hard as I could. But then his other arm snaked around my waist, tightened. His chest flexed against my torso as he moved, and I knew there was no way I'd win in a battle of strength – at least not using my regular muscles.

I forced my hands up, my arms around his neck, my voice to stay soft, steady. 'Do you like the beach?' I asked.

He nodded again, against my neck.

'Why don't we take a walk? It's such a nice day. I'd love to spend it with you outside.'

'Yes,' he murmured. 'Later.'

His lips grazed my collarbone. I swallowed a scream.

'How about now?' I managed.

He leaned into me, pushing my back against the shelf. His hands moved down my sides. When I tried to speak again, he silenced me with his mouth.

I tore my face away and squirmed beneath his weight. He didn't say anything as he pushed harder, searched for my mouth with his. The struggle zapped my energy, and I knew I'd be defenceless in a matter of seconds.

So I screamed. As loudly as I could. Only the sound wasn't sharp. It wasn't shrill or alarming.

It was soft. Sweet.

Effective.

Alex released me, stumbled back. Stunned by the reaction – and what had caused it – it took me a second to move. Finally, I bolted for the door. Tearing through the basement and up the stairs, I was only vaguely aware of a bright light flashing behind me.

I fought to compose myself as I flew through the kitchen. I didn't want to alarm diners, but I needed Paige. Simon. Someone to help me make sense of what had just happened.

Fortunately, I didn't have to go far. Simon and Caleb sat at the bar. Paige was pouring them coffee.

'Vanessa?' Simon jumped off his stool. Caleb followed close behind.

'Oh my God.' Paige dropped the coffeepot to the counter and grabbed a stack of clean dish towels.

'I'm okay,' I said, as they encircled me.

Which was a lie for three reasons.

My cut was so deep, blood trickled from my hand to the floor.

A wound like that should burn so badly, amputation would be an appealing alternative, but my body was completely drained. I felt nothing.

And most alarming of all, Alex the Portland fisherman wasn't in the basement.

He was at the table where I'd left him, eating pancakes.

CHAPTER 15

'You know, if you don't want to wait tables, you can tell me.'

Simon shot Paige a look.

'I'm sorry,' she said. 'But twelve stitches? I have to joke or –'

'She'll completely lose it,' I finished lightly. 'And it's too early in the summer for that.'

Simon turned to me. 'Are you comfortable? Do you need anything else?'

'I have food, pillows, blankets and my favourite people. What else is there?' I patted the couch next to me. 'Sit. Please. Eat.'

His frown deepened as his eyes lowered to my bandage.

'It's only my left hand,' I said. 'If I can still hold chopsticks, I can do anything.'

Doubt lingered on his face, but he sat down and took his plate from the coffee table.

'Security cameras,' Paige announced, biting into an

egg roll. 'Totally buying them next. I can't believe the restaurant's gone so long without.'

'Excellent idea,' Simon said.

'But not essential.' I wanted to reassure Paige, who I knew felt responsible. 'Betty's has never had a problem before, right? And plus, I was in the basement. You can't monitor every dark nook and cranny.'

'Yes, I can,' she said.

'Vanessa, will you just walk us through what happened?' Caleb asked, from the love seat. 'One more time?'

I bit back a sigh. I'd already recounted the events in the car on the way to the hospital, where I hadn't wanted to go but went anyway since we couldn't control the bleeding with plasters and gauze pads alone. I'd trusted doctors wouldn't need to take blood or do anything else that might alert them to the fact that I wasn't their average patient, and fortunately, I was right; we were there for less than an hour, no extra tests or exams required. Then, after leaving the hospital, I'd told the story a second time on the drive here, to the lake house. I knew my friends were just worried and wanted to make sure they had all the information, but I'd prefer letting it go, forgetting about it. Because the more we talked about it, the greater the distance between Simon's and my (mostly) happy date seemed to grow.

But it was either this or go to the police. Paige and I hadn't wanted to bring any more attention to the situation and had convinced the boys that alerting the WHPD wasn't necessary – yet. The more they knew, the better they'd feel about figuring out who attacked me and why, without involving the authorities.

'I went downstairs to get supplies for the restroom,' I said. 'While I was in the storage closet, a box fell, hitting and shattering the overhead light. I was trying to open the box with my keys when a guy, who I assumed was Simon since it was so dark, came in. He got a little rough, I cut myself on a piece of glass, he freaked out, and I left.'

'And he shoved you?' Caleb asked. 'That was it?'

I glanced at Simon. I'd omitted some details I thought would upset him unnecessarily, and his jaw was still tense as he stared at the untouched plate on his lap.

'That was it. So it was actually good that I cut myself and screamed. Because the big, tough guy couldn't handle the sight of blood.'

'But if it was so dark,' Paige said thoughtfully, 'how'd he *see* the blood?'

Our eyes met. Hers widened and she mouthed, 'Sorry!'

'Simon called,' I said. 'He saw it in the light from my cell phone, which had fallen to the floor.'

'But it was still too dark to get a look at him?' Caleb asked.

'I didn't really try,' I confessed. 'All I cared about was getting out of there.'

Simon's hand found my knee, squeezed.

'And no one else saw or heard anything?' Caleb directed this at Paige. 'The kitchen crew didn't notice some random, angry guy passing through?'

'The kitchen crew consisted of Louis and a busboy, both of whom were so crazed, they wouldn't have noticed a commercial jet land on the prep counter. There's no other way out of the basement, and he certainly didn't come back through the dining room, so he probably slipped right out the staff entrance.' She finished off the egg roll, chewed and swallowed. 'Hence the security cameras. Tomorrow.'

'He has to be with that group, right? The one stirring up stuff about last summer, whose camera we have?' He shook his head. 'That's the only thing that makes sense.'

'Or it could be one of those guys from the orange truck.'

Simon looked at Paige. 'What guys?'

'What orange truck?' Caleb asked.

Our eyes locked again. This time, she didn't bother with a silent apology. 'You know what? I told Natalie I'd call with an update, and it's getting late, so I should do that.' She stood, taking her plate of Chinese food with her. 'The reception's better outside. I'll be on the deck if you need me.'

She left. Caleb, Simon and I sat silently for several seconds before Caleb jumped up and headed for the door.

'Speaking of the camera, I haven't checked our e-mail today. Be right back.'

As soon as he was gone, I sat up and hooked one arm through Simon's.

'It was nothing,' I said.

'What . . . was nothing?' he asked, his voice strained.

'A few weeks ago, these two guys, fishermen, I think, talked to me at the hardware store when I went there for my dad. When I left, they followed me around town for a few minutes. It was no big deal.'

He put down his plate, pulled away, and shifted on the couch to face me. 'Vanessa, that is a big deal. It'd be a big deal even if the rest of it – what you heard at the open house, the camera, Carla, today – hadn't happened. Why are you making light of it?'

'I'm not.' And I wasn't – at least to myself. 'It's just – I'm fine. I'll *be* fine.'

He took my injured hand in his. 'Twelve stitches isn't fine. Something worse could've happened if I hadn't called when I did this morning. That's not fine either. We have to talk about these things.'

I didn't say anything. Only one word came to mind – *why?* – and I didn't say it because I didn't want to hear his answer.

'Did you recognise them?' Simon asked quietly, a moment later. 'The guys in the hardware store?'

'No.'

'But they drove an orange truck?'

I nodded. 'It was old. Boxy. With fishing poles hanging out the back.'

'Maine licence plate?'

'I think so. It was pretty dark.'

'Okay. I don't recall seeing it around, but most fishermen, local and not, pass through the marina at some point for bait and tackle. Caleb and I will keep an eye out. In the meantime, if anything else happens, even something as seemingly small as a random guy bumping into you on the street ... will you tell me? Please?'

He sounded so sad, I agreed, even though I knew I'd continue to edit as necessary. If we both wanted the same thing, what did it matter how one of us helped make it happen?

'There is actually something else I need,' I said, after we'd picked at our food without speaking for what felt like hours, 'that'll definitely make me feel better.'

His face brightened. 'Another blanket? More water?'

I stood and held out my good hand. He glanced at the back door, which remained closed, then took it. I led him across the living room and upstairs.

'Vanessa,' he whispered, 'where are we going? Isn't the second floor off-limits?'

'No more than the first.' Which, given the lake house's absence of parents, had become our unofficial late-night gathering place. 'And no one will know we were here. I just want to show you something.'

It was pitch-black upstairs, but I knew every inch so well, we reached the bedroom at the end of the hall without a single collision. I left that overhead light off, too, letting the moon's bluish glow guide us to the small window seat across from the doorway.

'What are we looking at?' He peered through the window.

'My favourite place.'

'The lake? It's a great view.'

'Best in the house. But that's not what I meant.' Still holding his hand, I tugged gently until he stood before the right side of the window seat, then pressed down on one shoulder for him to sit. 'Now look.'

He craned his neck. 'It's an awkward angle. All I can see are a lot of leaves and part of my house.'

'Which part?'

'The roof . . . and a den window.'

I hesitated, wanting to see if that meant anything to him. When he turned to me, I explained.

'You liked to work there. At the desk by that window. I know because I spent many summer nights reading in this exact spot. You'd be there, head lowered, calculating or measuring or analysing, when I sat down, and you'd still be there when I looked up a hundred pages later.'

'The light must be really good here.'

'Not the best in the house, actually.' When he turned for another look, I added, 'I didn't, like, stalk you or anything. It was just nice knowing you were there. Comforting.'

He seemed to study the view. As the seconds passed, I wondered if bringing up the past was a good idea. It certainly wasn't the obvious choice for convincing him I was someone else, but I thought it still might work, since the old Vanessa hadn't been bold enough to share this spot and secret.

Before I could really worry, he turned back and said, 'I wouldn't have minded if you did.'

He hooked one finger on the pocket of my jeans and pulled me into his lap. I nuzzled against his chest and brought my knees to mine. He wrapped both arms around me and held me close. Then, since it had worked well so far, I closed my eyes and shared some more.

'I want to be with you, Simon,' I whispered. 'I don't know if I'm supposed to say that . . . I don't know if you want to hear it . . . but I do.' I could feel his heart beat stronger, faster. 'When I think of you first thing in the morning, I want to be able to call and hear your voice. When something good happens, I want to tell you before I tell anyone else. When I can't sleep at night, I want to eventually drift off knowing I'll see you the next day.' I opened my eyes, found his. 'More than anything, I want to make you happy – not worried or concerned or protective. *Happy.* Every day, for as long as you'll let me. If you'll let me.'

These, too, were words I wouldn't have said a year ago, even though they'd been as true then as they were now.

'What if the longest I can let you is a month?' he asked quietly.

My heart sank. Was he going back to school early? Did he, like Charlotte, think it was best to cut ties sooner rather than later?

Did it matter?

'I'll take it,' I said.

He pulled me closer, lifted his chin so his lips were inches from mine. 'This summer?'

'Even better.'

His mouth neared mine. 'For ever?'

A ball of heat burst in my belly, shooting off waves of warmth. 'Please.'

The kisses that followed felt new, different – even from the ones we shared on the covered bridge. They were at once tender and urgent, soft and firm, sweet and passionate. And they probably would've lasted until we felt daylight on our backs as the sun came up the next morning – if a door hadn't slammed suddenly below us.

'Simon?' Caleb yelled.

'Vanessa?' Paige shouted.

We pulled apart, jumped up. Simon took my hand and held on tight as we ran out of the room and downstairs.

'What is it?' he asked, before we'd even cleared the last step.

Paige moved aside the take-out cartons littering the coffee table. Caleb put down his open laptop. They both sat on the edge of the couch and stared at the screen.

'We got responses,' Caleb said. 'To the camera post in the *Herald*.'

'You gave out your e-mail?' I asked, following Simon around the coffee table.

'I created a new address just for this.'

'Lostcamerainwinterharbor at gmail dot com,' Paige read from the screen. 'Clever.'

'Thanks.' Caleb's fingers flew across the keyboard as

he typed. 'I wasn't sure our Wi-Fi would reach here, so I downloaded all the messages without reading them.'

We were silent as we watched the e-mails load.

'They're all from different addresses,' Paige said.

'Which look as made-up as yours.' Simon leaned closer. 'Just a bunch of random letters and numbers at the same server.'

'And they all have attachments,' I said, noting the paper clip icons. 'What'd they do? Retake pictures with another camera to prove the one we have is theirs?'

'But they'd need only one e-mail address for that,' Paige said.

These questions were answered as more were raised. The attachments were pictures – each e-mail contained one photo and no message – but they weren't ones we'd already seen. There were a few nature shots, close-ups of other rocks and patches of grass, as well as several taken around town – at Eddie's Ice Cream, the miniature golf course, the library. People were in the latter, though they didn't seem to know their pictures were being taken. And the camera didn't focus on any one person in particular.

'That's all of them,' Caleb said, once the last had loaded.

'Can you map the locations?' Simon asked.

Caleb typed some more. 'No coordinates. They

must've wised up and disabled the GPS on their new camera.'

He scrolled slowly through the images. I was searching for a common link when Paige put one hand on Caleb's, stopping the cursor.

'That girl's in every people shot.' She pointed.

'How can you tell?' Caleb asked. 'You can't even see her face in this one.'

'Green handbag and pink shoes,' Paige said. 'They're hard to miss.'

She was right. The girl, who'd been caught buying a sundae, putting on the ninth hole, returning a book to the overnight bin, and running other errands, was in every picture that featured people.

'Why?' Simon asked. 'Who is she?'

As Caleb zoomed for a better look, the computer beeped.

'I guess our Wi-Fi reaches after all.' He minimised the photo and pulled up his e-mail, which was still open. 'There's a new message and another picture.'

The picture was also a people shot, but there was only one person in it. And she wasn't the woman with the green bag and pink shoes.

She was Carla. Bruised and unconscious, her body folded at the waist, her wrists tied together. Her eyes, half lidded and seemingly pleading, aimed at the camera.

A car door slammed outside. Simon and Caleb leapt from the couch at the same time and hurried to the hall window.

'It's a black Audi,' Simon announced. 'Your realtor.'

I stood, heart pounding, relieved for a reason to look away from the computer.

'Were you expecting her?' he asked.

'No, but that doesn't mean anything. She's probably just dropping something off for another showing.' I kissed his cheek as I opened the door. 'I'll be fine, but feel free to watch from here.'

'Thank you. I will.'

The Audi's hatchback was raised as I approached. It wasn't until it closed that I realised Anne wasn't behind it – Colin was.

'Vanessa, hey.' He grinned. 'I didn't know you'd be here.'

'Yeah.' I glanced back, waved to Simon. 'My friends and I were just having one last dinner. You know, reminiscing and stuff. We didn't tell my parents because we figured they'd tell us to stay out.'

'Totally understand and I won't say a word.' He held up a long ceramic planter filled with flowers. 'My mom asked me to drop this off. Thought it'd help with kerb appeal.'

'Sounds good. Put it anywhere you'd like.'

Where he liked, unfortunately, was on the front stoop, where Simon now stood. After introducing himself to Simon, who shook his hand cautiously, Colin peered into the living room.

'Is that . . . ?' Colin's voice trailed off as he looked at Simon, then at me. 'Sorry, can I just see something?'

'I don't know if –'

'Sure,' I said, interrupting Simon. I understood his concern, but Colin seemed harmless enough. Plus, I wanted to keep him happy so he wouldn't be tempted to spill the beans about our late-night gathering spot – or mention anything about what happened between us on the beach a week ago.

'It's okay,' I said, after Colin entered the house and I passed Simon. 'He'll be in and out.'

'Is that the new MacBook Pro? It is, isn't it?'

Simon and I reached the living room right as Caleb slammed the laptop shut and glared at Colin.

'Sorry.' Colin backed up, away from the coffee table. 'I didn't mean to intrude, I just hadn't seen one in person yet.'

'It's okay,' I said, before anyone said something he or

she would regret. 'Colin, was there anything else you or your mom needed?'

He shook his head and apologised again. I showed him to the door, left Simon to watch him drive away, and excused myself to the bathroom.

I avoided the mirror as I filled the basin and emptied the baggie of salt I'd stashed between two folded towels, which had been left in the linen cupboard for staging purposes, earlier in the evening. But then, too curious to know what the visible physical effects were of a day filled with such stress, both good and bad, I snuck a peek.

Beautiful.

It was the first word that came to mind, and I was the most insecure girl I knew. But I couldn't help it. Unlike my reflection in Betty's restroom mirror only hours before, my skin was soft and smooth, without the slightest wrinkle or crease. My hair shone as it hung in loose waves to my shoulders. My lips were pink, moist.

My eyes were wide. Bright.

And more silver than they'd ever been.

CHAPTER 16

One Week Later, No Leads in Marciano Case

Despite numerous requests for tips, Winter Harbor police have yet to hear from any witnesses who were on or near the scene of 18-year-old Carla Marciano's untimely death.

When asked if the incident – and lack of information – was reminiscent of last summer's string of water-related fatalities, Police Chief Green said, 'Yes and no. We experienced a similar lack of public feedback last year, but the nature of the deaths is very different.' Chief Green remained tight-lipped on how the situations differ, other than to say, 'This one was no accident.'

Miss Marciano's family is hopeful that the truth will eventually come to light, even though they, too, cannot contribute much. 'She was at work,' said Pamela Marciano, the victim's mother. 'She was home all day, she went to work – and got there safely, according to a text she sent shortly after –

and she disappeared on her break. That's all we know. But someone must've seen something. My Carla said Murph's had been even busier than usual lately. When they're ready, witnesses will come forward. They have to.'

Understandably, the tragedy has rattled local residents and visitors alike. Said Margot Davenport, a swimming instructor at the Winter Harbor Community Center, 'Am I scared? No. I'm terrified. This summer was supposed to be our chance to start over. But how can we ever move forward if we're constantly looking over our shoulders?'

The article ended with the police department's phone number, e-mail address, and website. I skimmed the other front-page headlines, then flipped through the rest of the paper. For better or worse, Carla remained the top news story, which meant hers was the only death to report.

'These are the biggest lobster rolls I've ever seen,' Charlotte said.

I pushed the paper aside as she walked towards the picnic table carrying two paper plates.

'Probably because with fewer customers, they have crustaceans to spare.' I took one of the plates and watched her round the table and lower herself, slowly, to the bench on the other side. Rather than climb over the seat, she kept her legs outside and sat at an angle. 'I don't know why you didn't let me get lunch.'

'Because I knew you wanted to save me the ten-foot trip from the Seafood Shack.' She smiled, spread a paper napkin in her lap. 'And that wasn't necessary.'

I sipped my water to keep from disagreeing. She still looked great in her long sundress, crocheted vest, and big sunglasses, but she was moving even slower than when she'd first arrived in Winter Harbor. Even now, after the twenty-foot-long round-trip, she breathed quickly. Her forehead was damp with perspiration. Her hands twitched as she raised the sandwich to her mouth.

'Can I ask you something?'

She chewed, swallowed. 'I feel fine, Vanessa. I promise.'

'Good. But that wasn't my question.' I wondered that to myself, of course, but didn't want to pry.

'Oh.' She sounded simultaneously surprised and relieved. 'Well, what is it?'

I was glad the cloudless blue sky made sunglasses necessary, so she couldn't see my eyes shift to the newspaper at the other end of the table. 'Have you heard anything . . . strange lately?'

She'd been about to take another bite but stopped. 'What do you mean by strange?'

229

'I mean, I don't know . . . voices? Singing?'

She lowered her sandwich and I knew she understood what I was asking. 'Why? Have you?'

'No . . . but I don't really know how to listen.'

She looked around to make sure we were far enough away from the few other people on the pier, then leaned towards me. 'How are *you* feeling? Have you been having headaches again?'

I hadn't, but this was a good segue to another question I wanted to ask. There were so many at this point, I didn't know how to raise them without overwhelming Charlotte – or me. Assuming she'd have been less surprised at my initial question if she had heard something recently, I decided to go with the second.

'I've felt better,' I admitted. When her face instantly tightened, I added quickly, 'My head's fine. No pain at all. But the rest of my body's another story.'

Her lips pressed together, as the skin around them softened. 'Go on.'

Not wanting to alarm her, I took a big bite of my sandwich before continuing. If eating came before what I was about to say, then it couldn't be that serious.

'It's been a little unpredictable lately,' I finally said. 'One minute, I feel strong and energised, and the next, I feel like I'm about to pass out.' She didn't need to know that I'd actually collapsed behind the lake house a few weeks earlier. 'I had a decent handle on it over the school year and knew that I'd need refuelling after a certain amount of time or a particularly stressful situation. I also knew how to refuel, either by drinking, bathing or swimming in salt water. But something's changed. What used to satisfy me now does or doesn't. If it does, the effect fades faster. In general, I get tired and feel cravings much sooner. I know you said I'd need more as a Nenuphar, but sometimes it seems like nothing's enough.'

'You're becoming stronger,' Charlotte said evenly. 'Even when you're weak, your body's still learning, developing, *growing*. What you describe is happening faster than it did for me and much faster than I'd hoped for you, but it's not unexpected.'

I couldn't see her eyes behind her sunglasses, but any hint of surprise was gone from her face. Even her lips had relaxed, turning down at the corners.

'Parker King.'

The name was like a slap in the face. I sat back, reached for my water bottle.

'What happened with him?' Charlotte asked.

'Nothing.' The word shot from my mouth. 'After Simon and I broke up, I told Parker we couldn't be friends – or anything else. We didn't say more than five words to each other before graduation.'

'What did you say to each other then?'

Defensiveness burned in my belly and I struggled to stifle the sensation. Charlotte sounded merely curious, not judgemental.

'He came up after the ceremony to say hi – and good-bye.' I didn't look at her as I picked at my sandwich. 'And to tell me he was going to Princeton after all, the way his father wanted him to.'

'How did you feel about that?'

'Terrible. He didn't want to go to Princeton. He wanted to get a boat – a small one, not the kind of yacht his family had – and sail up and down the coasts.' I frowned. 'At one point, he wanted me to go with him.'

We were quiet for a moment. The only sounds on the beach were the oldies music coming from the Seafood Shack and laughter from a group of guys playing Frisbee.

'You cared for him.'

'No, I didn't.'

'If that were true you wouldn't be so emotional now.'

'We were friends. Not for long, but still. I'd feel the same way about any girlfriend who told me she was do-ing something against her wishes, because her parents wanted her to.'

'Even if that girlfriend had come between you and the one person you loved more than anyone else in the world?'

I pushed my plate away, drained my water bottle. It

wasn't just what Charlotte said now that was upsetting. It was thinking back to graduation day, when Parker had given me a shy smile and hug – and I'd resisted holding on to him and refusing to let go. It was remembering the months before then, when we hadn't talked at my insistence, but exchanged fleeting glances in the hallways at school. It was being reminded of the time we'd spent together last fall, and how my body had been drawn to his, and the way my heart had started to follow. If he ever crossed my mind now – and he did, despite my best efforts – it was only as a reminder that Simon deserved as much as I could possibly give him, and more.

'I'm not trying to upset you, Vanessa,' Charlotte continued. 'I know you love Simon more than anything or anyone. But if you can, think about how you feel when you're with him and compare that to how you felt when you were with Parker. Physically, I mean. You don't have to share your answer with me, of course, but is there a difference?'

I didn't have to think about this. I didn't have to compare. I already had.

There was a big difference. Being with Simon was amazing and exciting and all I wanted.

Being with Parker had been amazing and exciting... and all I'd *needed*. We'd only kissed a few times, but those brief exchanges, which I hadn't been able to stop, no matter how hard my head tried to intervene, had energised me and set my body on autopilot for days.

'You know what I'm going to say.'

I looked up from my plate.

'I'm still not listening to your thoughts,' Charlotte said, 'which is a topic, by the way, that we'll come back to. But you're a smart girl. You might not have let yourself believe it . . . but you brought this up with me for confirmation only.'

'But Paige feels fine,' I said, still wanting there to be some other explanation. 'She told me she feels no differently here from how she did back in Boston.'

'Because, as I explained a while ago, the long-term efficacy of salt water fades with time. It's still necessary, but it's not enough to sustain you. Paige transformed months after you did, so her body's still adjusting.' Charlotte looked away, towards the harbour. 'Plus, it's unlikely that you'll respond the same way to various energy sources. After all, Paige isn't a Nenuphar. You'll always need more than she will.'

Before I could respond, a Frisbee landed on the table between us.

'Sorry!' A guy in board shorts and a sweatshirt jogged towards us. He appeared to be in his late twenties. 'Slippery fingers!'

'Watch,' Charlotte whispered. Or at least I think she did. The word came and went in an instant.

'Hey.' He slowed to a walk, motioned to our food. 'Hope I didn't ruin your lunch.'

'Not at all.' Charlotte picked up the Frisbee, removed her sunglasses, and smiled. 'Nice day for a game.'

'Yeah, my friends and I –'

He stopped, his eyes frozen to Charlotte's. Still holding the Frisbee in one hand, she pressed the other to his chest. A high-pitched note sounded; I tore my gaze away from them to look behind me, thinking the Seafood Shack must be experiencing technical difficulties with its outdoor speaker system, but the music played normally. The steady note grew softer when I turned away and louder as I turned back.

Charlotte. Her lips weren't moving . . . but somehow the noise was coming from her. It lasted five seconds, tops, growing in depth and volume and wavering at the end, but it was enough for her fingers to straighten, her skin to smooth, her white hair to darken to grey.

And then it was over. She dropped her hand from his chest and gave him the Frisbee.

'Thanks.' He blinked and took the plastic disc.

Charlotte put her sunglasses back on and returned to her sandwich. The guy stood there another second or two before backing away. There was another note, this one so soft and short, I thought I might be hearing things, and then the guy shook his head, turned, and jogged towards his friends. He didn't look back once as he returned to them, or after their game resumed.

'What *was* that?' I asked.

Charlotte, as though finally strong enough to feel her appetite, ate hungrily.

'He didn't even look at me,' I said. 'It was like I wasn't sitting right in front of him. That – and please don't take this as anything other than an appreciative observation – hasn't happened in a very long time.' I motioned to her arm. 'And look at your skin! It's so smooth, like you just finished a month-long swim or something.' I glanced back. 'He's totally oblivious. It's like nothing happened.'

'To him, nothing did.' She polished off the sandwich.

I thought of my reflection in the bathroom mirror at the lake house the other day. Is that why I'd looked so pretty? Because I'd screamed in the basement – or tried to, though the sound had come out very different – with my arms around that guy? And his response had energised me, shaving unnatural age from my physical appearance?

'Does he know he came over here?' I asked, returning to the present.

'Yes, but he'll remember only taking the Frisbee from the table. He won't remember our brief conversation.'

'But how's that possible? I mean, you actually touched him, and for several seconds.'

Charlotte placed her hands on the table, stood slightly, and lifted one leg, then the other over the bench. Her body was still frail, but steady. Our knees grazed under the table as she leaned closer.

'Vanessa, what you've been experiencing – the inconsistent energy levels, the sudden thirst, the debilitating fatigue – will continue. In fact, it will worsen. The only way to stave off the symptoms for longer periods of time is to invite the attention, both emotional and physical, of a member of the opposite sex – preferably someone who's interested in another girl, and whose attention you have to work for. This was the case with Parker, yes?'

'Yes, but I can't –'

'Do that to Simon again. I know. That's why I demonstrated a shortcut.'

'A shortcut . . . to what?'

'Your target's heart. Using physical contact and your inner voice. It will never provide the same long-term results as forging a more intimate relationship would, but it does a million times more than that bottle of salt water you just polished off. And if done correctly and often enough, it will get you from one day to the next without having to do anything more.'

I tried to make sense of this explanation and what I'd

just witnessed. 'But isn't that kind of hard? To go up to some random guy and do what you did – especially in public, with people around? Or do you wait for a beach to clear?'

'It's not easy,' Charlotte admitted. 'None of it is. It's up to you to decide which battle is worth risking the potential consequences.'

'So that's it? I start a relationship with some guy I care nothing about and lose Simon now and for ever, or I hypnotise lots of guys for short periods of time and hope no one notices? Those are my only two choices?'

Her head lowered. I hoped she was racking her brain or listening to another older, more experienced siren, one who could offer a more appealing alternative – preferably one that didn't involve *any* random guys.

Whatever she was thinking was soon interrupted. A scream pierced the air, drowning out the oldies music and making both Charlotte and me jump. I swivelled on the bench and scanned the shore. There were only a dozen or so people on the pier besides us and the Frisbee crew, and even fewer on the beach. It didn't take long to locate the noise's source.

It came from a couple near the bronze fisherman statue – the same one Paige said all tourists needed to preserve for ever via digital and cell-phone cameras. The girl, still yelling but not quite at the same pitch, shoved the guy. He reached for her, put his arms around her, pulled her towards him. She yelled again, squirming in his grasp.

I was so busy trying to decipher the words in her rant, I didn't notice what she was wearing right away. When I registered the khaki shorts, black T-shirt, and black apron, I leapt up from the bench and started running.

'Vanessa!' Charlotte called after me.

'Be right back!' I shouted back, yanking my phone from the pocket of my shorts. I opened it as I ran, keeping my thumb poised over the nine. The police department was so close to the pier, there was a good chance an officer could see the scuffle without getting up from his desk inside, but I didn't want to take any chances.

As it happened, I didn't need to call 9-1-1. The dispute broke up as I neared, and the guy stormed off to a blue SUV with Vermont licence plates. The girl strode towards the beach and dropped into the sand, covering her face with one hand and her neck with the other.

'Are you okay?'

Natalie gasped and looked up. 'Vanessa?'

I dropped to my knees. 'What happened? Who was that?'

She looked past me to the other people scattered across the pier and beach. 'Oh no,' she groaned, now using both hands to cover her face. 'I'm so embarrassed!'

'Don't worry about – ' I stopped when my eyes fell to the thin pink ring around her neck. Stretches were turning purple, already bruising.

'That was me.' Natalie held up a broken silver chain. 'My hands were shaking so hard, I couldn't undo the clasp, so I grabbed it and pulled as hard as I could. If only I were Sandra Bullock and this was a movie and not my life, it totally would've worked – without anyone getting hurt.'

My internal alarm quieter, I sat back on my heels. 'That was your fiancé?'

'*Ex*-fiancé.' She made a fist, pounded the sand once. 'I'm such an idiot. *Why* am I such an idiot?'

Remembering Charlotte, I turned and gave her a small wave to let her know everything was okay. Seeing other spectators, I waved to them, too.

'It's just – Will told me he wanted to talk. He said it was so important, we needed to meet in person. And then he drove seven hours to get here! *Seven* hours! Before today, the longest he'd ever driven to see me was forty minutes – and that was only because there was a blizzard and he didn't want to be snowed in at home without his iPod, which he'd left at my house.' She aimed her fist at the sand again, but it lost momentum and landed with a soft *plop*. 'Idiot me thought he wanted to get back together.'

'You're not an idiot,' I said, then paused. 'But that's not what he wanted?'

'Not even close.' She brought her legs into her chest and rested her forehead on her knees. 'He wanted the ring.'

'Your engagement ring? Why?'

'To give to his new girlfriend? To sell so he could buy something else for his new girlfriend? Who knows? Who cares?' She sighed. '*I* care. Because –'

'Because you're human,' I finished. 'Anyone else in the same situation would react the same way.'

She rolled her head to the left and looked at me side-ways. 'Really? Anyone else would scream and yell and put on a mortifying public display of epic proportions?'

'You thought that was epic?' I asked lightly. 'Please. This is a tourist town. This pier has seen way worse than that – especially when people who've spent too much time in the sun during the day decide to drink the night away.'

One corner of her mouth lifted, then fell. 'It was enough to make you come running.'

I nodded. 'Yes, well. After Carla and what happened at Betty's the other day . . . I guess I'm on high alert. But that's my issue, not yours.'

'Well, thank you anyway.' She sniffed, brushed at her eyes. 'Paige said you were a great friend. She wasn't kid-ding.'

Wanting to make sure she really was okay, I sat next to her and we fell into a comfortable silence. I thought about how suspicious I'd been, how wary of her friendship with Paige, and I felt bad. She was going through a tough time. Why *wouldn't* she want to latch on to someone else? And immerse herself in a totally different world to help forget her own? I knew better than anyone how tempting that was.

A few moments later, she sat up straight and slapped her palms to her thighs.

'That's it. I'm not going to waste one more second thinking about him. Guys just aren't worth the effort or inevitable agony.' She jumped to her feet and held out one hand to help me up. 'Except for maybe yours. What do you think? Is he worth it?'

I took her hand, started to stand – and immediately fell back. My legs, either from the emotional stress caused by what I first thought was happening to Natalie, the physical exertion it took to reach her, or simply my body's normal process, were exhausted.

As if on cue, a Frisbee landed in the sand next to me. Its owner left the group of twenty-somethings down the beach and ran towards me. My eyes rose slowly until they landed on his chest.

'Yes,' I said. 'He is.'

CHAPTER 17

'It's dark in here,' Simon said.

'It's a movie theatre,' I reminded him.

We were sitting in the back row. As the pre-show ads played, he scanned the other rows in front of ours. 'Maybe this wasn't a good idea.'

'It's a great idea. We haven't been to the movies together in years.'

'I know, but . . . wouldn't you rather watch a DVD at one of our houses?'

'And forgo the big screen? The ambience? The *popcorn*?' I shook my head – and the greasy container. 'Nope.'

He settled back in his seat and looked at me. He smiled but his eyes were worried. He wanted to be here and have a normal date, just like I did, but he couldn't help wondering who else was in the audience.

'Nothing has happened,' I said quietly. 'It's been days and not one new headline, e-mail, or trip to the ER for stitches.'

His eyes lowered to my injured hand, which was

clasped loosely in his. The wound was healing well and you wouldn't notice the bandage unless you looked directly at my palm, but Simon didn't need to see proof of the basement attack to remember that it had occurred.

'There's been no sign of the orange truck at the marina, right?' I asked.

His thumb stroked the top of my hand. 'Right.'

'And look – there are at least fifteen people in here. Who'd try anything with so many eyes and ears around?'

The ads gave way to trailers. Simon leaned across the armrest and tilted his face towards mine. We kissed just as the dim overhead lights went out.

'Did you see that?' he whispered, pulling back.

I did. It was a quick burst of white that lit up the theatre before fading. 'There.' I nodded to a group of kids a few rows down. They were laughing as they made faces and took pictures of one another with a cell phone. 'They're too young,' I added, before he could worry they were the ones I'd seen by the lake a few weeks ago.

The movie started a few minutes later. The Winter Harbor Cinema had only two screens and between our choices of a comedy or a drama, we'd gone with the former. It was a good move because Simon seemed to relax, putting his arm around me and pressing his lips to my temple in between funny scenes.

I was at ease, too – at least at first. But we weren't

even half an hour into the movie when the familiar discomfort began to take over. I shoved salty popcorn in my mouth by the handful and drank Simon's soda after finishing the water I'd sneaked in my bag, but it wasn't enough.

This is ridiculous, I thought to myself. *I'm not even* doing *anything. I'm just sitting here.*

It didn't matter. So I stood before I no longer could.

'Ladies and refill,' I explained softly when Simon sat up. I took the empty paper cup, kissed his cheek, and climbed over his feet. 'I'll be two minutes.'

I was briefly blinded again when I reached the lobby, and it took a second to remember it was the middle of the afternoon. Blinking against the daylight, I tossed the cup into the trash and made a beeline for the ladies' room.

Which, unfortunately, wasn't empty. Of three stalls, two were occupied. To buy time, I entered the third and took care of business.

When I came out, a girl was at one of the basins, washing her hands. Our eyes met in the mirror on the wall, and I thought I saw something flash across her face. Was it surprise? Recognition? Had I seated her at Betty's lately? Whatever the expression, it came and went too quickly to tell. I offered a smile just in case, and her mouth turned up for an instant as her gaze dropped.

I went to the basin one down from hers and turned on the water, which, thankfully, took several seconds to warm up. By the time it did and I washed my hands, this girl would be done and gone and the other still in the stall would be on her way.

Or maybe not. Because this girl, who looked to be a few years older than me, was in no rush. She rinsed and dried her hands, took lotion from her handbag, and moisturised her palms for what seemed like minutes. Then, apparently too moisturised, she washed her hands again and repeated the same process with a smaller amount of lotion. Each time, she took not one but two turns at the dryer, which was understandable since the ancient appliance had always blown more cold air than hot.

Once her hands were appropriately moistened, she re-did her make-up. She took one item – lip gloss, mascara, blush – at a time from her bag, and lined them all up on the small metal shelf beneath the mirror. She spent several seconds on each facial feature, which wasn't quite as understandable since her make-up already looked per-fectly – and recently – done. After all that, she moved on to her long brown hair, brushing and arranging and spraying like she was preparing for a professional photo shoot.

Unwilling to leave the room without doing what I'd

come here to do, I did my best to stall. My bag, however, wasn't as well stocked, and it took some quick creative thinking to come up with reasons to linger. I was buttoning and unbuttoning the long cashmere sweater I'd borrowed from Charlotte and examining my appearance in the mirror when the girl turned to me.

'You look familiar,' she said. 'Have we met?'

'I don't think so. But have you been to Betty's Chowder House lately? I'm the hostess there.'

Her green eyes narrowed and her pink lips puckered. 'I don't do seafood.'

'Are you from Winter Harbor?' I asked. 'My family's been coming here for ever, so maybe we've seen each other around town.'

'Maybe.' She sounded doubtful.

My face warmed as she studied me. A long moment later, she shrugged and turned back to her mobile make-up counter. I swallowed a sigh of relief as she brushed all of the cosmetics back into her bag at once. A few minutes more and I might've passed out before I could rehydrate.

'*I* know!' She spun back, her smile wide and eyes bright. 'You're that girl.'

I paused. 'What girl?'

'The one from last summer. Whose sister fell off a cliff and died.'

As she beamed, clearly proud of her supreme powers of recall, I grabbed the handbasin to steady myself.

'I'm amazed you came back.' She took her jacket from the side of the basin and started towards the door. 'I mean, most family members dread returning to the scene of the crime . . . or at least that's how it goes in the movies, right?'

A sudden loud noise echoed through the room. She stopped, facing the door, and I bent down to pick up her cell phone, which must've fallen from her jacket pocket. The phone was open, and as I handed it to her, I caught a glimpse of shiny red floor tile moving across the small screen.

'Thanks.' She grabbed the phone and disappeared into the lobby.

Too afraid to waste time and energy by crossing the room to lock the door, I leaned against the basin, turned the water on full blast, and plugged the drain. I took the snack bag of salt from my bag and emptied its contents into the small, swirling pool.

'You'd think we'd all share the same basic set.'

I gasped, turned off the water, and spun around. I'd been so taken aback by the brunette's comment and distracted by my weakening body, I'd forgotten about the room's other occupant. She stood, a pretty, heavier-set blonde, in the open doorway of the third stall, dabbing at her eyes.

'But some people are just born without, I guess.' She sniffed, stepped out of the doorway.

I inhaled, exhaled. Inhaled, exhaled. 'Without what?' I asked, when I could finally speak.

'The most rudimentary set of social skills. The kind that keeps you from blurting out terrible things to a complete stranger in a public bathroom – or at least makes you aware that's what you're doing and prompts you to apologise, if you absolutely can't stop yourself.' She took a deep breath and blew her nose. 'Also the kind that keeps you from standing up the poor, pathetic woman who finally worked up the nerve to invite you to a movie after seeing you at the same coffee shop every morning for a month.'

For a brief moment, I forgot my own problems. 'I'm sorry.'

'Me, too.' She balled up the tissue, tossed it towards the trash can. It missed and landed on the floor. 'Normally, I would've burst out and given that brat a piece of my mind, but I knew I'd just start blubbering all over again. And that wouldn't have done anything for anyone – except for maybe the rude girl who probably would've gotten a good laugh.'

'Is there anything I can do?' I asked. 'Want me to

stand guard outside and not let anyone in until you're ready to come out?'

She smiled. 'Thank you, but that could take a while and I've already been hiding out for twenty minutes.' She shuffled across the room, picked up her discarded tissue, and dropped it in the trash. 'But there is something else you can do.'

'Name it.' I started to take my phone from my jeans to text Simon and let him know I was fine but needed another few minutes.

'Be careful.'

My fingers froze in my pocket.

'It doesn't matter what they tell you or what you want to believe . . . guys cannot be trusted.'

She gave me another sad smile, yanked a handful of paper towels from the wall dispenser, and left the room.

I turned back to the basin, which was nearly empty despite being full moments before. The remaining salt water gurgled past the old rubber stopper and slid down the drain.

'Great,' I muttered. I'd been in a hurry to meet Simon earlier and had brought only one bag of salt.

I turned on the tap, cupped my hands beneath the water, and drank. Regular water didn't do for my energy what salt water did, but it was still something. And I needed whatever I could get if my legs were going to carry me all the way to the concession stand.

'Vanessa.' Simon strode across the lobby when I entered it, cell phone in hand. 'Are you okay?'

Not trusting my body to remain upright, I stopped and let him come to me. 'Of course,' I said.

'You've been gone ten minutes.'

This was surprising to me, too. It hadn't felt like that long. 'I'm sorry.' I gave him a quick, reassuring hug when he reached me. 'There was a situation.'

He held me at arm's length. 'What do you mean? What kind of situation?'

'The red-eyed-girl kind.' I nodded towards the cinema exit, where the blonde was heading for the double doors, her arms filled with the bags of candy she'd apparently bought while I was still in the Ladies. 'Poor thing was stood up.'

Simon's arms relaxed. 'That's terrible.'

'It is. That's why I offered her a listening ear. If I hadn't, she probably would've set up permanent residency in stall three.'

He leaned closer, kissed my forehead. 'You're sweet.'

'And I still owe you a soda, which I was just about to get. Meet you inside?'

'That's okay, I don't need it.'

I held firm when he tugged gently on my good hand. 'I insist.'

'All right,' he said, giving me an uncertain grin. 'Then I'll come with you.'

'But I don't want you to miss any more of the movie.'

Normally, this wouldn't be enough of a reason for him to leave me unattended when he was already worried. But just as I was trying to be braver, he was trying to be less overprotective. So he gave my hand another squeeze before releasing it.

'See you inside,' he said.

I waited until the theatre door closed behind him before moving as fast as my body would allow towards the snack counter. Because both movies were well under way, there was no queue and only one employee manning the concessions.

I ordered a large popcorn, a large soda, and a bottled water. My presence seemed to throw off the employee, a tall, gangly boy who looked no older than seventeen. According to his name tag, his name was Tim. He dropped my money, gave me too much change, and bumped into the candy case before finally making it to the beverage counter. Returning to me took even longer as he dumped half the soda en route and had to go back for a refill. When he left the drinks in front of me and turned towards the popcorn machine, I opened the water, emptied a saltshaker inside, shook the bottle, and drank.

By some miracle, the popcorn was easier for Tim to handle, and he came back with the bucket while I was still guzzling.

'Extra butter,' I said, coming up for air. 'Please?'

'Sure.' His face broke into a smile, like I'd just asked him to ditch this part-time gig and run away to Vegas with me.

I tried to return his smile but couldn't. As I continued drinking, I realised something was very wrong – the salt water wasn't working. The white spots popping across my vision faded with each swallow, but the instant the water reached the bottom of my throat, they reappeared. The more I drank, the more they multiplied and the faster they moved. Soon my head joined them, spinning so quickly, I couldn't make sense of my thoughts.

'Is this enough?' Tim asked. 'Or do you want –'

He stopped. I couldn't see much through my blurred vision, but I saw enough.

Like his brown eyes, wide, unfocused. My good hand, reaching out. My fingers grabbing his yellow polo shirt. My palm pressing against his chest.

An explosion of silver, swallowing my entire field of vision.

'Vanessa?'

At Simon's voice, my hand fell to the counter. I blinked, and my vision cleared.

'Did you hear that?'

I did. There were two soft, high-pitched notes. The first lasted several seconds, and wavered at the end. The second ended almost as quickly as it began. Both seemed to come from inside my body and nowhere near it at once.

But this unearthly music, it turned out, wasn't what Simon was referring to.

'That girl,' he said, when I turned around. 'The one who was stood up? I knew there was something familiar about her and I just figured out what it was.' He stepped towards me, not even glancing at Tim, who I assumed was still behind the counter. 'She had blonde hair. Her shoes were pink and her bag was green. Just like –'

'The pictures,' I finished, not believing I hadn't put it together myself. 'From the e-mails.'

'Do you think it's her?' he asked.

I didn't answer. I didn't have to.

The scream outside said it all.

CHAPTER 18

The victim's name was Erica Anderson. She was twenty-eight and had grown up in Winter Harbor, gone to college in upstate New York, and returned to Maine after working around the north-east for a few years as a professional nanny. She'd got a job at Waterside Nails and Tails, the local salon, to pay rent, but often talked about going back to school for a master's in education. She'd adored Poppy, her cocker spaniel, which would now be looked after by her parents and younger brother, who still lived in Winter Harbor.

'That's all?' Paige asked. 'What about her shoe size? Or her love of macaroons and Trivial Pursuit? Or the fact that years before she was a professional nanny, she was the most popular babysitter in town?'

'This isn't your fault,' I said gently, not for the first time.

She sat back, away from the *Herald* website displayed on the computer screen. 'I should have recognised her.'

'She babysat Simon and me,' Caleb said, 'and we didn't recognise her, either. The pictures never gave a clear shot. And with the weight gain and dyed hair, she looked totally different.'

'I talked to her minutes before and didn't put it together. Even if one of us had, would it have mattered? We couldn't know for sure that this was going to happen.' That's what I'd been telling myself anyway. I had yet to believe it.

'Paige has a point, though.' Simon scrolled down the page. 'There's a lot of information about Erica . . . but nothing about what happened to her.'

'Maybe the police want to investigate more before they say too much,' I said.

'Or maybe they're so exhausted from last summer, they've simply given up.' Paige shook her head. 'I mean, it was the middle of the day. In the middle of town. How were there no witnesses?'

It was a good question, and we didn't have an answer. Erica had been discovered lying by a rubbish skip in an alley between the cinema and a bagel shop. The scream we'd heard inside the lobby had come from the older woman who'd spotted Erica's leg sticking out from behind the metal bin, while walking with her grandson. Simon and I beat the police there by minutes; I'd stayed back, unable to look away from the discarded pink kitten heel, but he'd gone right up to the body. After checking for a pulse and obvious signs of struggle, he'd sprinted down the alley and around the block in search of her attacker.

But the attacker had escaped – somewhere, it seemed, with a computer. I knew because Simon had been standing next to me, still catching his breath, when Caleb had texted to let him know they'd received a new e-mail.

Neither of us was surprised when the attachment was a photo of Erica's lifeless face.

'It had to be the guy who stood her up.' Simon looked at me. 'Don't you think? He probably even agreed to the date with the intention of doing what he did.'

'Maybe,' I said. 'She did say *she* asked *him* out – and after seeing him at the coffee shop every day for a month. And it's only July tenth. The group I saw at the lake house looked pretty young – college-aged, tops – so would they have already been in town that long?'

'The pictures on the camera they dropped were taken three weeks ago.' Caleb shrugged. 'Another few days wouldn't be too big a stretch.'

'What about that other girl?' Simon asked. 'The one with all the make-up? She knew who you were, right?'

I nodded, glad I'd come clean this time and shared (almost) everything about what had happened in the cinema restroom. 'But she had a delayed response, just like you guys did with Erica. She seemed to recognise me, but it took until she was leaving for her to remember why.'

'But how could she know who you were?' Caleb asked. 'Some of the articles last summer mentioned Justine having a sister, but your picture was never included.'

This was another good question without an answer. There was also the fact that the brunette had taken for ever to do her hair and make-up. Had she been waiting for Erica to come out of the stall? For me to leave? Both?

'Well, if she had something to do with it,' Simon said, 'she didn't act alone. The bruises on Erica's neck are too wide. Someone bigger and stronger helped.'

Paige groaned lightly, stood, and walked to the deck railing. 'If it is the crazy stalkers doing this . . . why? If they want to get our attention, or expose us to the world, or whatever, why aren't they going after men, to alert us and bring us out of hiding? Or since they seem to know something about Vanessa's involvement, why aren't they targeting us directly? Do they think all women in Winter Harbor are like us and deserve to be punished? And if that's the case, should we, I don't know, make some kind of announcement? To save the rest of the female population?'

The more Paige spoke, the faster the words came. I started to go to her, but Caleb beat me to it. He stood next to her and put one arm loosely around her shoulders. We were quiet for a moment; the only sounds came from seagulls and Louis's banging pots around in the kitchen, below the employee break deck.

Then I registered something I'd just said.

'It's July tenth.'

Simon's eyes met mine. 'And?'

'And yesterday was the ninth.' I reached for the laptop on the table before him. 'May I?'

He slid the computer towards me. I typed 'drowning timeline' in the *Herald*'s search box and scanned the results. Finding the correct link, I clicked on it and turned the laptop back to Simon. He stared at the screen without moving.

'What?' Paige asked, stepping towards us. 'What is it?'

'Charles Spinnaker,' I said.

'The second guy found last summer.' She nodded. 'What about him?'

'He died July ninth,' Simon said quietly.

Her eyes widened. 'And the first male victim? Paul Carsons?'

'June thirtieth.' Simon frowned.

'The day Carla was found,' I added.

Paige reached behind her for Caleb's hand. 'So these

people . . . whoever they are . . . are following last summer's schedule? Only with women instead of men?'

Before one of us could respond, a door slammed down below. Footsteps raced up the stairs. Natalie leapt onto the landing; her smile fell when she saw us.

'I'm sorry,' she said. 'I didn't mean to interrupt – I didn't know you were all here. I just wanted to let Paige know that the first guests have arrived.'

Paige dropped Caleb's hand, like it somehow suggested what we'd been discussing. She smoothed her skirt and straightened her blouse as she hurried to Natalie.

'Are the display areas ready?' she asked. 'How about the music? Are you sure two menu options are enough?'

They started down the stairs, Natalie leading the way. Before her head disappeared behind the stairwell wall, Paige caught my eye and mouthed, 'We'll talk more later.'

'I wish you'd planned this little party for a night we could be here,' Simon said, when they were gone. 'We can't really bail on Dad's birthday.'

I glanced at Caleb. He stood up straight from the railing and headed for the stairs. 'I'll be in the car. Take your time.'

'Vanessa –'

'I love you.'

Simon stopped. Smiled despite his concern.

I closed the laptop, stood, and held out one hand. He hesitated before taking it, and I led him to the far corner of the deck, which offered the best view of the harbour below.

'Can we just focus on that for a minute?' I pulled him close, rested my head on his chest. 'Please?'

His chin brushed against the top of my head as he nodded. Then, precisely sixty seconds later, he said, 'I love you, too. That's why I want to be here tonight. So I can watch over you and make sure nothing else happens.'

I pulled back and looked up at him. 'Even if you could be here tonight . . . what about tomorrow? And the night after that?'

'I'll figure something out.'

'What about in the fall, when we leave for school? Are you going to drive to Dartmouth from Bates to tuck me in every night?'

He lifted a loose strand of hair away from my cheek, kissed the space it had just occupied. 'Would that be so bad?'

My chest warmed. 'It'd be amazing. But probably hard to pull off.' I moved my face so his mouth met mine. I hoped my words reassured him, because they had the opposite effect on me. 'I'll take care of myself, Simon. I have to. Like it or not – and I don't – we can't be together every second of the day.'

He kissed me, pulled me close. 'Why not?' he whispered against my lips.

I kissed him harder in response. When we separated a few minutes later, I did my best to offer more immediate consolation. I told him that, with the help of Natalie's dad, we'd invited only a few select guests. And that, as promised, Paige had installed security cameras around the premises. And that she'd also bulked up on male waiting staff – not because we were going to be that busy, but just in case anyone grew rowdy and we needed to quell potential disputes with bigger bodies. I finished by showing him my cell phone, which now had the Winter Harbor police department on speed dial.

'I hate that,' he said, looking at the phone. 'I mean, it's a good idea . . . but I hate that it's a good idea.'

I kissed him once more and we went downstairs. When we reached the lobby, he continued outside and I stepped behind the hostess stand. As I was straightening the menus Paige had made for tonight's event – which featured fewer than ten items, including appetisers and desserts, and a picture of a flying fish Paige had drawn herself on photocopied paper – I discovered a bottle of water by the phone. A Post-it note was stuck to the label.

Fishermen can be chatty. This should help! — Natalie

I'd gotten over my initial suspicion of Betty's new

waitress after our encounter on the beach, so my first thought was that this was a thoughtful gesture. Then I remembered the salt she'd served with my coffee a few weeks earlier. Without my asking, Paige had explained that the busboy had gotten the salt and sugar containers mixed up while refilling shakers and bowls the night before, but that instance had stayed with me anyway.

Now I took the water, opened it, and sipped.

No salt. I smiled in relief.

Fortunately, I'd taken enough precautions earlier in the day that rehydrating wasn't necessary. Because for the next hour, I barely had time to grab more menus and turn around each time I returned to the lobby after seating diners. The front door never stopped opening and closing as more fishermen arrived, hauling coolers and paper-wrapped packages. As I led them to their seats, I pointed out the long tables arranged at one end of the dining room and the banner above it, announcing the FIRST EVER BETTY'S CHOWDER HOUSE SURPRISE O' THE SEAS CONTEST. I watched for their reactions, still not quite buying the universal appeal of Mountaineers' marketing methods, but the majority seemed to be excited, curious. Those who looked like they'd rather be elsewhere were prodded along by enthusiastic wives and girlfriends – of which, I was happy to see, there were many.

Soon the tables were full and I seated guests at the bar. When I ran out of stools and diners continued to arrive, I flagged down Paige, who was overseeing the contest display area.

'Don't turn anyone away,' she said, joining me behind the hostess stand.

'But there isn't a single chair left,' I said. 'And the people who are already here aren't leaving anytime soon.'

'So we'll go with standing room only. Let's pack them in wherever they'll fit – in the bar area, on the porch, on the back patio.'

'Isn't that a fire hazard?'

'Maybe.' She nodded to a nearby table. 'But there's the safety inspector.'

The safety inspector apparently had a fishing gig on the side. From here, I could hear him telling his friends about the best catch he'd ever had in between big gulps of beer.

'What are all these people doing here anyway?' I asked. 'I thought you and Natalie invited only a few select fishermen? As a trial.'

'We did.' She shrugged. 'But I've been distracted by other things, as you know, and didn't monitor the guest list that closely. I guess she asked a few more. That, or the ones we invited spread the word – which is exactly what we wanted them to do.'

Eventually. That's what we wanted them to do *eventually*, after we'd figured out what worked and what didn't.

'By the way,' Paige said, with a smile, 'have I told you how pretty you look tonight?'

She was called away by a waiter before I could answer. I turned to the next set of waiting fishermen and asked them to follow me. As we passed through the dining room on our way to the bar area, I sneaked a peek at my reflection in the mirror over the fireplace.

Paige was right. Before Simon and I had started seeing each other, I'd been rather self-conscious and never paid much attention to my appearance. I'd paid more since then, but focused primarily on my flaws – probably because I hoped they'd be enough to keep other members of the opposite sex from noticing me. Since arriving in Winter Harbor, I'd been seriously taken aback twice by my reflection. The first was in the lake-house bathroom the night of my Betty's basement encounter. And the second was last night, when I was mentally replaying the afternoon's events as I got ready for bed. As bad as I'd felt in the movie-theatre Ladies, and as upset – and scared – as I'd been by Erica's death, I should've been too weak to stand before the bathroom mirror.

But I'd felt solid instead. And when I looked at my reflection now, I lost my breath in surprise, not fear.

There was one explanation. When I used my inner

voice on men, as I had in Betty's basement and at the movie theatre, my body somehow harnessed their energy in ways it never had before. Not only was I infinitely stronger, my eyes shone and my skin glowed, as if I were so filled with life and love, the two radiated light from the inside out.

I couldn't deny the result since I was experiencing it first hand.

It was breathtaking.

'Vanessa?'

I'd just left the fishermen and spun around to find Oliver standing with one arm around Betty.

'What is all this?' he called out over the din. 'What's going on?'

'It's a party!' Betty answered happily. 'Even I can see that.'

'But Paige said you were hosting a small gathering. That's why we stopped by, to have a bite to eat and say hello.'

'And it's so nice that you did.' As I gave them quick hugs, I tried to catch Paige's eye. She was too busy talking with the fishermen by the contest tables to notice. 'I guess after such a quiet start to the summer, people were ready to let loose. I'll find you a seat, but can I get you a drink in the meantime?'

I asked one waiter to bring them iced tea and two

others to drag down chairs and a small table from the employee break area. I was heading back towards the lobby when I passed Natalie on her way to the kitchen. She grabbed my arm and pulled me towards her.

'Isn't this great?' She beamed. 'The place is packed!'

'It's something – definitely a bigger crowd than we expected.'

'And everyone seems to be having a great time.' She lifted her chin. 'Including our favourite manager.'

I looked behind me. Seconds ago, Paige had been talking to individual fishermen as they surveyed the catches displayed in ice bins. Now they all formed a circle around her and ignored the contest entries. She stood in the middle of the group, smiling, laughing and occasionally reaching forward to pat an arm or squeeze a shoulder.

'Maybe I should do that,' Natalie said. 'Hook up with a bunch of cute, random guys so I forget about Will.'

'She's not hooking up,' I said quickly.

'Not this second. But by the looks of it, she's open to the possibility.'

I didn't say anything. Because Natalie was right. Paige was flirting like her life depended on it . . . and even though in a way it did, it still bothered me to see. I didn't want my best friend to have to do what I had to do. I especially didn't want her to do it in public, with a hundred sets of eyes watching her every move.

'I better check on my tables,' Natalie said. 'Don't want to rock the boat with lacklustre service.'

She left and I weaved through the crowd back towards the lobby. Still feeling energised after yesterday's exchange with the movie-theatre guy, I kept my eyes lowered and crossed my arms over my chest. I felt curious gazes follow me and wanted to avoid engaging and encouraging unnecessarily.

'Vanessa?'

In the lobby doorway, I stopped and looked up. An older man with white hair, a kind smile and a wedding ring stood by the hostess stand.

'Yes?' I asked.

'I was asked to give you this.' He held out a long package wrapped in brown paper. 'It's a late contest entry.'

I stepped towards him and took the package. It was softer and lighter than I expected.

'This is a fish?' I asked. Judging by the filled bins in the other room, most of the entrants had decided longer and heavier was better.

'I assume so, though the gentleman didn't say. He just stopped me on the porch, asked me to give it to you for the contest, and left.'

I turned the package over. The brown paper offered no clues. 'He asked for me specifically?'

'If you're Vanessa Sands, then, yes.'

'Do you know who he was?'

'No idea.'

Wary of overwhelming the elderly messenger with questions, I lowered the package and returned his smile. 'What did he look like?'

'Not sure. My back was to him when he thrust the package at me, and by the time I turned, he was gone.'

I thanked the man and showed him and his friend to the bar. They'd been the only patrons still waiting to be seated, so I took advantage of the lull to check on Betty and Oliver, who were still puzzled but fine; Louis, who was frantic in the kitchen but elated to have so much to do; and Simon, who'd already texted me twice. I typed back:

WE'RE BUSY BUT GOOD, EVERYTHING'S UNDER CONTROL. ENJOY DINNER, I'LL CALL YOU LATER. XO

Back in the dining room, Paige stood before a microphone belonging to the local rock band she'd hired. She welcomed everyone to the first-ever Betty's Surprise o' the Seas event, thanked them for their contest contri-

269

butions, and began introducing the entries. There were no monster fish like the kind Natalie had described, but there were still some unusually heavy catches; a few boasted unique characteristics, like misshapen fins or odd colouring. Paige spoke naturally, easily, and played off the fishermen when they called out questions or comments from their seats. I didn't want to interrupt her so I waited until she spotted me by the bins of fish, before holding up our last entry.

She motioned for me to join her. I shook my head.

'Have you all met Vanessa?' Paige practically sang into the microphone. 'Our delightful hostess.'

The fishermen clapped and cheered. My face turning cherry red, I forced a smile and waved.

'What do you have there?' Paige asked.

Glancing over my shoulder, like the front door would come to me, I tried – and failed – to think of a way to get out of this.

'A late contest entry,' I finally said.

She cupped one hand to her ear. 'What's that?'

I repeated myself, louder.

'Fantastic! Bring it on up!'

You owe me, I thought.

If Paige heard, she didn't let on. Her expression remained unchanged as I walked towards the small stage.

'There she is! Let's give our lovely hostess another round of applause!'

I gave her the package, smiled and waved again, and darted to the back of the room. My skin burned with the heat of the intense gazes that followed me.

'Let's see what we have here. . . .' Paige handed the microphone to the male lead singer, who gripped it tightly with both hands, seemingly terrified of dropping it and disappointing the mesmerising girl before him. Her smile grew as she undid the tape and gently tore open the paper. She leaned towards the microphone. 'It looks like we might need a bigger stage – there's a comedian in our midst!'

She held the soft toy animal, a killer whale, over her head for all to see. I thought it was more strange than funny, but the room swelled with laughter as the fishermen cracked up.

'Please don't tell me this is a representation of the real deal,' Paige continued. 'Our new front porch is pretty, but it won't hold a ten-thousand-pound beached orca.'

This prompted a fresh wave of laughter. Paige joined in, and the effects of her voice made the fishermen only happier. The ladies in the audience appeared to be less pleased, but Paige didn't seem to notice.

Or maybe she did. A second later, her smile froze, then faded.

But she was no longer looking out at the crowd; she was looking down at the stuffed animal. She turned it over, brought it closer. As it moved beneath the portable stage lights, something glinted around its neck. The flash was like the spark a match gives off when lit, only it shone silver instead of gold.

As Paige dropped the stuffed animal and hurried offstage, I heard her voice . . . but her mouth didn't move.

Raina.

CHAPTER 19

'Thank goodness.'

I stood in the kitchen doorway, car keys in hand. Mom flung herself towards me, one hand over her chest.

'It's after midnight,' she added.

'I called three times,' I said, 'to tell you I was going to be late, to tell you I was going to be even later, and to let you know when I was finally leaving the restaurant.'

She threw her arms around me and squeezed. 'You're a good daughter. But it's been forty-five minutes since your last call.'

As I hugged Mom, I looked into the living room. Dad stood between the couch and coffee table, gripping a wineglass so tightly, I could see his knuckles turn white from the next room.

'Sorry.' I pulled away from Mom so she couldn't hear my heart race inside my chest as I lied. 'Paige's car wouldn't start so I gave her a ride home.'

Mom sighed. Dad nodded. I thought of the truth, which was that I'd been so paranoid each time a pair of headlights appeared behind me, I took eight different detours to throw off potential pursuers. I lost them all easily, which meant they probably weren't following me in the first place, but the fifteen-minute drive from Betty's still ended up taking three times as long.

'But I'm here.' I forced brightness into my voice. 'And exhausted. I think I'll take a quick swim and go to bed.'

I kissed Mom's cheek and headed for Dad to do the same. When I reached him, he put one hand on my arm. The gesture was gentle yet firm at the same time.

'We'd like to talk with you for a moment,' he said.

'Can it wait until morning?' I asked, because he sounded serious and I didn't know how much more drama I could take tonight. Plus, I'd told Simon I'd call him the second I got home, and just as my parents were worried, I knew he was, too.

'I'm afraid it can't.' Dad motioned to the armchair on the other side of the coffee table. 'Please. Sit.'

I glanced at Mom, who reached for her wineglass as she joined Dad on the couch.

'Are we celebrating something?' I asked, sinking into the chair. My parents enjoyed a glass of wine with dinner, but that meal had ended hours earlier. They usually switched to tea or decaf coffee later in the night.

'In a way,' Mom said.

'You don't sound happy,' I said.

'We got an offer.' Dad put down his glass, leaned forward, and clasped his hands between his knees. 'On the lake house.'

The mixed signals sent by their sombre expressions and beverage choice now made sense. My heart lifted and sank at once.

'That's good news, right?' I asked. 'I mean, it's sad, too, since it won't be ours any more . . . but at least it's one less thing to worry about.'

'It is good news.' Mom rubbed Dad's back. 'And it means our business here is done.'

I was confused again. 'What do you mean?'

'With the lake house sold, we don't need to be here any more.' Dad offered this like it was a real explanation.

'Here?' I asked. 'As in this house? Or Winter Harbor?'

'Both,' Mom said.

'I'm sorry.' I shook my head. 'I'm not following. We just bought this place. Mom, you just finished decorating. If we were only hanging around until the lake house sold, why go through all that trouble?'

I was trying to stay calm, logical. It was that or get back in the Jeep, drive to Simon's, and handcuff my wrist to his.

Instead of answering, Mom lifted the wine bottle on the coffee table. As she did, I noticed the newspaper that had been serving as a coaster. The headline screamed from the front page.

Erica Anderson, 28, Found Dead by WH Cinema. Visitors and Residents Panic, Police Scramble for Clues.

'You want to leave?' I asked. 'Because of this?'

'Can you think of a better reason?' Dad asked quietly.

I could think of different reasons – like there being male victims instead of female – but not better.

'We wanted to wait a little while after the first girl was found,' Dad continued, his voice wavering, 'but after this, we can't wait any more.'

'Vanessa.' Mom leaned towards me. 'We thought all this was behind us.'

'But it's not si–' I stopped myself. 'It's not like last summer.'

'It doesn't matter,' Mom said. 'It shouldn't be happening. And had there been the slightest indication it would be, we never would've come back.'

'We simply can't put you in harm's way,' Dad added.

'I'm not in harm's way. I'm fine. I'm better than that – I'm great.' I reached for the lamp next to my chair, turned it on. 'Look. Don't I look great? Healthy?'

'You look wonderful,' Mom conceded, 'but –'

'That's because we're here. It's because I get to swim in the ocean and breathe salty air whenever I want. This is where I'm supposed to be, where I *need* to be. Going back to Boston would be more dangerous than staying.'

'We don't have to go back to Boston.' Dad looked at Mom, who nodded. 'We thought we could try California or Oregon, or maybe even Hawaii. We can still spend the rest of the summer by the ocean – just the Pacific instead of the Atlantic.'

My eyes welled. 'But what about Paige?'

'She's your best friend,' Mom said. 'She'll understand. She can even come with us if she wants.'

'She can't leave the restaurant.' I took a deep breath, blinked back tears. 'And what about Charlotte?'

'She didn't plan to stay much longer anyway,' Dad said. 'You know that.'

I looked down. Tears fell from eyes and landed in my lap. I barely noticed.

'As for Simon,' Mom said softly, guessing – correctly – what I was really thinking and too afraid to say, 'he'll also understand.'

'Can he come with us, too?' I asked.

Mom hesitated. 'I don't know if that'd be such a good idea. And you two were going to have to say goodbye eventually. Maybe it'll be easier this way.'

277

It wouldn't be. Saying goodbye to Simon, even for a day, would never be anything but painful.

But I couldn't explain this to my parents. Even if I found the words, I knew they wouldn't understand. And though they'd feel sorry for me and bad about the situation, that wouldn't be enough to convince them to stay.

There was only one thing that might work.

'Justine,' I whispered.

Dad sat back. Mom gasped lightly.

I pictured my sister, imagined her infectious grin and her blue eyes glittering in excitement. I could almost see her hiding in the next room, talking into a small microphone that fed to an invisible speaker in my ear. I'd feel guilty for what I was about to say if it wasn't partially true – and if I wasn't 100 per cent sure that Justine would've encouraged me every step of the way.

'I miss her,' I said.

Mom jumped up, hurried around the table, and perched on my armrest. 'Of course you do. We all do.'

'And I guess that, I don't know . . . being here makes me feel closer to her. Maybe because it was the last place we were together? It doesn't make sense, but –'

'Yes, it does.' Mom put one arm around my shoulders, kissed the top of my head.

I took a deep breath. 'That's why it would be really hard to leave. I can't imagine spending the summer somewhere I've never been with Justine, especially when we've only ever spent summers here. It was one thing to move out of the lake house and into this one, but leaving Winter Harbor completely? That'd just feel . . . wrong, somehow.'

Mom pulled me close until my head rested against her chest. My eyes were still watering so I couldn't make out Dad's expression as he and Mom shared a silent exchange, but I wouldn't have been surprised if he was on the verge of tears, too.

A moment later, Mom sighed and said, 'Well, we don't have to start packing tonight. Why don't you get some rest and we'll talk more in the morning?'

I sniffed, nodded. She gave me one more hug then stood up and rejoined Dad on the couch. I dried my eyes with the sleeve of my denim jacket, said good night, and started across the room.

'Oh, and sweetie?' Mom called out, just as I entered the hallway.

I stopped. Turned.

'We'll need you to quit your job at Betty's.'

'But –'

'That one's not up for discussion. We can't have you driving around alone, at all hours of the night. Your father and I will cover your expenses.' She shifted in her seat and blew me a kiss over the top of the couch. 'Good night!'

I opened my mouth to protest again, but then closed it. Compared to leaving town, this was a fair request. And I didn't want to push my luck.

Back in my room, I grabbed two bottles of salt water from the fridge in the bathroom and drank as I called Simon. He answered halfway through the first ring.

'Do you want to go out tomorrow?' I asked, before he could ask where I'd been, if I was okay.

He paused. 'Out?'

'On a hike or something? We could pack a picnic.'

'Don't you have to work?'

I sat on my bed, shrugged off my jacket. 'I'm taking the day off. Can you? From the marina?'

'Probably . . . I'd just need to clear it with Monty and Caleb in the morning.'

He sounded pleased but confused. I kept talking to help the former feeling override the latter.

'I know I saw you a few hours ago, but it still feels like too long. And all I want is to spend the day together. Don't you think that'd be nice?'

'Considering that's all I want every day, absolutely. I'll do my best to make it happen.'

I could hear the smile in his voice. Despite the upsetting conversation that had just transpired in the living room, it made me smile, too.

We talked for a few minutes more. I told him about the evening at Betty's, carefully editing out some of the more alarming moments, since those would be better discussed in person, and he told me about his dad's birthday dinner.

'I wish you'd been there,' he said.

'Me, too.' I finished off one water bottle, opened the second. 'Next year?'

'Definitely.'

We agreed to work out date details in the morning, said good night, and hung up.

The effects from my moment with Tim, the movie-theatre employee, certainly not helped by my stressful night, were fading. My body was fatigued and my skin dry enough that pale flakes dusted the waistband of my black skirt. Deciding a quick swim wasn't a bad idea, I returned to the bathroom to get my swimming costume hanging from the hook on the door. Before changing, I went to the window to lower the shade – and noticed Charlotte's bedroom light still on.

She was in bed, but I couldn't tell if she was reading or sleeping. A book was open in her lap, but her head was resting on the pillow and turned to one side. I watched her a minute; when there was no movement besides her chest's rising and falling, I took the shade cord in one hand and pulled.

I'm awake.

I froze. I didn't breathe as I slowly raised the shade.

Charlotte was sitting up. Her eyes were open . . . and looking right at me.

Would you like to come visit?

Like Paige's hadn't earlier, Charlotte's lips didn't move.

I swallowed. Nodded.

She was still in bed when I reached her room. I stood in the doorway, uncertain whether to step inside. I hadn't been in this guest room since she started staying there, and I couldn't help feeling like I was trespassing – even though this was my family's house.

'Hello,' she said.

'Hi.' I didn't move.

'Would you mind bringing me my sweater?' she asked, after a moment. 'Please? It's on the window seat.'

Now that it had a specific task, my body thawed. I entered the room, retrieved her sweater, and handed it to her. Up close, I saw that she wore only a cotton night-gown, and I looked away as she put on the sweater.

'I'm sorry, I don't mean to be a bother . . . but would you mind? Do you think you could . . . ?'

I turned back. Breathing quickly, Charlotte struggled

to lift her back from the pillow. Her hands and arms shook as she tried to slide them through into the wool sleeves. Her face twisted, like the small effort caused great pain.

'It's okay,' I said, hoping my voice didn't betray my concern.

I went to the bed and held up the sweater. When she still had difficulty moving her quivering limbs, I pressed gently on one arm until she lowered it, and then I guided the sleeve to her shoulder. I offered her my hand and she took it with both of hers. She held on and pulled herself up just enough for me to drape the material behind her back with my other hand, and then she fell against the pillow with a *whoosh* and closed her eyes. I finished the job while she recovered, sliding the other sleeve up her right arm.

'Do you want me to close the window?' I asked.

'No, thank you. The cold air feels nice.'

I lowered myself to the edge of the window seat, waited. I looked around the room, at the new dresser, overstuffed chair, and ottoman. The beach-scene painting done by a local artist. The pale blue rug. The white roses on the nightstand. It was the kind of guest room you'd see in a magazine, that most people would love to replicate in their own homes and most guests would never want to leave.

Except our guest, it seemed, had other plans.

'Your suitcase is out,' I said. It sat on the floor by the door. Her shoes and handbag were next to it, her jacket laid across the top.

Charlotte's eyes opened. Her head turned slowly towards the luggage. 'So it is.'

'Why?'

She sighed – or tried to. The breath stuck in her chest, prompting a coughing fit that rattled the bedposts.

I jumped up, dashed into the bathroom, and brought back a glass of water. Mom hadn't installed another mini refrigerator for Charlotte's stay, but she had made sure a pitcher of fresh salt water was always available.

Charlotte reached for the glass. I faced her as I sat on the bed, pressed on her shoulder until she sat back, and brought the glass to her lips. She sipped in between coughs and I watched her mouth, cheeks and forehead. They should've flushed and smoothed instantly . . . but they didn't.

At least the fit abated – after a second glass of water. When it did, Charlotte rested her head against the pillow and tried to smile.

'Did you go swimming today?' I asked.

'Yes.'

'You should go again. Right now. I'll help you down to the beach.'

'Thank you, Vanessa, but that's not necessary. I'm just tired. You understand.'

I would understand if that were what was really wrong. But I didn't believe that it was.

'I'm leaving in the morning,' Charlotte continued. 'I've already stayed much longer than I'd planned, and I can't delay my appointments any more.'

'But you're sick – or more tired than I've ever seen you. And it's late. You can't drive to Canada on so little sleep.'

She slid her hand from her chest to the blanket between us as if to reassure me. 'I'll be fine.' She inhaled, exhaled. The breaths were dry, scratchy. 'I want – I need – to tell you a few things before I go.'

'They can wait,' I said automatically, wanting her to conserve her energy. 'You already shared something that's made a huge difference in my day-to-day life. Whatever else you want to tell me can wait until the next time I see you.'

'But as I explained –'

'You don't know how long you'll be gone. I remember. And I can wait.' She started to protest again so I added, 'If I have any other questions in the meantime, I can always ask Betty.'

Her eyelids fluttered closed and, for a second, I

thought she was crying. But then they lifted again and her eyes were even clearer than they'd been before.

'You need to leave this world,' she said.

'Excuse me?'

'When you listen. You need to tune out everything around you – conversations, passing cars, waves crashing – until your thoughts still and your mind clears. Until it's just you totally alone, even in a room full of people. Complete focus is absolutely necessary.'

'I'm not sure I'm following.'

Still on the bed, her fingers stretched towards me. 'You want to know how to hear others like us, don't you? At will and not just when spoken to?'

I did want to know this – at some point, maybe in the very distant future. Now wasn't the time.

Unfortunately, Charlotte continued before I figured out how to say this convincingly. As she spoke, I became too curious to try to stop her.

'You must listen for her voice, and to do that, you must know it in its natural form. You need to have heard it laughing, crying, screaming, or used in some other purely emotional way. You need to be able to hear that sound again, as clearly and exactly as if it were happening right then, right there in front of you.'

She paused to catch her breath. I tried to stand to get

her another glass of water, but she slid her hand on top of mine, stopping me.

'And then you need to choose one note to focus on. Stretch it out, blow it up, let it fill your head until the pressure is almost too great to bear. The thoughts will follow.'

I studied her face as I listened. She didn't appear to be weakening further, and she'd made it clear that she wanted to share this information now. So even though I was tempted to leave and let her rest . . . maybe it wouldn't hurt to ask a few questions first.

'When I've heard sirens in the past,' I began carefully, 'without intentionally listening for them, how did that happen?'

'Like at the bottom of the lake? When you heard me speaking to you?'

I nodded.

'Sirens are born with the natural ability to silently communicate with each other. The difference between that and what I just described is that the dialogue needs to take place in person. We automatically tune into one another; our bodies sense commonalities even when we don't. As long as a siren's close enough that you can reach out and touch her, you should be able to speak to her without saying a single word out loud. Focus is still required on both parts – each needs to intend to speak to the other – but the effort needed is much less. And after an initial exchange, communication becomes even easier. Close proximity isn't as necessary. That's how you and I can speak silently from different rooms in the house.'

This could explain how I'd just heard Paige say Raina's name at the restaurant, and how I'd heard her whisper her unborn baby's name the night of the Northern Lights Festival last summer. It also explained how I'd heard Zara on the bottom of the ocean at the base of Chione Cliffs, and at the lake last fall.

There was one thing, however, that didn't match up.

'Last summer,' I said, 'I heard Justine. Talking to me, after she was gone.'

The corners of Charlotte's mouth turned down. 'I remember. You told me that last fall.'

'But she wasn't a siren . . . was she?'

'No.'

'So how was that possible?'

Charlotte's fingers moved lightly across the top of my hand. 'It wasn't,' she said. 'At least not the way it seemed.'

Outside, a wave crashed into the rocks below the house. Already on edge, I jumped.

'This might be difficult to understand,' Charlotte

continued, 'and even harder to accept. Are you sure you want to know?'

Heart thudding in my chest, I settled back down on the bed. 'Yes. Please.'

'The voice you heard, though it sounded identical to the one you'd heard every day for seventeen years, didn't belong to your sister.' She paused, letting this sink in. 'It belonged to you.'

The thudding in my chest fell silent.

'Justine seemed to speak to you in moments of distress, yes? When you were feeling particularly sad or scared or confused?'

I thought back to last summer. I'd heard her my first day back in Winter Harbor after the funeral, when I pulled into the lake-house driveway and thought I saw flashes of silver light behind me. She'd encouraged me to follow other silver light streaming from beneath Zara's bedroom door, and to keep looking through Zara's scrapbook of conquests and targets when I ached to throw it and run. She'd guided me towards Caleb when he was fleeing his pursuer's hold. She'd reached out every time I needed her, just as she would've if she'd still been alive.

Charlotte took my silence for agreement and continued.

'Our bodies can act without instruction, as we know, and when you heard Justine, yours was doing two things unprompted. The first: it was manipulating your grief by making you hear a voice that wasn't there. This could happen to anyone, siren or not, who has suffered a tragic loss.'

'But she – the voice – knew things I didn't. Like that Caleb was running down the road, towards a gas station. That helped me find him. If I was just talking to myself, how would I have known where to look?'

'That's the second thing your body was doing,' Charlotte said. 'It was already tuning in to the sirens around you without your knowing, taking the information they provided, and sharing it with you via Justine's voice so that you'd listen.'

I shook my head, struggled to make sense of this. 'So when I heard Justine say Caleb was running down the road . . . I was translating information my body picked up from Zara?'

'Precisely. She and Caleb had been physically close just before he ran, correct? So they were still connected to some degree, and she could sense his whereabouts. Your body picked up on that. Unlike hearing the voice of someone you've loved and lost, only sirens have this ability.'

I turned my head, looked out the window. Charlotte was right. This was hard to hear – and even harder to accept. This whole time, I didn't know how it was possible, but I still liked believing that it was. I liked knowing

Justine had still been with me for a time even when she no longer was physically.

'You stopped hearing her after the Northern Lights Festival, right?' Charlotte asked gently. 'After you'd faced your fear of jumping off the cliff and successfully stopped the sirens' attack?'

I hadn't stopped them for long, it turned out, but the rest was true. Anytime I'd heard Justine since then, there was no question I was only remembering her speaking to me.

'You transformed that night, and you no longer needed Justine to be the brave one,' Charlotte said. 'Your body could sense on its own without tuning in to other sirens, and your mind was healing. You didn't need her –'

'Of course I did.' My head snapped back. 'I'll always need her.'

Charlotte gave me a sad smile. 'I wasn't finished. I was going to say you didn't need her in quite the same way.'

I wanted to disagree but couldn't.

'There's something else, Vanessa,' Charlotte said, a moment later. Her voice was soft, serious. 'I don't really know how to –'

She was cut off by another coughing fit. This one started with a jolt and quickly grew stronger. I leapt from the bed and grabbed the pitcher of salt water from the bathroom. I tried to hold a glass to her mouth but her body writhed uncontrollably. Each time her lips neared the water, her lungs seemed to explode inside her chest, shoving her head back against the pillow.

'Vanessa, what –?'

I looked up. Dad stood in the open doorway, his eyes wide, locked on Charlotte.

'Help!' I gripped her hand, lifted the glass again. 'She's choking and I can't – I don't know how to –'

He was in the room in an instant. He sat on the bed next to her and put one arm around her shoulders. She leaned into him until his body shook as much as hers. He wrapped his other arm around her torso and held her as tightly as her coughing would allow. Her knuckles threatened to crack their thin covering of dry skin as her fingers dug into his leg.

For a split second, I was taken aback by their contact. It was uncomfortable. Wrong, even.

In the next, I encouraged more.

'Take her hand.'

Dad looked at me, confused.

'Press it to your chest. Please!'

He did as I asked. I took Charlotte's other hand and leaned close.

'Sing, Charlotte,' I said, my eyes meeting hers. 'You have to sing. Just like you told me to.'

The sound that came from her mouth was nothing like the one she'd made when mesmerising the Frisbee player on the beach a few days ago. It was low. Loud. Garbled, like, as hard as it tried to get out, her body tried to keep it inside.

It also didn't work. Dad's eyes were clear as he held on, completely unaffected.

Eventually, when she was simply too exhausted to cough any more, the fit faded. Dad stayed put, rocking her gently and brushing her hair back from her forehead. Wanting to give them space and needing my own, I sat on the window seat. We were quiet for several minutes. The only sounds were waves rolling onto the shore below, and Charlotte's shallow, sporadic breaths.

I was trying to decide whether to stay or go when Charlotte spoke.

'That's what I wanted to tell you, Vanessa,' she whispered. 'It's not enough.'

I held my breath. 'What do you mean?'

Her head shifted slowly towards me. Her eyes met mine. When she spoke again, her voice filled my head, but her lips didn't move.

Sharing a life, she said, so only I could hear. *It's not enough. If you want to save your own . . . you must take someone else's.*

CHAPTER 20

My legs burned. My chest stung as my heart and lungs did double time. Sweat lined my brow and trickled down my temples.

But I wasn't tired. I *refused* to be tired.

'We might want to save some energy for the trip back,' Simon called out behind me. 'Are you sure you don't need a break?'

I shook my head, pushed harder, moved faster. I had no idea how long we'd been hiking or how much further we had to go, and I didn't care. In fact, the further, the better. Because I was savouring every breath and muscle contraction. I was basking in the warmth of the sun and chill of the breeze. I was inhaling the sweet scents of trees, flowers and dirt, and listening to the birds, bugs and leaves. I was committing it all to memory without thinking about why.

Because if I let my mind go there, my legs would buckle. My heart and lungs would stop. I'd die right then and there, on the trail.

And compared to the alternatives, that option was too tempting to entertain.

After Charlotte had dropped that bomb last night, I'd gone to my room without asking another question. That wasn't because I didn't have any – you can't hear something like that and not have a million questions. It was because I didn't want to know any more than I already did. The more I knew, the realer it became . . . and I wasn't prepared to accept that.

I'd stayed in my room, ignoring Dad's knocks and even Paige's phone call. Earlier in the night, I'd cornered Paige in the restaurant kitchen, after she'd fled the small stage, leaving the stuffed animal, and she'd confirmed the necklace around the toy whale's neck had belonged to her mother. This was especially alarming because, according to Paige, Raina had been wearing the jewellery the night the harbour froze during the siren attack at the Northern Lights Festival last summer – and not when she'd gathered forces at the bottom of Lake Kantaka and attacked Simon and me last fall. Which meant she'd either lost it that first night, or it had been taken. Either way, whoever had delivered it to the restaurant knew more about Raina, those events and us, than anyone outside our immediate circle should.

Before I could wrap my mind around this, Paige had excused herself to attend to a party-related matter and said she'd call me later. But after my conversation with Charlotte, I didn't want to talk about it – about *any* of it. All I wanted was to pretend like it wasn't happening. So I let the call go to voicemail.

To aid my denial, I got up extra early that morning, went for a long swim, and drove to Harbor Hike House. I arrived at the gear shop before it opened, and when the male manager finally unlocked the door, I warmed him up by asking for trail suggestions. Then I did what Charlotte had been unable to do with Dad hours earlier. The adrenalin rush was instant – and so strong, I almost cried in relief.

But I didn't. Because that would've been like admitting something was wrong.

Simon's text came as I was leaving the store. He'd got out of work and was free all day. We agreed to meet at the pier an hour later and drive to the trailhead together. We'd been climbing since.

The sun shone directly overhead by the time the trees started to thin and the path level out. Soon there was enough room for Simon and me to walk side by side. He jogged up next to me and reached for my hand. His touch yanked me from my hiking hypnosis and slowed me down for the first time since my sneakers had hit dirt.

We wandered around the summit without speaking.

Eventually, we came to a large rock formation that rose up twenty feet from the ground. I kissed his hand before releasing it, then wedged my sneakers wherever they fitted as I scaled the boulder base. The natural structure was solid, despite a few loose rocks that sent me sliding back twice, and I reached the top no more tired than I'd left the bottom.

'Wow.' Simon came up behind me, swigged from a water bottle. 'I've lived here all my life . . . and I've never seen Winter Harbor like this.'

I hadn't spent nearly as much time there, but I still understood. The top of the rock formation offered a perfect three-hundred-and-sixty-degree view of the town and outlying areas. Turning slowly, I saw Main Street and the harbour. Lake Kantaka. Camp Heroine. The lighthouse. The ocean.

'It's beautiful,' I said.

'I didn't even know this trail existed. And considering we're the only ones on it, not many other people do, either. How'd you hear about it?'

I hesitated. 'The Hike House. Where I went this morning to get some of these.' I swung my backpack around, opened the front pocket, and took out a handful of trail-mix packets. The manager hadn't seemed the least bit suspicious after I removed my palm from his chest, but I thought returning the favour by giving the store some business was only fair.

Simon took a packet. 'Funny, when you mentioned a picnic, this isn't what I thought you had in mind.'

He smiled, but I felt terrible instantly. 'I'm sorry, I was in a rush when I left the house and didn't think to take anything from there, and I'm kind of tired of Betty's food, and Harbor Homefries doesn't take debit cards, and the bank wasn't open yet, and –'

I stopped when he held up a large brown paper bag. I was so busy trying to be convincing, I didn't notice him unzipping his backpack as I lied.

'You brought food,' I said, my chest warming.

'I figured we should do it right or not at all. And I thought you might be too tired after your late night at work to put something together, so I took it upon myself. I hope that's okay.'

I smiled. 'It's more than that. Thank you.'

He lowered to a squat, took a blanket from his bag, and spread it across the rock. 'It might be too soon for gratitude. Since I made most of it myself, the thought really could be the only thing that counts.'

I sat across from him on the blanket and watched him take a cooler bag from the paper bag.

'I don't think I've seen one of those since kindergarten,' I joked.

'Yes, well. Mom said if I fed you cold pancakes, she'd never let me come home again.' He winked at me. 'You were always her favourite.'

My eyes smarted with tears. I was glad I remembered to bring sunglasses so he couldn't see.

We ate breakfast, which in addition to pancakes included eggs, bacon, fresh fruit and tea. We didn't talk much, and that was fine with me. Just as I'd savoured every muscle contraction and heartbeat on the hike up, I now savoured this time with Simon. It was so simple, so normal. The only way it could be better was if it never had to end.

When we were done, we packed up our rubbish. Without discussing what to do next, he used his backpack as a pillow, stretched out on the blanket, and held out one arm. I lay next to him, resting my head on his chest.

'So the party last night went well?' he asked, a few minutes later.

I nodded, tried to sound casual. 'We had a great turnout. Hopefully it'll translate to more regular business.'

'And the customers . . . they were okay? Nothing out of the ordinary happened?'

I pictured the stuffed animal, Raina's necklace. I didn't want to keep anything from Simon and had vowed to talk to him about that today . . . but I'd made that promise to myself before my conversation with Charlotte.

Would delaying the truth a few minutes more be so bad? In the end, wouldn't we both be glad I had?

I lifted my head, brought my mouth near his ear.

'I'm not really in the mood to think about anything or anyone but you right now,' I whispered. 'Would it be okay if we talked about last night, and everything else, a little later?'

Simon's mouth met mine in response. I smiled against his lips and slowly lifted myself up and over until I was lying on top of him. His hands slid down my back, under my tank top. I lifted his T-shirt, kissing his chest and stomach. He gently raised one knee between both of mine, and I shifted my legs until they hugged either side of his waist. Our kisses grew stronger, more urgent; soon our breaths came as quickly as our lips moved.

'We're pretty exposed,' Simon said softly. 'Maybe we should hike back down and continue this someplace more private?'

'There's no one here.' I kissed his ear, his neck. 'And I don't want to stop. Do you?'

He shook his head, lifted his torso so we both sat up. I could feel his breath, warm and moist, through the thin cotton of my shirt. Wanting to feel it against my skin, I took off the tank top and tossed it to the side. I closed my eyes, wound my fingers through his hair as his mouth travelled across my shoulders, down my chest, towards my abdomen. His fingers followed, eventually lingering on the button of my shorts. I lifted my hips slightly towards his.

He'd just unbuttoned my shorts when my cell phone rang inside my backpack.

'Do you want to . . . ?' he asked.

'Not even a little.' I pressed my chest against his, took off his shirt as we lowered back to the blanket.

The ringing stopped.

A second later, it started again.

'Are you sure –'

'Positive.'

The ringing stopped. Started again.

'Sorry.' I sat up, reached for my backpack, and took out my phone. In addition to the missed calls, I had three new voicemails and seven new texts, but I silenced the ringer without checking whom they were from.

I tossed the phone back in my bag and settled against Simon again. We were still kissing a few minutes later when his cell phone rang.

'Do you want to . . . ?' I asked.

'Not even a little.'

The phone stopped after two rings. Almost instantly, it rang twice more.

Simon's hands tensed. His lips slowed.

'What?' I asked, just as the phone beeped. 'What is it?'

He stopped kissing me, looked over his shoulder at his bag. 'Our signal.'

I was lying on the blanket and lifted myself up on my elbows. 'Whose signal? For what?'

He turned back. His lips, which had just moved so easily against my own, pressed together. His eyebrows lowered. 'Caleb's and mine. For emergencies.'

My breath stuck in my throat. I swallowed it down. 'What kind of emergencies?'

He didn't answer. He knew that I already knew.

'I should call him,' he said, sounding sorry.

I nodded and lay back as he jumped to his feet and lunged for his backpack. He wandered several feet away, either in search of a stronger signal or to save me from trying to guess what the emergency was from his side of the conversation. The latter was unnecessary; I had no interest in knowing what was wrong. I felt guilty as I thought it, but I almost hoped whatever it was was so bad Simon wouldn't want to tell me. Then maybe I could keep pretending for at least a little while longer.

'You didn't tell me Raina made an appearance last night.'

I shot up, held one arm in front of my face to shield it from the sun. Simon stood at the edge of the blanket, clutching his closed cell phone.

'She didn't,' I said.

'That's not what Caleb said.'

'Caleb wasn't there. How does he –'

'Paige. That's who was just calling you. When you didn't pick up, she figured you were with me and tried him.'

Biting back a sigh, I reached for my discarded tank top and pulled it over my head.

'Someone entered a stuffed animal wearing Raina's necklace into the contest,' I explained. 'I was going to tell you, I promise. I was just hoping we could have a nice, normal time before the entire day became about that.' Then, registering what he'd said, I stood and faced him. 'There's something else. I already knew about the necklace . . . so Paige was calling to tell me about something else.'

He looked down, and I knew he was trying to decide which thing – my silence about last night or this latest news – to talk about first. After a moment, he went with the news.

'The restaurant's security cameras caught the guy who

303

delivered the necklace. It's not a clear shot, but Paige has a guess that she thinks you can confirm.'

As this sank in, I crossed my arms over my stomach and turned away.

'Vanessa, this is good news.' Simon stood next to me. 'It's not an ideal way to spend the afternoon, and believe me, I'd like nothing more than to pick up right where we left off a few minutes ago. But if we know who delivered the necklace, we probably know who's sending the e-mails – and doing everything else. The sooner we have that information, the sooner we can stop them and move on. For ever.'

He was right, of course. About everything, minus the very last part.

Regardless of what happened after we watched the security footage, or if we found out who killed Carla and Erica and stopped them tonight, I'd never move on. Simon and I . . . would *never* move on. Charlotte had confirmed that last night.

But I couldn't feel sorry for myself now. There wasn't enough time for much else, but there'd be plenty of time for that later.

'Okay,' I said, my eyes fixed on the harbour in the distance. 'Let's go.'

Simon took the lead down the mountain. I wasn't in as big a hurry to get to the bottom as I'd been to get to the top, and I was also moving slower. My body felt sluggish, like my hiking shoes were weighted down with some of the rocks we'd just left. If Simon were someone else, someone who hadn't fallen in love with me before I'd transformed, our latest make-out session would have energised me so much I could have flown down the trail. Instead, it seemed to have the opposite effect.

The thought was so upsetting, I forced it from my mind and tried to focus on the task ahead.

When Simon offered to drive as we neared the Jeep parked on the side of the road, I assured him I was fine and got behind the wheel. We didn't talk as we headed back to town, but the trip passed too quickly anyway. Before long, we were pulling into the Chowder House car park– which was nearly full.

'In that sense, I guess the night was a success,' Simon said, as I found an empty spot in the staff parking area.

He reached for my hand when we got out of the Jeep. We'd just started up the steps leading to the kitchen door when Paige leaned over the railing of the employee break deck and called down to us.

'Sorry to break up the lovefest . . . but you guys definitely want to see this.'

Simon and I exchanged looks. He released my hand to hold open the door.

'We know him,' Paige said, as we stepped onto the

deck. She sat in front of a laptop, Caleb on one side, Natalie on the other. 'I couldn't tell you how, exactly . . . but I know we know him.'

Natalie smiled at us, then leaned closer to the computer screen. I glanced at Simon, whose brows were furrowed, his eyes narrowed in confusion. I knew he was wondering the same thing I was.

What was she doing here?

Paige turned the laptop around so it faced us. 'What do you think?'

We'd have to figure that out later. Now we hurried to the table and studied the black-and-white footage. It was from the camera located above the restaurant's main entrance and showed various fishermen on the porch, talking, smoking, and laughing. Ten seconds in, a guy emerged from the shadows the camera didn't reach. He wore jeans, a cargo jacket and a baseball cap. His head was lowered and his hands were stuffed in his pockets. A lumpy package was tucked under one arm. His stride was quick, purposeful.

'How can you tell that we know him?' I asked. 'His face is hidden.'

But then he bumped into one of the other men on the porch, who appeared to bark something in response. Our stalker turned towards the man, and for a split second, the camera caught his side profile.

'Let's go back.' Simon leaned forward and ran his thumb across the computer's track pad. 'We can freeze the frame for a better look.'

'That's okay,' I said. 'We don't have to.'

Because Paige was right. We knew the stalker. *I* knew the stalker. And I'd spent enough time with him that a split second was all I needed to identify him.

He was Colin. The realtor's son.

I opened my mouth to share this just as my cell phone rang. It was a long, old-fashioned ring, like the kind Dad's office phone back in Boston still made. The sound was comforting, familiar – which was why I'd assigned it to our new beach-house number.

'Sorry,' I said, taking my phone from shorts pocket, where I'd stowed it for easy access before hiking back down the mountain. 'That's my parents. I better take it.'

Grateful for the excuse to process what I'd just seen, I turned away and walked to the balcony railing.

'Hey, Dad. What's up?'

'Vanessa, it's me.' Mom's voice was tight with worry. 'You need to come home now. Please.'

Before I could ask why, Charlotte's voice filled my head.

Take care, my dear, sweet Vanessa.

I know you're strong . . . now you just need to decide what it really means to be brave.

CHAPTER 21

'Honey, trust me,' Mom said. 'You don't want to go in there.'

She stood before the guest-room door, clutching a crumpled tissue. I stepped to one side, then the other. She copied my movement as if her body were a wall I couldn't break through.

'Yes, I do.' My voice was calm. Even.

'Vanessa,' Dad said quietly, touching my arm. 'She doesn't . . . that is, she's not . . . you don't know how . . .'

His voice wavered, then trailed off. His head dropped and he pushed up his glasses with his pointer finger and thumb. He pressed into the corners of his eyes, but the tears managed to slip through anyway.

'She looks different from what you remember.' Mom's eyes watered, too, but she gave Dad her tissue.

'I just saw her last night,' I said. 'And I don't care how bad it is. I'm sure I've seen worse over the past year.'

Mom blinked, sending a fresh stream of tears rolling down her cheeks. 'That's all the more reason not to go inside.'

'You called me fifteen minutes ago and said I needed to come home right away. I assume so I could see her. What changed between then and now?'

Dad released a long, shaky breath and looked up. 'A lot.'

Mom reached forward and brushed my hair off my face. 'Why don't you go lie down for a while? Your father and I will handle the situation.'

I looked away. I hadn't seen her this sad since last summer and thought I might start crying, too. And if I was going to convince them I was emotionally sound enough to see whatever lay on the other side of that door, I had to hold it together.

The doorbell rang. Mom sniffed, stood up straight, and tugged on the hem of her blouse. I didn't watch it happen, but I knew her eyes told Dad that he'd better restrain me in her absence.

'Charlotte asked that you not see her like this,' he said, when Mom was gone.

'Charlotte had her way for eighteen years.' I looked up. Our eyes locked. 'I think that's long enough.'

'You're upset. Don't let your emotions make you do something you'll regret later.'

And with that, I'd had enough of other people telling me what I should and shouldn't do.

'I'm going in.' I stepped towards the door. 'When I'm ready to come out, I will.'

He held my gaze for a second more. A sharp pang pierced my chest – I knew he was in pain, too – and I worried I might lose my nerve. But then he nodded and shuffled towards an armchair down the hall.

'I'll be here if you need me,' he said.

I waited until he was seated and then faced the door. I put one hand carefully on the knob, expecting the metal to be either so hot or cold it scalded my skin . . . but it felt cool. Normal. Strangely reassured, I gripped it tighter, turned and pushed.

The stench engulfed me instantly. It was a mixture of salt, rotting fish, and decaying flesh, and it was so thick, I could feel it weaving around my limbs, entering my pores.

Gagging, I covered my mouth with one hand and clutched my stomach with the other. If Dad wasn't sitting ten feet away, I'd have yanked the door shut and bolted for the nearest exit. Since he was, I stifled my shock and forced my feet across the threshold, closing the door behind me.

The air inside the room was still. Heavy. Warm. Perhaps in an unconscious effort to avoid the bed, I looked to the windows, which were closed. Keeping one hand clamped over my nose and mouth, I hurried across the room. When I needed both hands to throw up the glass, I reluctantly released my face. I held my breath until I felt the cool ocean breeze on my face, then I closed my eyes, pressed both palms to the screen above the same window seat I'd sat on while talking to Charlotte only hours before, and inhaled.

The nausea passed a moment later. I opened my eyes and watched the waves rolling onshore. I didn't realise it right away, but I wasn't simply stalling; I was listening. For Charlotte to tell me that everything was okay, that *she* was okay.

But she didn't. I heard only the rush of water.

I turned slowly, keeping my gaze averted until I faced the bed. From here, everything looked fine. The wood floor shone. Charlotte's fuzzy white slippers sat before the nightstand, as they had last night. The sheet hung at an angle, crisp and new.

Maybe there's been a mistake, I thought, as I raised my eyes. *Maybe she's just sleeping, or too weak to communicate. If I bring her some water, or soak her blankets in salt water, maybe . . .*

My mind fell silent. There was no mistake. The sheet was pulled over a long, thin, unmoving figure. Her chest didn't rise and fall. The cotton didn't lift where it covered her mouth as she breathed. When I stepped towards the bed, her head didn't turn towards me.

My last hope was that it was someone else – and not the woman who'd given me life – lying there. Because the figure seemed too slender to be Charlotte.

There was only one way to know for sure. Remembering what she'd said about being brave, I took another step towards the bed. And another, and another. Then, careful not to nudge her slippers with my feet, I leaned forward, pressed the corner of the sheet between two fingers, and pulled.

A blizzard of white flakes filled the room.

'No.' I fell back. Reached for the sheet and missed. 'No, no, *no*!'

Despite the floating white flecks clouding my vision, I could tell immediately that it was Charlotte. She had the same long white hair, the same blue-green eyes. She wore dark jeans, a short-sleeved blouse, and jewellery, like she'd been getting ready to go out when she fell suddenly ill. And given how she'd planned to leave today despite being so sick last night, maybe she had.

But her skin was grey. It cracked and peeled, exposing dried flesh, muscle and, in some places, bone. Her lips were gone, her nose sunken. Her right foot was bare and split across the middle so that the top of her foot flapped over, and the backs of her toes pressed against her heel.

There was no blood, though. Her body was completely dry. She looked like she'd been lying there, dead and unattended, for months. Maybe years.

Except she'd still been alive when Mom called. Which meant she hadn't been gone more than fifteen minutes.

The breeze shifted. As the air streamed through the open windows, it spun the white flakes. They swirled around me, coating my hair, my clothes, my face.

It wasn't until I brushed them off my mouth that I realised what they were.

They were pieces of Charlotte. And they were everywhere.

I cried out, ran for the bathroom, threw the door shut. I ran to the basin, turned on the water, and scrubbed my face. I jumped up and down and shook out my clothes and hair. Still feeling her on me, I kept scrubbing and moving long after the last flakes had settled on the tile floor. Finally, exhausted, I lowered myself to the edge of the tub.

You're not alone, Vanessa . . .

I looked up. The voice was familiar. Too shaken to know if I'd heard it out loud or inside my head, I held my breath as I waited for more. A soft scraping sound came from the other room; I stood and walked slowly to the door.

'Betty?'

She sat in a chair in the corner of the room, her hands

folded in her lap, her lightly clouded eyes aimed at me. Oliver stood between the bed and window seat, sweeping the fallen death dust into a neat pile. When I stepped into the room, he paused to give me a sad smile before continuing.

'I'm very sorry, my dear,' Betty said.

I nodded. Then, remembering she might not be able to see me, I said, 'Thank you.' As I leaned against the dresser, I noticed that the sheet had been pulled back over Charlotte's face. 'Did my parents call you?'

'Yes, but I was already on my way. Charlotte had reached out earlier and asked me to check on you.'

'Did she say she was . . . did you know that she . . . ?'

'Was dying?' Betty frowned. 'Yes.'

'Do you know why? I mean, she seemed pretty weak when she got here a few weeks ago, but not to the point that . . . this . . . seemed possible.'

Betty's head turned towards Oliver. He glanced up when she didn't respond, saw her looking at him, and rested the broom against the wall. He squeezed my arm on his way to the bedroom door, which he opened and closed gently behind him.

'Sit, Vanessa. Please.'

'I'm fine standing.'

Her lips pressed together but she didn't protest. 'Did Charlotte tell you what she came here to tell you?'

'She didn't come here to tell me anything. She just stopped by on her way to Canada. She said she wanted to see me because she didn't know how long she'd be gone.'

'She didn't want you to worry.'

'About what?'

In the brief silence that followed this question, I understood.

'Charlotte . . . wasn't going to meet with the Nenuphars?' I asked.

'She wanted to. She hoped to see if reconciliation was possible, and if they'd forgive her transgressions quickly enough to help her. But she also knew that time was critical, and that the longer she stayed here, the less chance she had of making it there.'

I tried to process this. 'She didn't just stop by Winter Harbor on her way up? She planned to come here?'

'Yes. She wanted to give you the space you'd asked for last fall, but she also wanted to tell you things you needed to know before she no longer could. She made it look like a spur-of-the-moment decision so that you'd be more willing to welcome her.'

'So by staying here, for me . . . she risked her life?'

Betty's head tilted to one side. 'She risked her life long ago, Vanessa. For a time, you gave it back.'

Slightly aware that my legs were growing numb

315

beneath me, I walked around the bed and sank onto the window seat.

'But what about last fall?' I asked. 'At the bottom of the lake, she was so strong. She looked so young, so healthy.'

'She looked her age. Because she'd taken a life to give her the strength to stop Raina and the other sirens.'

I forced my mind past this part. 'That wasn't that long ago. What happened?'

Betty hesitated. 'Before I go on, Vanessa, I need to know . . . did Charlotte tell you about your future? And what you'll need to do in order to –'

'Yes.' I cut her off, not wanting to hear her say it out loud. 'She did.'

'Very well.' Betty's eyes shifted towards the bed, rested somewhere above Charlotte's hidden face. 'She never wanted to do that herself, hence sparing your father and hiding out in Boston. As a result, the ageing process happened quickly, and that's why she looked like a grandmother, and not a mother, when you first met her. As you now know, Nenuphars have greater physical needs than normal sirens. This being the case, she actually looked even older than an ordinary siren would under similar circumstances.'

I pictured Charlotte at the coffee shop months earlier, remembered the seaweed drink she'd served me before

I knew who she was. The memory prompted tears; I blinked them away.

'When she took a life, the clock turned back instantly, giving her seemingly boundless energy and vitality,' Betty said. 'But the first time is always the most effective.'

My breath caught. 'The first time?' I practically whispered.

Her head turned towards me. 'So she didn't tell you everything.' Betty sighed. 'Yes, to experience long, seemingly normal lives, we depend on those of others. Taking one man might sustain us for a few months, but once its effects wear off, the ageing process begins again – and accelerates. In order for Charlotte to have had a different fate, she would have needed to kill again. And though she loved you more than you'll ever know and was beyond elated to spend time with you . . . she couldn't bring herself to do it. That wasn't who she wanted to be for you.'

Fresh tears brimmed. I didn't bother blinking them away. 'So death was the best option?'

'She thought better hers than someone else's.'

I turned and faced the windows. Pressing my forehead to the cool metal screen, I focused on breathing.

'So you,' I whispered, 'you've . . . ?'

'I have. It's not something I'm proud of, but I had

a daughter and, eventually, two granddaughters to care for. When it became clear that Raina intended to use her powers maliciously and teach Zara and Paige to do the same, being there for them was even more important. So I did what I had to do.'

It was too much. All of it – Charlotte, Colin, girls dying, my friends and family suffering, our uncertain futures. It was all too much. I didn't think I could handle it.

'Whatever you do, Vanessa,' Betty continued gently, 'do not blame yourself. You're not responsible for her death. The only other thing Charlotte wanted besides your health and happiness was for our legacy to magically disappear. At the very least, she wanted the public to never know about us or suffer by our hands. She couldn't control the greater siren community, but she could control her own actions.' Betty paused, took a deep breath. 'So even if your paths had never crossed, this was bound to happen – and sooner rather than later.'

Tears streamed down my face and neck as we fell into silence. Several minutes later, I asked, 'What about a funeral?'

'She didn't want one. Besides, her body won't last long enough for arrangements to be made. Most don't.'

'So what do we do with . . . how do we . . . ?'

Betty's voice was soft, apologetic, when she answered.

'We return her to the sea one last time. I'd be honoured to take her whenever you're ready.'

'I can do it.'

'It's lovely of you to offer, dear, but –'

'I *want* to do it.' I turned, saw Betty's chin lower towards her chest in resignation. 'When?'

'As soon as you feel up to it. Oliver and I will just need a few minutes to prepare.'

I stood up and crossed the room. 'I'll send him in.'

In the hallway, Oliver stood next to Dad, who still sat slumped in an armchair. I went to them and touched Dad's shoulder.

'She didn't want a funeral,' I said gently. 'Do you want to take a moment with her before . . . ?' I couldn't finish the sentence.

His frizzy white hair floated on air as he shook his head. 'I already did.'

I looked at Oliver. He nodded once and returned to the guest room.

'Your friends are here,' Dad said. 'Simon, Paige, Caleb. And a nice blonde girl I'd never met before.'

Natalie. That was strange. Why would Paige invite her along?

'They wanted to make sure you were okay,' Dad said. 'Do you want me to get them?'

I was tempted to ask for Simon and Paige, but I was

afraid I'd lose my nerve if I saw the concern and sadness on their faces. So I thanked him but said I'd wait until I was back to see them.

Fifteen minutes later, Betty and Oliver joined us. Betty reached for my hand, and I gave it to her.

'Swim as long as you'd like and rest her wherever feels right. Don't worry about the container – it will disintegrate before night falls.' She squeezed my fingers. 'We'll be here when you're done.'

Which was what Charlotte had said the day she showed up at the restaurant a few weeks ago and I'd left her on the dock to talk to Simon. A lump formed in my throat; I forced it down into my chest.

Dad stood and the three of them left for the living room. I went to the guest room, which had been cleaned up and looked as if no one had stayed there in some time. The bed was made. Charlotte's belongings were gone. Sunlight streamed through the sheer curtains, which hung straight and even. The only evidence that the room had been recently occupied was a square bag on the window seat.

That, I thought, *is my mother.*

The bag was silver and crinkled, like heavy-duty cellophane. It had a zipper on top and two straps attached to the back. It was lighter than I expected, and I almost unzipped it to check its contents, but didn't. Instead of wearing it on my back, I hugged it to my chest. I held it like that down the hall, outside, and all the way to the beach. I put it down only to take off my hiking shoes and socks, and then I picked it up and hugged it again.

I never wore the bag like a backpack. In the water, I paddled with one arm, using the other to hold the bag close. I didn't know how long I swam or how far. But I didn't stop until I reached a large coral reef near the ocean floor. My eyes had adapted to darker water over the past year, and I could see that the structure teemed with colourful fish and plant life. It was a bright spot in an otherwise black world. Deciding that this suited Charlotte, I swam to a small crevice and carefully set down the bag.

And that was it. There was no ceremony. No sad music or fond speeches. A woman's challenging life had come to a difficult end, and this was all she got. A biodegradable bag at the bottom of the ocean.

I stayed there for as long as I thought I could without worrying everyone waiting on land. Then I pressed one hand to the bag, pictured a young, healthy, smiling Charlotte, and said goodbye.

My head stayed clear as I returned to the surface. Back at the house, I found my friends and family gathered in the living room. Mom had switched into hostess mode and served tea and sandwiches, most of which sat untouched. I assured everyone I was fine, then asked for a few minutes alone with my friends. As Mom, Dad, Betty and Oliver retreated to the kitchen, I sat on the couch next to Simon, who put his arm around me instantly.

'I'll do it,' I said. 'I'll stop Colin.'

CHAPTER 22

About a week later, Paige fiddled with her cell phone on my bed while I prepared for my date. Getting ready was taking much longer than I'd planned because my body wasn't co-operating. It had been six days since I'd stolen the charge of energy from the Hike House manager, and it showed.

'Who *is* she?' Paige groaned lightly. 'How come I can't place her?'

'Maybe you don't know her.' Standing before the bathroom mirror, I rubbed a third layer of moisturiser into my face, neck, and hands.

'I knew Carla and Erica. And this girl, at least from the back, looks familiar.'

I didn't answer. Caleb had been sent three new photos of our stalker's latest target, a petite brunette, which he'd forwarded to Paige at her request. She'd been driving herself crazy trying to place the girl since, without success.

'Did I go to school with her? Has she been to the restaurant?'

As Paige racked her brain, I finished off a gallon of salt water and waited to see if it made a difference. When my skin stayed pale and dry and the slight creases around my nose, mouth, and eyes didn't smooth, I reached for my last line of defence: make-up. It took blush, lipstick, mascara, eyeliner, and half a bottle of foundation, but eventually, I thought I could pass for eighteen again.

'Wow.' Paige's eyes travelled from my head to my toes as I came out of the bathroom.

'Is it too much?' I turned towards the freestanding full-length mirror. 'I don't want to look like I tried that hard. It might make him suspicious.'

She got up from the bed and stood next to me. 'You look just amazing enough.'

As I smiled at her reflection, I couldn't help but think the same about her. Paige had always been a head-turner, even before her transformation, but she was even more beautiful now. Her long hair shone, and her creamy skin was smooth. Her blue eyes were lighter and brighter than I'd ever seen them. She didn't wear a stitch of make-up – and she didn't have to. We were the same age, but she looked younger now than she did a year ago, while under my cosmetic disguise I looked much older. According to Charlotte, this was partially because I'd transformed sooner, but also because I was a Nenuphar and Paige wasn't. A small part of me was envious. But mostly, I was relieved. I didn't want my best friend to have to deal with what I'd been going through. Ever.

I gave my reflection another quick review. The rest of my body was as dry as my face, so I'd borrowed a long linen skirt from Mom to cover my legs. I'd paired that with a tank top, my denim jacket, and sandals. I'd left my hair down and let it air-dry so that it looked natural, wavy.

As long as Colin didn't look too closely, I should be okay.

'Are you sure you don't want me to come with you?' Paige asked. 'We could tag team and totally blow his mind.'

I'd actually considered this but decided against it. I hadn't broached the topic yet, but for whatever reason, Paige had been fairly reckless with her abilities lately. So although back-up would be nice, I didn't trust her to do something that might alert him and ruin our chance.

'Thanks,' I said, 'but I'll be fine. Plus, you guys will be right down the road, so if anything goes wrong –'

'Which it won't.'

'Which it won't . . . but if I need you for any reason, you won't be far away. And the best part is, I won't even have to use my cell phone.'

The suggestion that I might reach out to her the way

Charlotte had taught me seemed to appease her. She pulled me into a tight hug.

'Be careful,' she whispered. 'Or I'll never talk to you again.'

We headed for the kitchen, where Mom was baking and Dad reading, and told them we were having dinner and watching a movie at Paige's. They still looked concerned as I kissed them goodbye, just as they now did anytime I left the house, but they didn't protest or try to convince us to stay.

And then we got in our cars and drove to town. When we reached Main Street, Paige turned right and continued to Betty's Chowder House. I stayed straight and found a parking spot across the street from Murph's Grill.

'I'll sit at the bar.'

Still in the Jeep, I gasped and dropped the lip gloss and compact I'd been using. 'Simon. What are you doing?'

He stood next to the driver's side door, his hands in his jeans pockets and his forehead wrinkled with worry.

'He'll never know I'm there,' he said.

Heart still racing, I reached through the open window and gently tugged on the front of his T-shirt so he stepped closer. 'But I'll know.'

'Vanessa,' he said quietly. 'I'm not sure about this.'

'We discussed our options,' I reminded him. 'Over and over again. And we all agreed this was the best one.'

'But why won't you let me come with you? I'll stay out of sight and only intervene if necessary.'

I hesitated, debating my response. I'd already tried reassuring him with the fact that we'd be in a public place, surrounded by people; that no matter what, we wouldn't go anywhere else; that I'd abort the mission at the first sign of trouble; and that I had him, Caleb and the police on speed dial. That had been enough – until now.

Finally, trusting that it was the only thing that might work, I went with the truth.

'I don't know what it'll take.'

'What do you mean? You said you'd use your –' He stopped himself, looked around to make sure no one was listening, and tried again. 'You said you'd be so convincing, he'd have no choice but to confess.'

'And I will. I just don't know what I'll have to do to be that convincing.'

His face fell.

'There's a line,' I added, my face flushing. 'Obviously. But . . . there will probably be flirting. Some minor PDA. Do you really want to watch? Especially if it might make you lose focus of the ultimate goal?'

'What if I don't lose focus?'

'Is that possible?'

It wasn't. We both knew this, so he didn't bother answering.

'It's July seventeenth,' I reminded him softly.

He looked down, nodded. 'Can you please promise me one thing?'

'Of course,' I said, thinking this request would be related to the aforementioned PDA.

'Don't be too brave.' He raised his eyes to mine. 'Okay?'

The memory of Charlotte's voice filled my head. I pushed it aside.

'Okay,' I said. 'See you soon.'

He lingered for another few seconds before walking away. I was relieved when he didn't try to kiss me first. I wouldn't want – or be able – to resist, and if Colin somehow saw the exchange, our plan would be over before it even started. Apparently, Simon agreed.

I waited until the Subaru drove past and turned on to Main Street, then checked my appearance once more in the rear-view mirror. Satisfied, I hopped out of the Jeep and hurried to the restaurant. Colin was already there, at a table in the back room. Spotting me, he stood and waved.

You can do this, I told myself as I made my way through the bar crowd. *He's just another guy.*

My body wasn't buying it. The closer I got to the back

room, the harder my legs trembled. When I reached the table, I dropped into a chair and drank the glass of water that had already been served before saying hello.

'Hey,' Colin said, giving me his glass next. 'Let's get some refills.'

He motioned to the waitress, who left us a pitcher.

'You feeling all right?' he asked.

'Absolutely.' I resisted taking the pitcher in both hands and forced a smile. 'How are you?'

'Great.' He grinned. 'I have been ever since you called.'

I tried to casually search for deeper meaning behind his words and expression. The one concern that Simon, Caleb, Paige and I had all shared was that Colin would think my asking him out meant we were onto him and would be instantly on the alert. And even though he seemed to be asking for the attention, we weren't sure what he planned to do once he had it. I was encouraged by how quickly he'd responded to me that morning on the beach, when he saw me emerge from the ocean after a long swim and I'd held on to him for support . . . but I was still wary.

If Colin were harbouring sinister thoughts, however, he didn't show it. He seemed happy. Excited. Maybe a little nervous, as suggested by the pink around his shirt collar and the fact that he couldn't pick up a utensil without dropping it to the floor, but even that seemed innocent enough.

My own nerves easing slightly, I started with small talk. In no time, we'd addressed the weather, movies and favourites, including colour, food and holiday. I asked most of the questions, which he answered easily.

After we'd ordered and received our food, I decided to steer the conversation towards more personal, serious topics. Before beginning, I scooted my chair closer to his until we sat so close, our arms brushed together.

'Do you mind?' I asked, when he looked pleased yet surprised. 'It's pretty loud in here and I don't want to miss a single word.'

The pink on his neck spread to his cheeks. 'I don't mind.'

'Good.' I smiled and let my knee rest against his. 'So remind me how long you've lived in Winter Harbor?'

He picked up his fork – and dropped it again. As he bent down to retrieve it, I reached into my bag, slung across the back of my chair, found the digital voice recorder in the small pocket, and turned it on.

'About two months,' he said, sitting back up.

'That's it?'

'And I won't be staying much longer, either.' His smile faltered as he caught my eye. 'Unfortunately.'

A small ball of energy warmed my stomach. I wanted to look away but held my gaze steady. 'Why not?'

'College.'

My pulse quickened. 'Where do you go?'

'Pomona. It's a small school in California.'

'That's a long way from here.'

He nodded, once again looking disappointed. I pressed on before I lost him to the feeling.

'So does your mom live here? And you're spending the summer with her?'

'Yes. My parents split two years ago, and she moved to Winter Harbor a few months later – right in time for winter in summer.' He paused. 'Were you around for that?'

I'd just taken a bite of salad and focused on chewing and swallowing. 'Yes,' I said.

'Was it insane? It sounded totally insane. I mean, the storms and the bodies and the ice? What *was* that? My mom was so freaked out, she wanted to bail. Too bad she couldn't afford to move somewhere else. She'd just spent her savings on a house and didn't have the money – and no one was going to buy it while all that was going on.'

He was talking fast, growing animated. Was this how all murderers spoke about their psychopathic passions?

'It was pretty crazy.' I watched him out of the corner

of my eye as I picked at my food. 'And this summer's not off to such a great start.'

'You mean with the girls?' He shook his head, picked up his burger. 'I know. It's awful. I forbade my mom from going out by herself at night. That's why I brought that stuff to your family's house a few weeks ago, when you and your friends were hanging out.'

He chewed, wiped ketchup off his chin, slurped his soda. Once again, if my question threw him off, he was very good at hiding it.

'Can I tell you something?' he asked.

My breath caught. His voice sounded different. Quieter, but there was something else, too. Was it more nervousness? A touch of fear?

I forced the puzzlement aside and smiled. 'Of course.'

'Even if it's completely crazy? And might make you think *I'm* completely crazy? So much so that you write me off and we end what could've been a blissful, perfect relationship right here and now?'

I turned slightly so that I faced him more directly – and gave the hidden voice recorder a clearer shot. 'A perfect relationship, huh?' I leaned forward, rested one hand on his knee. 'I'm so happy you think this is going as well as I do.'

This stopped him for a second. His bottom lip fell away from his top, but nothing left the space between.

Thinking I'd gone too far too fast, I removed my hand. He lowered his burger to his plate, took a deep breath, and continued.

'You know how the news chalked everything up to the weird weather? Global warming, cranky Mother Nature, whatever you want to call it?'

I breathed. Nodded.

'Some people disagree. They think there's more to it than that.'

Unable to fight the urge, I reached for my water glass and took two long sips. 'Like what?' I asked.

Now his hand was on my knee. The contact sent a fast jolt shooting up and down my leg.

'Did you ever read *The Odyssey* in school?'

I hadn't, but I knew why he asked. 'Once.'

'You remember who – or what – Odysseus encountered on his journey to Ithaca? That almost killed him?'

I started to nod but then caught myself. 'Not really. It was a while ago.'

He leaned closer. His blue eyes glinted as they held mine. 'Sirens,' he breathed.

I expected the word but somehow, it still caught me off guard. I sat back so fast, the entire chair moved.

'I know. It's almost too ridiculous for fiction, so how

could it be possible in real life? But believe it or not, some people think it is.'

I struggled to stay composed. 'Which people?'

'My friends, to start. A few of them came out from California a few weeks ago and I made the mistake of mentioning it. They latched on to the idea and wouldn't let it go the whole time they were here.'

'Your friends . . . left?' I asked, remembering the voices I heard behind the boathouse.

'They wanted to stay all summer after that, but they had jobs and significant others to get back to.'

'Have you made other friends here?' I asked.

'Present company excluded?' He winked. 'Not really. Despite the down market, Mom's doing pretty well in real estate, so I've been busy helping her.'

And following you. And stalking other pretty girls. And killing in the bright light of day. All on my own, apparently.

'Who told you?'

'Sorry?' he asked.

I forced the air down my throat, tried again. 'You said you mentioned it to your friends. Who told *you*? Who else thinks this is a possibility?'

'It's the strangest thing, actually. A week or so before my friends arrived, I got this e-mail –'

I leapt up. My knee slammed into the table, the back

of my chair into the wall. I yanked my bag free and stumbled towards the hallway dividing the rear dining room from the bar.

'Vanessa, where –'

'Be right back!' I called over my shoulder.

The white spots were back, ballooning and bursting across my field of vision. I rubbed my eyes as I walked, but that only seemed to make them multiply.

Nearly blind, I was frantically feeling my way towards the restrooms when something hard knocked into my left shoulder.

'Well, hi, there, pretty lady.'

Recognising the voice instantly, I stopped, flung one arm forward. My hand landed on a firm, flat surface.

Beneath my fingertips, the fisherman's heartbeat sped up.

'Ready for round two?' He leaned into my hand. 'I wouldn't mind a more formal invitation . . . but I'm still game if you are.'

A high-pitched note filled the space between us. I braced for the rush of energy, the same kind I'd received from the movie-theatre and gear-shop employees . . . but it didn't come. When I tried a second time, the white spots dulled and thinned enough that I could see the familiar scruffy face before me, the same one I'd first seen at the hardware store weeks before, but that was all.

'Everything okay here?' a burly male waiter, on his way to the men's room, asked.

The fisherman stepped back. 'Everything's dandy.'

'Miss?'

I shook my head. 'Yes. I'm fine.'

The waiter blocked the fisherman. I continued down the hall and slipped into the single-person ladies' room. I locked the door and leaned against it, gasping for air and trying to calm down.

Colin knew that I knew. He had to – that was why he was messing with me. And I had to get it together if I wanted to play him the way I'd planned and get enough of a confession on tape that we could turn it – and him – over to the police.

But could I? My body had begun to go downhill at the first mention of sirens, and plummeted after Colin lied about the e-mail. And when I tried to steal energy from the fisherman just now, something I hadn't wanted to do again unless absolutely necessary, in hopes of delaying what Charlotte and Betty insisted I had to do for my long-term survival, it hadn't worked.

Because I couldn't think of my future without also thinking of Simon, I fumbled through my bag for my phone. I knew his worry worsened with each passing second and I wanted to reassure him. My hands shook so hard as I typed, a text that would normally take five seconds to write took a minute.

EVERYTHING OK SO FAR. GETTING CLOSER TO WHAT WE NEED. WILL KEEP YOU POSTED. LOVE, V.

The small connection to Simon was comforting. After sending the text, I felt calm enough to go to the small mirror over the handbasin. It was smudged and blurred, but I could still see that my make-up was cracking as my skin dried out underneath it. Trying not to panic, I turned on the water, added salt from my bag, and washed my face. Then I put on more moisturiser and redid my make-up. I was just about to brush my hair when there was a knock on the bathroom door.

'Vanessa? Are you okay? Can I get you anything?'

Colin. He sounded concerned. Sweet, even. Was that how he'd been with Carla and Erica? Had he won their trust before taking their lives?

The thought was motivating. I put away my make-up, adjusted the voice recorder so it was near the top of my bag, and opened the door.

'Can I ask you a small favour?' I asked.

He smiled, seemingly relieved I hadn't passed out before he could suffocate me. 'Name it.'

I opened the door wider and raised my eyebrows. He hesitated briefly, then stepped inside.

'Not very spacious, is it?' he asked, once I'd closed the door.

It wasn't. The bathroom was so small, we couldn't stand before each other without our torsos touching.

'So,' Colin said, looking around as his face reddened, 'did you need help with something, or . . . ?'

Since Charlotte's trick hadn't worked on the fisherman, I opted to save time and go with the next best thing.

I rested my fingers lightly on the side of Colin's face until his eyes found mine. The burst of energy was slight, but it was there, travelling down my arm. Encouraged, I stood on my toes and brought my mouth near his ear.

'I want you to tell me,' I said softly.

He inhaled. Exhaled. 'Tell you what?'

'What you've been doing.'

'What I've been doing . . . when?'

'The past few weeks. With the girls.'

'What girls?' He tried to pull back. 'Vanessa, I know you didn't have to twist my arm to come in here, but trust me – I don't just do this kind of thing. The second I saw you on that beach . . . I don't know how to explain it. I just . . . felt this thing. This connection . . . you know?'

This wasn't the confession I was hoping for – but somehow, it was exactly what my body wanted to hear.

I wouldn't tell anyone about what happened next. I wouldn't tell them how I moved my mouth from Colin's ear, across his jawline, and to his lips. Or how we kissed for minutes on end, without once coming up for the air we so desperately needed. I wouldn't tell them how he'd lifted me up until I sat on the edge of the basin, and stood between my legs, and kissed wherever his mouth could reach. Most importantly, I wouldn't tell them how good – how *amazing* – it felt.

Natalie, on the other hand, was another story.

'Oh my God.'

I sat up, shoved Colin. He stumbled back, confused. Natalie stood frozen in the open doorway, her mouth agape.

'Sorry.' She stepped back. 'I didn't know – I didn't meant to – the door was unlocked and – '

'It's okay.' I slid off the basin, grabbed my bag. 'And I can explain.'

'You don't have to. Really.'

She darted into the hall, and I ran after her. As strong as I felt, Natalie was stronger – and faster. It wasn't until she was swallowed by the bar crowd that I remembered

Simon's finding out wasn't the worst possible consequence of what I'd just done.

But by the time I made it back to the restroom, I was too late.

Colin was gone.

CHAPTER 23

Breaking News: Third Body Found

Gretchen Hall, 29, was discovered by joggers in Seaview Park early this morning. Police said her fatal injuries were similar in nature to those suffered by recent victims Carla Marciano and Erica Anderson, and urged all residents, particularly women, to practise caution when travelling throughout town.

Story developing, check back for updates.

'Can you please close the computer?' Paige asked.

I didn't answer. My eyes moved from the words to the accompanying photo of a white gazebo encircled by yellow crime-scene tape, and back.

Paige reached over and closed the laptop. 'We get it.'

Simon, seated next to me on the employee deck, took my hand. I sat back and looked towards the harbour.

It was July eighteenth. The anniversary of another death, and yet another day I'd never forget. Only this time, the date wouldn't stick simply because an innocent girl had died.

It'd stick because I'd helped kill her.

'We have to go to the police,' Caleb said.

'With what evidence?' Paige asked.

'The e-mails,' Caleb said.

'You and Simon, like, broke the entire Internet yesterday trying to track the IP addresses,' Paige reminded him. 'And what'd you find?'

Caleb sighed. 'That each e-mail was sent from a different place.'

'Where?' Paige prompted.

'All over the country.'

'So that would help the police how?' When no one answered, Paige continued. 'What it *would* do is tell them that we've been sitting on potential clues to the identities of future victims. And correct me if I'm wrong, but I don't think they'd be especially grateful to us after the fact.'

'What about the recording?' Caleb looked at me. 'Let's listen to it. I know you didn't get an outright confession, but there could still be something on there we can use.'

'The stairwell door's locked,' Paige said. 'No one else will come up and accidentally hear anything.'

I didn't argue or try to talk my way out of it. There

342

was no point. I squeezed Simon's hand before releasing it, then took the voice recorder from my bag, placed it on the table, and pressed Play. As Colin's and my voices filled the air, I watched Simon's face, noting every wince and cringe. The expressions were fleeting, which I knew took conscious effort on his part . . . but they were still there.

'Vanessa, where –'

'Be right back!'

I reached forward, clicked off the recorder.

'You texted me right after that?' Simon asked. 'From the bathroom?'

I nodded.

'And he was gone when you got back?' Caleb asked.

'Yes.' My voice was surprisingly steady. 'And again, I can't tell you how sorry I am for leaving right then. I was so surprised by the way he talked around things, and when he said he'd gotten an e-mail . . . I just needed a minute to get myself together.'

Simon leaned towards me, lowered his voice. 'You have nothing to apologise for. You did what you were comfortable doing, and now we'll come up with another plan. It's okay.'

Behind my sunglasses, my eyes welled briefly, then dried. My body was too depleted to cry.

'So should we share this with the police anyway?' Caleb asked. 'It might –'

'*No*,' Paige and I said at the same time.

'It would raise way too many questions we don't want to answer,' she added.

I agreed. I was also more determined now than ever to keep the secret Charlotte had wanted kept between sirens – and sirens only.

'Can I at least send them an anonymous tip that these dates match the ones from last summer?' Caleb asked. 'Just in case they haven't put that much together on their own?'

No one could argue that. We were silent as he composed and sent an e-mail. When he was done, he closed the computer and checked his watch.

'It's almost seven.' He nodded to Simon. 'We should probably get down there.'

Betty's was hosting another fishermen's dinner and contest that night. Simon and Caleb, hoping Colin would make another appearance, had insisted on attending. They were going to stake out the car park and watch guests arrive.

'We'll be right outside if you need us.' Simon kissed the top of my head as he stood.

'Be careful.' Caleb aimed this at Paige, who promised she would.

'I don't get it,' she said, when they were gone. 'What's this guy trying to prove? That he's just as strong, if not stronger, than us?'

'I'm not sure.' I took a bottle of salt water from my bag and drank. 'But if someone has it in him to kill another person, he probably also has it in him to do so with no good reason.'

'I guess.' Paige watched me finish off the bottle. 'Vanessa, are you okay? Physically, I mean. You seem a little . . . tired, or something.'

She was being generous. I'd examined my appearance in the mirror that morning. I'd seen my skin flaking and the bags under my eyes. I'd even found a single strand of grey hair, which I'd instantly plucked from my scalp. Paige was either too kind to tell me how terrible I looked, or too distracted. 'I've been feeling a little off,' I admitted. 'I guess my body's been having a hard time dealing with everything that's going on.'

'Of course it is.' Paige reached across the table and rested one hand on my arm. 'You should go home and rest. We'll be fine.'

'And risk being locked up for ever by my parents? Who, after reading today's paper, have probably already put up an electric fence lined with barbed wire? I don't think so.' I didn't add that I'd already made matters worse when I'd lied about where I was going when I left the house earlier. I'd planned to quit Betty's as they'd asked but had put it off in light of recent events. 'There is something else I could use, though. And I'll need your help to get it.'

I wasn't even halfway through my explanation when Paige agreed.

'You're my best friend,' she said simply. 'And I know you'd do the same for me.'

Back downstairs, she stayed in the kitchen to talk to Louis and I headed for the hostess stand. Most of the guests had attended the first dinner and were more than happy to seat themselves when I gave them menus and asked them to sit anywhere they'd like. This saved me energy while allowing me to stay put – and not miss a single person walking through the door.

I left my post only once, when Natalie walked by on her way to the Ladies. I excused myself to the two men who'd just come in and followed her.

'Hi,' I said, when she came out of the stall.

She stopped, then continued to the basins. 'Hi.'

'I just wanted to thank you,' I said, heart racing. 'For not telling anyone about yesterday. I really appreciate it.'

'Yes, well. You were nice to me during my meltdown on the beach.' She shook the water from her hands, patted them on her apron. 'Not to mention it's none of my business.'

'Still. Thank you. And I'm so sorry for putting you in that position. If you have a second, I'd be happy to –'

'Vanessa, honestly. It's not necessary. Relationships are complicated.' At the door, she turned and smiled. 'Believe me, I should know.'

She left. I still felt uneasy, but, reminding myself that this was my problem and not hers to fix, I tried to shrug it off as I returned to the lobby.

Ten minutes later, Paige joined me at the hostess stand.

'I found him,' she said quietly.

My heart leapt against my ribs. 'Colin?' I whispered.

'No, but a way to ruin the mood.' Our eyes met. 'The thing you asked me to do? I picked a guy to do it with. He's cute, too.' She wiggled her eyebrows. 'We'll be on the back patio if you want to watch.'

I started after her as she walked away, tempted to tell her to forget it, that I'd changed my mind. But my legs moved so slowly, she was out of hearing range before I could. I lingered by the contest table for a few minutes, pretending to check out the catches as she got situated outside, and then weaved through the crowd and towards the French doors at the back of the dining room.

Paige hadn't wasted time. She leaned against the stone wall enclosing the patio, her back to me. An attractive guy who looked to be in his early twenties faced her. He had light brown hair and wore khakis and a red plaid shirt, unbuttoned, over a white T-shirt. They talked, laughed, grew closer. I was twenty feet away, but I could still see the glimmer in his eyes as Paige's power took hold and the world around them began to disappear. When his head lowered towards hers, I turned away. I was embarrassed to watch them kiss, and felt guilty, too. Paige had agreed to help without reservation, but I couldn't help thinking I'd put my best friend in an uncomfortable situation.

Not that she *seemed* uncomfortable. When she found me standing there a few minutes later, still inside the dining room, her smile lit up her whole face, her blue eyes gleamed silver, and her skin radiated pink.

'His name's Jaime. He's twenty-four, from Bar Harbor – and all yours.' She handed me a glass of iced tea. 'I told him I'd be right back with this.'

'Thank you.' I hugged her.

'No problem. Anytime you need me to do that again, I'm more than happy to help. Trust me.'

She headed for the microphone on the other side of the room. I stopped by the bar for a quick shot of salt water, then went outside. As Paige started the contest festivities, the fishermen hanging out on the patio congregated near the open French doors to watch and listen.

Grateful for their distraction, I straightened my skirt, smoothed my shirt, and went to Jaime.

'Hi, there.'

He looked up, his hazel eyes slightly unfocused. 'Where's Paige?'

'She had to take care of something inside so she asked me to bring you this.' I held out the iced tea. He studied it for a moment, as if trying to remember whether he was thirsty. When he didn't move to take it, I rested it on the wall behind him.

'Is she coming back?' He peered over his shoulder.

'I'm not sure. She's pretty busy.' I waited for him to turn back. He didn't. 'I'm Vanessa, by the way.'

'Nice to meet you,' he mumbled, without looking at me.

I stepped towards him until I was so close, I could see his chest lift with each breath. 'The pleasure's mine.'

For a split second, his chest stopped.

'It's such a nice night,' I said quietly, hating each word more than the last. 'Would you like to take a walk?'

He turned back. His eyes, slightly clearer, narrowed and searched my face. Guessing he needed a bit more encouragement, I leaned into him and sang a single note so softly, I knew no one but us could hear it. It was a variation of what Charlotte had taught me, and given how that had failed with the fisherman at Murph's yesterday,

I didn't think it'd work. The most I hoped for was that it would help shift Jaime's focus from Paige to me.

Which was why I was stunned when his eyes widened and locked on mine. And my body felt a surge of life so unexpected, I gasped and grabbed his shirt for support. Taking this as an invitation, he reached for my waist.

'Let's walk,' I whispered.

He followed willingly. My head spun as we crossed the pier and headed down the beach, away from Betty's. Part of me wanted to take the energy I'd just gotten and return to the restaurant immediately. But a bigger part wanted to keep going. Charlotte had said that attracting the affection of a guy who was interested in another girl was the best way to stay strong – at least, I assumed, until more was required. If that was true, and if Paige had done her part well enough, then a few more minutes with Jaime wouldn't hurt. If anything, they should give me the strength I'd need to correct yesterday's mistakes.

So I looked behind me only once more, to make sure we'd gone far enough. As I turned back, my gaze lingered on the line of cars in the car park where Simon hid with Caleb.

This is for him, I told myself. *It's for all of us.*

I lowered myself to the sand and smiled up at Jaime. He sat next to me. I mentioned I was cold, and his arm was around me instantly. I huddled against him, which led to snuggling. Soon we were lying next to and holding on to one another. I didn't kiss him – I refused, no matter how much my body ached to – but he kissed me. As his lips moved across my face and down my neck, I closed my eyes. I listened to the water rush towards us and retreat. I gave into the exhilaration and let my body have this moment, as if the physical me and emotional me were two separate, opposing forces struggling to come together for the good of the whole.

I was so consumed, I didn't realise we weren't alone until it was too late.

'Hey!' The voice was familiar, but also distant. Muffled. Like its source was buried beneath a thick blanket. '*Hey!*'

And then the moment was gone. Jaime was jerked to his feet before being thrown back down in the sand – several feet away. When he tried to stand, he was knocked over again. I sat up, head spinning. Between the darkness and my confusion, it took me several seconds to figure out what was happening.

When I did, I scrambled to my feet and lunged at Simon.

'Stop! He didn't do anything!'

'Stay back, Vanessa!' he shouted, without turning around. 'Let me handle this!'

'There's nothing to handle!' I grabbed his arm and

pulled when he moved to shove Jaime a third time. 'I'm fine!'

Simon yanked his arm from my grip. '*He* won't be by the time I'm done with him.'

Feeling more powerful than they had in weeks, my legs bolted. I flew around Simon and threw myself between him and Jaime.

'He didn't do anything,' I insisted. 'This is my fault.'

Still focused on the cowering figure behind me, Simon opened his mouth to protest. But then something distracted him . . . and his attention shifted to me.

'Vanessa?' He straightened. His arms relaxed. 'Your eyes . . . you look . . .'

'Different?' I guessed.

He shook his head. 'Beautiful.'

I didn't say anything. Simon's awe quickly turned to confusion.

'You're okay?' he asked. 'This guy wasn't attacking you?'

'I'm fine. And, no. He wasn't.'

He looked from me, to Jaime, still lying on the ground, and back to me. 'But if you're . . . if he wasn't . . .' He raised his arms, let them drop to his sides. 'What were you doing?'

I held up one hand, asking him to give me a second,

and then turned and offered the same hand to Jaime. He took it, and I helped him stand.

'You should go back to the restaurant,' I said. 'Paige will be happy to see you.'

He hesitated, and I thought he might not go. But he nodded a moment later and then shuffled away.

When I turned back, Simon was pacing. He'd put it together. Maybe not everything – like why – but enough to know what Jaime and I had really been doing when he'd assumed I was being attacked. I stood there, wanting to go to him, to stop him, and throw my arms around him, but I was too uncertain whether he wanted the same thing.

Finally, he said, 'You were kissing him.'

'He was kissing me,' I said calmly.

'Does it matter?'

A few minutes ago, I thought it did. Now that I saw just how upset Simon was, I wasn't sure.

'I needed him,' I said.

This stopped him. 'You what?'

'Not necessarily him, specifically . . . but I needed to be with a guy. Physically.'

'And – what? You couldn't wait long enough to make the huge trek to the car park?'

His voice was loud, accusing. It hurt so much, I had to look away.

'This is part of it, Simon.'

He stepped towards me. 'Part of what?'

Now that my body was sufficiently refuelled, the tears fell easily. I brushed my eyes as I faced him. 'My life.'

His face relaxed but his shoulders remained tensed. I knew he was torn between his anger and wanting to comfort me.

'Haven't you noticed how I've looked lately?' I asked. 'Tired? Weak? Older?'

'Tired, yes. But a lot's been going on. It'd be strange if you *weren't* exhausted.'

'It's not just that.' I searched his face, wished I could wipe away his pain. 'I'm sick.'

He took another step towards me. 'Sick . . . how?'

'My body's failing. Because of what I am. It needs things other people's don't.'

'Like salt water. And swimming.'

'And what you just saw.'

He looked at me, waited, like he expected me to say I was kidding. When I didn't, he clasped his hands on top of his head and turned away from me, towards the ocean.

'It doesn't work with you.' My voice cracked and the tears fell faster. 'Not in the same way. I wish it did . . . you can't know how much I wish it did. But because you love me –'

'I can't give you what you need? Do you know how that sounds? How it *feels*?'

I took a deep breath, released it. 'Yes. I do.'

He released his hands and his head lowered. I walked over and stood next to him. The tide was rising, and the water stalled inches from our feet before rolling back.

'I love you, Simon,' I said, fixing my eyes on the dark, distant horizon. 'Which is why you need to know that this will only get worse. It already has. I thought I had everything under control when my family and I first got here – I wouldn't have pursued getting back together otherwise. Then when we did and I started feeling worse, I pretended I was fine. I thought that if I just drank more and swam further, I would be. But now I know that's not the case . . . I can't ask you to be with me. It's too hard. It's not fair.'

For a long moment, he didn't speak. Part of me hoped that this was enough, that I wouldn't ever have to tell him what Charlotte had told me before she'd passed away. I hoped that one day I'd just disappear and he wouldn't have to know, because to him, I'd already been gone a very long time.

But he kicked off one sneaker, and then the other. He took off his socks. He walked through the foamy run-off, hopped a breaker, and waded into the ocean. He

355

stood there, watching the water, then turned around and reached out one hand.

I held my eyes to his as I walked towards him. I took his hand, and he pulled me close. We stood like that, our arms around each other, my cheek against his chest and his chin on top of my head, until the tide rose so high, we could no longer feel the sandy floor beneath our feet.

I knew then that it wasn't enough.

Nothing would be.

CHAPTER 24

When the next e-mail clue arrived four days later, Simon and I were sitting in the coffee shop in town, hoping to catch Colin stopping by for his morning caffeine fix. I'd called and texted several times since our date at Murph's, apologising profusely and offering to make it up to him on a second date, but he never answered and my messages went unreturned. I'd considered getting his address through my parents, whom I thought might know where their realtor lived, but I couldn't come up with a reason for wanting to visit him that wouldn't invite questions. Plus, no one was entirely comfortable with cornering the killer on his home turf. The plan was for me to reel him in for another shot at a confession, this time with Simon, Caleb and Paige nearby to intervene as needed, but giving him a home-field advantage didn't make sense.

That had left public stalking . . . and waiting.

'Here we go,' Simon said, when his phone buzzed with a new text from Caleb. 'Right on time.'

I leaned closer and we watched the picture load.

'She's in the supermarket, wearing a black shirt, and not looking at the camera.' He sighed. 'As helpful as always.'

'Wait,' I said, as he started to close the phone. 'Can you zoom in? On her wrist?'

The photo blurred slightly as her arm grew bigger, but it was clear enough for me to see what I needed to. I sat back, vaguely aware of the blood leaving my face, the feeling abandoning my body.

'What?' Simon brought the camera closer. 'What is it?'

The bell over the door rang as a customer walked in. My head snapped in that direction and I grabbed my empty coffee cup, as if a ceramic dish was all it'd take. When the customer was an older woman, I lowered the cup but held on to it, just in case.

'Her bracelet,' I said quietly.

'What about it?'

'It's actually a necklace. See how it's looped around a few times?'

'Yes,' he said. 'And what are those things hanging from the chain?'

'Charms. Two birthstones and two initials.'

'One's a *Z*,' he said, squinting, 'but the other's partially hidden behind her arm.'

He was right. But I didn't have to see the whole thing to know what it was.

'It's a *P*.' I paused, not believing I was going to say what I was about to say. 'For *Paige*.'

Simon put it together instantly. 'Why is she wearing Raina's necklace as a bracelet?'

Because you can't help who your mother is – who she was. Because you still feel some sort of connection to her, no matter the terrible things she's done. Because, sometimes, it's nice to pretend that nothing's wrong and that your family's like everyone else's.

'I don't know,' I said. 'But we have more important things to worry about.'

'Are you absolutely sure it's her? Maybe we should wait for other pictures before we –'

His phone buzzed. Her face was still hidden in the next photo, but the girl getting out of the SUV in the Chowder House car park was definitely my best friend.

He closed the phone and lowered his voice. 'We're going to the police. Even without solid evidence, we can at least put Colin on their radar. And they can protect Paige.'

I couldn't argue. We'd just have to deal with whatever potentially uncomfortable, revealing questions our leads prompted the best we could.

We stood, delivered our dirty dishes to the service

counter, and hurried to the door. The police station was only a few streets over, but we headed for the Subaru, which was closer than my Jeep. I'd just buckled up when my eyes caught the time on the dash.

'I can't go,' I said, bringing one hand to my forehead. 'I'm supposed to be home in three minutes. I promised my parents I'd have brunch with them.'

'Brunch?' Simon looked at me. 'Really?'

'That was the only way they'd let me out of the house this morning to see you. They've already threatened leaving here for good, and all they need is one more freak-out to turn that threat into realty. And I can't tell them what's going on for the exact same reason.'

He reached over and kissed my cheek. 'It's fine. Go. I'll have Caleb come with his laptop, and you can meet us when you're done.'

We said goodbye and I got out. He waited until I was in my car and pulling away from the kerb before making a U-turn and heading in the opposite direction.

As soon as he was out of sight, I parked again and called Paige. I hated to scare her, but she needed to know she was being targeted. Maybe fear would convince her to stay home with the doors locked until tomorrow – which, according to last summer, was the next scheduled attempt – had come and gone without incident. After three calls went to voicemail, I texted instead.

The message sent, I threw the Jeep in drive and punched the gas. I didn't get far before having to hit the brake for a black sports car. Its driver was in no hurry, and I was debating whether to pass him on a double yellow line when the car stopped short for a pedestrian crossing the street. I slammed the brake to avoid running into him; as I did, I registered the rounded sticker in the car's rear window. It was a college sticker, like the Dartmouth one Mom had proudly stuck on her SUV the day we'd found out I'd been accepted.

And it was for Pomona. The small school in California.

I barely breathed as my eyes travelled to the Audi logo beneath the back window. The two kayaks strapped to the roof. A tanned, bare arm resting on the driver's side door.

Colin was right in front of me. Cruising through town like this was any ordinary Sunday. Like he wasn't hours away from taking his fourth victim.

Keeping my eyes glued to his car, I grabbed my cell from the cup holder and dialled Simon. It went right to voicemail, probably because he was on the phone with Caleb. I left a quick message, then called my parents and explained that I'd lost track of time, apologised, and said I'd be home as soon as I could.

And then I gripped the steering wheel and followed the Audi.

It drove through town and turned onto a county road that paralleled the coast. The further it went, the louder the voice in my head warning me to turn around grew, but I kept going, keeping a safe distance behind. I didn't think about what I was doing or what would happen when the Audi finally stopped. All I thought was that this person wanted to take someone else from me. Someone good and pure and loved by everyone she met. And I couldn't let him out of my sight.

Fifteen minutes outside town, the Audi turned into a small dirt car park. I turned, too, without hesitating. I felt some small trepidation when ours were the only cars there, but then Colin saw me, and it didn't matter. I took the digital recorder from my bag and slid it in my jacket pocket.

'Hi.' I forced a smile as I hopped out of the Jeep.

'Hey.' He stood next to his car, eyeing me warily. 'What are you doing here?'

'I followed you from town.' Not exactly subtle, but we didn't have time for that. 'I wanted to see you.'

'Why?'

I stepped towards him. 'Because I haven't seen you since our date. And you never returned my calls or texts.'

His eyes narrowed. He turned away from me and started working the kayak cords. 'You shouldn't be here.'

My heart beat faster. *Why* shouldn't I be? Did he have another target we didn't know about?

'I'm sorry', I said, as my stomach turned, 'if I made you uncomfortable or did anything inappropriate the other day. I guess I have a hard time expressing my feelings . . . especially when they're so strong.'

I placed one hand on his arm. His muscles flexed, then froze, beneath my fingers.

'But I was hoping we could start over,' I said. 'Maybe give things another shot.'

He considered this. Finally, he said, 'I do still owe you a kayaking lesson.'

The wind shifted then and I smelled it. Salt. I'd been so focused on him, I hadn't paid attention to where we were.

The ocean. Talk about home-field advantage.

'I'm ready if you are,' I said.

His face softened slightly, but he still seemed sceptical and I wasn't sure why. He'd certainly made out with me willingly enough in the restroom at Murph's . . . so was it because we'd been caught? Was he worried that I knew the truth about him? But didn't he *want* me to know the truth? Wasn't that why he sent e-mails with images of future victims?

Or was it simply because he preferred to be the one calling the shots, and that hadn't happened this time?

Encouraged, I helped him untie the kayaks and lift them from the car roof. Not wanting to chance a technological malfunction in the event of unpredictable waves, I claimed thirst and popped back into the Jeep. As he fiddled with paddles, I drained a water bottle, dropped in the voice recorder, tightened the cap, and placed the bottle in my inside jacket pocket. It wasn't perfect waterproof protection, but it was better than nothing.

Back outside, Colin and I carried the kayaks, one at a time, down a steep, rocky path that led to the beach. A third trip was made for paddles, and then we dragged all the equipment towards the water.

'It's all about upper body strength,' he said. 'The waves will kill you if you let them. The trick is not letting them.'

If this was a lesson, Colin was a questionable instructor. Good thing I was already well learned in wave manoeuvring.

'Got it,' I said. Then, 'I just need one thing before we get started. If it's okay with you.'

He turned to me. I held open my arms, relieved when they didn't shake.

'It's going to be us against the water, right? So as teammates, I think we need to start over. With a clean slate.'

He frowned and his chin lowered towards his chest. He looked at the ground like he was trying to work out something in his head. A moment later, he looked up, offered a tentative smile, and let me put my arms around him. I tried not to tense as his arms encircled my shoulders – or think that in this position, he could easily snap my neck if so inclined.

Fortunately, he didn't kill me right then and there; in fact, his body relaxed against mine, and I considered this progress. Even if I couldn't get a direct confession out of him, I hoped to use my abilities to either earn his trust or make him feel so strongly about me, he eventually agreed to whatever I asked – including an afternoon trip to the Winter Harbor police department.

'Are you sure you want to do this?' he asked once we'd separated.

'Can you think of one reason I shouldn't be?'

His gaze shifted and focused on something behind me. I turned – and was startled to see the sky darkening to grey in the distance. It was the first time it had been anything but blue in months.

'We'll be fine,' I said, turning back. 'There are no

clouds here, and it's barely drizzled all summer. I'm sure that'll clear up long before it reaches us.'

'If you say so.'

He continued towards the water. I took off my sandals, rolled my jeans up to my knees, and followed him in. It took some effort getting the heavy plastic boat past the break, which kept shoving it back to shore, and I was glad Paige and I had practised our new, weird version of spin the bottle twice more since our first attempt with Jaime. I still fatigued easily, but felt better than I had in weeks. And our game participants, two waiters at the Lighthouse Resort, where Paige and I had enjoyed a few meals, had been happy to play and none the wiser.

Once the kayaks were far enough out, we hopped in and started paddling. I kept my focus on Colin, who stayed a few feet ahead of me. I followed his lead when he turned to travel parallel to shore and was surprised to see how far we'd gone. Our cars were barely visible on top of the cliff we'd climbed down, and the beach was a narrow beige strip about a quarter mile away.

'Am I doing this right?' I called out, intentionally adjusting my technique so that the paddle cut too deeply and my rhythm was off. The kayak swerved all the way to the right, a little to the left, and all the way to the right again. By the time Colin reached me, my back was nearly to him.

'Not bad for a beginner.'

He demonstrated how to hold the paddle and I noticed he seemed even more relaxed now. Maybe I wasn't the only one who benefited from time spent on the water. I asked him a few more questions about proper form and positioning, as well as how he'd come to know so much. The more he talked, the easier the words came – and the surer I felt that this could work. For good measure, I made sure our hands brushed together, and sat incorrectly so he had no choice but to reach over and correct my posture by touching my back or shoulders. Not only did these brief moments of contact seem to help him warm up to me, but combined with the occasional salt-water splash, they kept me energised enough to keep going.

I felt so solid physically, when he asked if I'd like to head out to a sandbar another twenty yards away, I agreed.

Unfortunately, the storm we saw in the distance half an hour earlier was coming closer as we paddled, and the waves were growing taller. By the time we reached the sandbar, the blue sky had been taken over by fat, dark clouds. Cool droplets began to fall, the wind to pick up.

'Maybe we should turn back!' I called out. 'Save this for another day!'

Up ahead, Colin didn't answer. Perhaps he hadn't

heard. He rode the waves, paddling every now and then as he watched the water beneath him. After a few minutes, he gripped one end of the paddle and shot the other end into the water like a spear. The paddle anchored and Colin held on, triumphant. Using his free hand, he tied what looked like a surfboard lead around the paddle, then climbed out of the kayak. The boat bobbed on the ocean's surface, tethered to the paddle that was lodged in the sandbar. Under normal conditions, I guessed he could stand with the water lapping around his ankles; under these, the water knocked against his knees.

'That's not going to hold!' It took all my strength to cut through the water towards him. 'The waves are too big!'

He opened his mouth to answer just as a bolt of lightning shot into the horizon, slicing the sky in half. A ground-shaking *boom*, which I felt despite my distance from the ocean floor, followed three seconds later, suggesting the storm wasn't as far away as it looked. The deluge came next, washing the salt water from my skin and making the dark green Atlantic pop and bubble as if flames burned somewhere below.

'I'm sorry!'

'What?' I yelled. Nearing the anchored paddle, I reached out to grab it – and missed. A wave started to carry me away, and I flung the paddle in and out, in and out, struggling to not drift too far.

'I didn't mean to do it!'

My head snapped up. It was hard to hear anything over the rush of wind and water . . . but had Colin just said what I thought he did? Was he confessing here, in the middle of the ocean, in the middle of a thunderstorm?

'I didn't know what was happening!'

He was. I released one end of the paddle and reached into my jacket pocket. The voice recorder was soaked, but I felt for the largest button and pressed it anyway.

'If I knew . . . if I had any idea . . .'

I took the paddle in both hands again and pumped my arms as hard and fast as they'd go. 'If you had any idea . . . *what*?'

He looked at me, rain streaming down his face. His eyes were clear, sad. He shook his head and said something else, but I couldn't read his lips in the flash of lightning, and his words were drowned out by a second, louder clap of thunder. Before I could ask him to repeat what he'd said, a wave rushed from behind, slammed into his back. He managed to stay upright, but the anchored paddle was torn from its post and tossed away, taking his kayak with it.

For a split second, Colin froze. He stared at the boat, his eyes and mouth wide in panic.

In the next second, his face relaxed. And he dived headfirst into the water.

I sat there, breathless, watching the ocean's surface, waiting for his head to break through. When it didn't and his kayak continued to drift farther away, I climbed to my knees, gripped the sides of my boat, and scanned the dark depths. But the pouring rain and sloshing water made it impossible to see anything else.

At which point, I had two options. I could either paddle or swim back to shore and leave him there to accept whatever fate he had coming . . . or I could save him. So that he suffered a different fate, one that punished him for as long as the legal system deemed appropriate, later.

I still hadn't made up my mind when a swell of water lifted my kayak and threw it back down. I toppled out before the small boat capsized, and was instantly sucked into a powerful current. It took hold of my waist and jerked me to one side, then the other. Before I could swim out of it, it grabbed my chest. My mouth. My forehead. It snaked around my neck and took hold, squeezing the water from my throat. Beneath my feet, I saw a second pair, kicking.

The water wasn't dragging and choking me.

Colin was.

And he was strong. I elbowed him in the gut and freed my neck. I was spinning around for a better shot when he grabbed my arms and twisted them behind my back. The water was so rough, I couldn't see his face, but it lightened overhead. Every few seconds, he gave a hard kick and gasped for air above the surface before sinking back down.

My arms burned as he clenched one hand around both my wrists. He clamped his other hand over my nose and mouth, trying to suffocate me. I shot both legs up and behind me, aiming for his groin, but the angle was too awkward. I couldn't reach him. After several seconds of wriggling and writhing, the only thing keeping me from passing out was the water seeping between his fingers. I inhaled it greedily, hoping he didn't notice.

I didn't think he did, but either way, this was taking too long. I could feel it in his fist, the slight ease in pressure around my wrists. Soon he removed both hands. Before I could make a break for it, they were back around my neck, squeezing tighter this time. So tight, the white spots I'd become familiar with over the past several months reappeared. Only now they fizzled instead of brightening. The pain was so intense, I thought my head might just snap off and float away.

This was it. I was going to die. Here, in the water. Just

like Justine had. And all those men last summer and fall. Was this what it had been like for them? So dark? So cold?

There was another *boom*. And another and another. Bright white flashes lit up the ocean. Convinced the end was imminent, I started to close my eyes against the glare . . . but something stopped me.

A paddle. From one of the kayaks. It had been sucked beneath the surface and now spun and spiralled near my feet.

Carefully, gently, moving so slowly Colin wouldn't notice, I gripped the flat paddle end between my toes and lifted it up. I brought my arms forward. My fingers wrapped around the hard plastic pole.

And I swung behind me, as hard as I could. The paddle slammed into his back. His hands fell from my neck and I shot forward, away from him and into deeper, darker water.

My first instinct was to get as far away as fast as possible. But then I did a somersault and circled back towards the sandbar.

I found him, clinging to the hard stretch of sand that, by the end of this storm, would likely be broken up and resettled on the ocean floor. I could see him, too, his face reaching towards the surface, his cheeks bulging as he fought to keep the pockets of air from bursting. Tiny air bubbles streamed from his nose and pressed lips, and I knew if I left him alone, he'd be gone in seconds. He'd die certain he almost had me, never knowing I'd returned for him.

It might be what he deserved, but I couldn't let it happen.

That didn't mean I couldn't teach him a lesson. So I sang. To get his attention. To let him know that I knew what he'd done, and that I'd make sure everyone else did, too. The note started softly, sweetly, and quickly grew louder. It stretched towards the sandbar, the ground, the horizon behind me, and overhead. Soon I could no longer hear the thunder roaring or the water rushing past my ears.

Neither, it seemed, could Colin. His fingers straightened. He released the sandbar and, despite the currents, drifted towards me. His cheeks flattened. His lips parted. Still singing, I kicked once and shot towards him. If necessary, I knew I could force the ocean from his lungs, but we didn't have to go that far. He needed to be okay – physically, at least. So that on the drive back to Winter Harbor, we could discuss exactly what he'd tell the police.

It was a good plan. A *great* plan.

But then the current shifted, yanking him deeper. Pulling him away from me. I kicked faster, paddled harder, but it seemed the more I tried the greater the distance between us grew.

Until, several long seconds later, he smiled.

I stopped. The ocean fell silent. Colin continued towards me, arms outstretched, looking happier than I'd ever seen him. His hand had just grazed my stomach when the light in his eyes went out. His entire body fell limp.

At the same time, somewhere in the back of my mind, Paige's voice was pleading.

Vanessa, help me. Please. Now.

I'm at Betty's . . . and he's after me.

CHAPTER 25

I tried to save him. I brought him back to shore. I pounded his chest and forced air into his lungs. Each time I pulled away and saw his lips turned up, I thought he was coming to, that his face was contorting as his body struggled to hang on . . . but he was only smiling.

'*No.*' I squeezed his nose between two fingers and pressed my mouth to his. His chest rose, fell, and stopped. I did it again, and again.

He grinned the whole time.

Vanessa . . . please hurry . . .

I breathed more. Pounded harder. Rain poured down, blending with the tears streaming down my face, but I didn't feel it. I didn't feel anything.

Neither did Colin. Every few seconds I checked for a pulse, but his veins were still. His heart was done.

Oh my God . . . he's in here. . . .

I sat up and looked down the beach, in the direction of the restaurant. It was a few miles away, so I wouldn't have been able to see it on a clear day, but I hoped Paige could somehow sense me tuning in, reaching out.

I pictured her pretty smile, imagined her laugh, and answered.

Where?

I waited. When all I heard was the rain thrashing and water roaring onto shore, I tried again.

Keep talking, Paige. I'll be there as soon as I can.

Still listening for her, I leaned towards Colin. I lowered my mouth to his ear and spoke softly.

'I don't know how you were involved with those girls . . . but I do know what you just tried to do to me.' I brushed at my eyes, which wouldn't stop crying. 'And I'm still sorry. You would've faced consequences eventually . . . but not this. Not from me.'

Unable to look at him, I kept my gaze averted as I climbed to my feet, pulled off my soaked denim jacket, and used it to cover his vacant eyes. I offered one more silent apology, then shoved my feet into my sandals, which were still on the beach where I'd left them before entering the water, and ran up the steep path to the car park.

The next several minutes were a blur. I reached the rain-filled Jeep and called the police to report a found body, give them the location, and tell them something was going on at Betty's. I called Simon and left a hurried message saying that I was fine but Paige was in trouble, and asked him to go to the restaurant as soon as possible.

As I started the car and gunned it backwards, I called my parents and assured them that I was okay and would be home as soon as I could.

I didn't think about what I'd just done. I couldn't. If I did, I'd stop. I'd sit right there in my car with the top down, and let the freshwater pummel my skin until it began to slowly poison my body.

And Paige needed me. I couldn't save Colin . . . or Justine or Charlotte . . . but I could still save my best friend.

I was so focused on this I almost peeled out of the car park without noticing the car parked between a skip and a sand dune. When I saw it, I hit the brake so hard, the Jeep lunged forward.

It was an empty orange pick-up. With fishing poles hanging out the back. The fact that Paige was in danger even though Colin could no longer hurt her meant he hadn't acted alone the past few weeks. Did he have help here, too? Were the fishermen lurking somewhere around the lot, waiting to finish the job?

Vanessa!

I shook my head and hit the gas. The tyres spun in mud before gaining traction and shooting backwards. I flew out onto the road, slid into a turn, and headed for town.

The storm worsened as I drove. The sky turned as

black as night and the rain was a thick grey wall my headlights couldn't break through. I was actually grateful for the lightning, which managed to illuminate the darkness – and the road – every few seconds. I gripped the steering wheel and stared straight ahead, thinking only of Paige. When my cell phone rang, I checked the number on the screen; but it was only my parents, so I let it go to voicemail.

Nearing town, I spoke again.

I'm almost there. Are you okay?

There was a long beat. I held my breath as I stared through the blurred windscreen, following the fuzzy double yellow line. I was about to repeat myself, louder, when she answered.

Yes, she said, voice trembling. *But he's here.*

Who? Where?

She spoke again but her voice was lost in an explosion of thunder. A shard of lightning lit up the sky before striking a tree to my right, splitting it in two. Seeing the halved trunk tilting towards the road, I punched the gas – but it was no use. The tree gained momentum on the way down and hit the road before I could pass. I skidded to a stop, avoiding a collision by inches, then backed up and tried to go around it.

But it was too long. It blocked the entire road and its top branches tangled in the woods twenty feet away. I threw open the door, jumped out of the car, and ran to the tree, determined to create a passable lane. I leaned into it with all my weight; it rocked slightly, but didn't budge. Because it sat at an angle, it was too tall to simply drive over. On the other side, the road remained dark. This was the kind of storm people pulled over to wait out, so chances were slim that anyone besides the police would come this way and, when they couldn't get through, give me a ride back to town.

I was still a mile away.

Inside my head, Paige whimpered softly.

There was only one option. I moved the Jeep to the side of the road. Grabbed my phone, bag and keys. And ran.

My legs pumped beneath me. My feet flew over rocks and twigs. My heart beat quickly but consistently. Before I knew it, the dim lights of Main Street appeared.

Are you still at Betty's? I asked Paige.

Yes . . .

Where?

In the –

She fell silent.

Paige? Are you okay?

Nothing.

I moved faster, sprinting through town. As Betty's came into view, I grabbed my phone from my bag and

379

tried Simon again. He didn't answer, so I left another voicemail saying I was at the restaurant with Paige and asking him to please hurry and meet us there.

I charged up the porch steps and lunged at the front door. It didn't give. I gripped the knob tighter and tried again.

The door was locked. In the middle of the day, when the restaurant should be serving lunch. Betty's was open 365 days of the year and didn't close for any reason. Paige liked to say that if a blizzard shut down the rest of the town, you could always snowshoe to the pier and know you'd find a hot bowl of chowder waiting for you. This storm, though bad, wasn't worse than that . . . so what was going on?

And then I saw it. A handwritten sign, taped to the other side of the door's small window.

Betty's is closed today for a private party. Please come back tomorrow!

Paige hadn't mentioned anything about a private party. But I could hear the music from here. And as I moved down the porch and peered into the dining-room windows, I saw what appeared to be some sort of celebration. I recognised many of the fishermen who'd become recent regulars. They milled about, talking and laughing with several girls I didn't recognise. Nobody sat at the tables and ate; they mingled like they were at a cocktail party. Maybe that was because no one was serving them – in a quick scan of the room, I didn't spot a single employee.

Paige, I tried again, hurdling down the porch steps. *I'm here. Where are you?*

Nothing. I bolted around the side of the building and headed for the kitchen door. I wasn't surprised to find it locked, too, and was relieved to see the room empty when I peered into the adjacent window. I glanced around to make sure I wasn't being followed, then unlocked the door with the key Paige had given me when I'd started hostessing.

I checked the basement next. No one was there so I went back upstairs and tried the pantry, the utility closet, the freezer. All were empty. I was hiding behind stacks of dishes, trying to figure out how to infiltrate the dining room without anyone noticing, when something thumped overhead. It was followed by a light scraping that started to my left and travelled to my right.

A knife lay on the counter next to me. It rested by a half-sliced tomato, like whoever had been preparing it had been interrupted. I grabbed it and headed for the stairs.

I heard voices as I climbed. Paige's soft moaning

seemed to grow louder, and I soon realised that was because I now heard it both inside and outside my head.

At the top of the stairwell, I tightened my hold on the knife handle and stepped onto the employee break deck.

I didn't have a plan, but if I had, it wouldn't have mattered. The second my eyes registered the scene before me, I was too stunned to move.

Like the dining room downstairs, the deck was decorated for a party. Paper globe lanterns were strung from the ceiling and bobbed in the wind. Candles, their flames protected by clear glass domes, were scattered across the tables, floor and railings. In the centre of the table that my friends and I had sat at countless times, a large silver bucket held ice and three bottles of champagne. Glass flutes surrounded the bucket.

Paige sat in a plastic chair in the far corner of the deck, her wrists tied with rope and her mouth taped shut. Her head lolled to one side, like she was too tired to hold it upright. Jaime, the cute, young fisherman we'd manipulated a few days ago, stood next to her. Simon and Caleb, also bound and gagged, huddled together on the floor in the opposite corner. When Simon saw me, his entire body jerked, like it automatically wanted to run to and protect me; I managed to shake my head so he stayed put. I didn't want him to alert their captor, whose back was to me.

Paige, are –

'Vanessa!'

Paige's head lifted. I stepped back.

Natalie turned around.

'So nice of you to join us.' She slid off the guy's lap she'd been sitting in and hurried across the deck. She wore a soft red sundress with a skirt so long, it trailed behind her. 'Care for some bubbly?'

I didn't answer as she reached me, pulled me into a hug, and kissed my cheek.

'Poor thing. You're soaked!' She started to pull back – and stopped when her eyes met mine. A second later, her lips turned up. 'And you've had some morning, haven't you?'

She let out a small squeal and practically skipped back to the table. I glanced at Simon, who looked at me. His eyebrows were lowered as his gaze travelled slowly from my feet to my face. Caleb watched me curiously. Across the deck, Paige, now alert, did the same thing.

'How do you feel?' Natalie asked. She popped a strawberry in her mouth with one hand and poured a glass of champagne with the other.

Somehow, I found my voice. 'Fine.'

She glided back towards me. 'That's all?'

I started to say yes, and then realised it wasn't true. I'd kayaked. Swam. Been attacked and freed myself.

Dragged a hundred and eighty pounds up the beach. Absorbed a ton of fresh rainwater. Sprinted a mile. Between my recent physical exertion and the accompanying emotional stress, I shouldn't be here. I should be back at the beach, passed out, perhaps left for dead.

But I wasn't. Because Colin was.

I felt stronger, healthier, than I ever had. And I knew this was why. The effects of my unthinkable actions were likely apparent in my appearance, which was why my friends were examining me like they wanted to make sure it wasn't someone else standing before them.

I tried to channel this superhuman energy now.

'What's going on, Natalie?' I asked calmly.

She shrugged, grinned. 'What does it look like?'

'Kidnapping?'

'And here I was going for bohemian chic,' she said, with a pout.

She came back towards me and held out the champagne glass. When I didn't take it, her eyes fell to my hands.

'Oh. You won't be needing that.'

Before I could react, she grabbed my arm and twisted it so that I dropped the knife. The guy whose lap she'd been sitting in jumped up, ran over and snatched it from the floor.

'Thank you, dear,' she said.

As they kissed, I realised I'd seen him before. On the beach. The day Natalie had broken down and I'd comforted her.

'That's your ex-fiancé,' I said, as he returned to the table.

'Actually, he's my husband. Going on what? Five years?' She looked to him for confirmation, and he nodded. 'I made up all that drama because girls love to bond over shared heartache, and that's what I wanted you and me to do. But if all goes well, you and Simon will be as happy as Will and I are. For ever.'

A door slammed. Heavy footsteps thudded up the stairs. I stepped aside, prepared to see police officers charging . . . but it was the fisherman. The one with the orange truck.

'Sam?' Natalie asked, when he cleared the landing. 'What are . . . ?' She frowned, then cringed and sipped the champagne she'd poured for me. 'So it was Colin, not you. That wasn't in the script, but, oh well.'

I was about to ask what script, when Sam lunged towards me. He was soaking wet, his eyes unfocused but aimed at mine. Before I could get out of the way, a short, high-pitched sound that resembled a ringing bell pierced the air, temporarily silencing the wind, rain and thunder. For a split second, I saw white and my mind was completely clear.

When the deck came back into view, Sam was sitting next to Natalie's husband, his expression blank as he stared straight ahead. Natalie stood before me, smiling.

'You're a . . .'

She raised her eyebrows, cupped her hand to one ear. 'What's that?'

I tried again. 'You're . . . a siren.'

'Of course I am.' She looked at me like I was being silly.

'But my head . . . it's been fine.' Despite how terrible I'd felt the past few weeks, I hadn't experienced the sorts of migraines that had previously indicated a siren's presence.

'Do you really think I'd give myself away so easily?' She glanced at Paige. 'Though I must admit, I'm surprised your good friend – your *best* friend – didn't tell you.'

My eyes locked on Paige's.

I'm so sorry, Vanessa. I didn't –

'Quiet!' Natalie shouted.

As Paige winced and fell silent, I tried to put the pieces together.

'You took the pictures,' I said. 'And sent the e-mails.'

'Wrong.' Natalie took another sip. 'And wrong.'

She waited for me to take another guess. When I

386

didn't, she flitted across the deck and leaned against the railing.

'I've waited a very long time for you,' she said. 'Although I didn't know I was waiting for you specifically . . . but after last summer, there was no question you were the one.'

I swallowed. 'The one?'

'To join me,' she said, her silver-blue eyes glittering, 'in leading the next generation.'

CHAPTER 26

A lightning bolt tore through the sky. Thunder roared. Everyone but Natalie and me jumped.

'Listen,' she said casually, waving her glass around, 'I'm not knocking centuries of hard work. The ladies who came before us did well enough with what they had. We wouldn't be here otherwise. But their focus was narrow, their scope limited. Their primary concern was, and for the most part remains, survival.' Her mouth lifted in a slow smile. 'But we're capable of so much more than that.'

I yearned to look at Simon. I wanted him to focus on me, to ignore everything Natalie was saying. But I was afraid she'd mistake the gesture for something more and hurt him in response, so I kept my gaze level as she continued.

'Raina's attempt last summer was impressive, if flawed. That said, she was the first one, at least that I know of, to use her powers to try to make a larger statement. It was a bold move, and if it had worked, I can only imagine what else she'd have accomplished.'

Now I wanted to look at Paige, but didn't.

'I'd been monitoring the activity of the more powerful communities for years, and when word of Raina's successes reached me – in northern California, by the way, not landlocked Vermont – I started paying closer attention. Then, when it became clear what – or who – had gotten in her way, I was hooked. So I decided to spend this summer on the East Coast.' She grinned. 'Great lobster, by the way.'

'I don't understand,' I said. 'What does that have to do with the e-mails? The pictures? The girls?'

'You were reluctant. You didn't want the gift you'd been given. I had to get your attention and make you see how valuable it is, how special you really are. It was the only way you might join me.'

'But if last summer didn't convince me, why would all this?' I asked.

'Because this summer's victims were young women – not men. And up until a few minutes ago, you thought their attacker was male, yes? And deserved to be punished accordingly?'

'So you did it?' I asked. '*You* killed the girls? To try to get me to see something I never will?'

Natalie frowned. 'You'll have to learn not to leap to such conclusions if we're going to have a successful partnership.'

'We're not going to –'

The note sounded again. I saw white. My thoughts vanished.

'I didn't kill anyone,' Natalie said, when the light faded. 'Not this time. I didn't have to.'

She was still by the railing and motioned for me to join her. As I did, I thought of the police. Where were they?

'All I did', Natalie said, when I reached her, lowering her voice, 'was orchestrate.'

She looked over the railing, to the beach. I did, too, and saw all of the guests from downstairs trickling towards the harbour. The female guests, I now knew, weren't ordinary women.

'I controlled them all,' she said softly, happily, like we were two friends sharing secrets. 'I had young sirens from both coasts send the e-mails so they couldn't be tracked to anyone here. A select group joined me and was put in charge of the camera you found, which was purposefully loaded with pictures significant to last summer's events and left for you to find. You recognised those clues as I hoped you would, and were instantly suspicious of the crazed siren stalkers.'

'What about the people I overheard at the lake house?' I asked.

'Happy accident. Colin was sent an anonymous tip

about the truth behind last summer because I knew you'd be in contact with him and hoped he could serve as a distraction while I worked with the other men. That his friends were around and excited was a pleasant coincidence.'

'And the other men were the fishermen?' I guessed.

'Indeed. Colin's involvement was to have been minimal, but the fishermen, under the spells of talented though slightly inexperienced young sirens, were more aggressive than I liked. They knew you were the ultimate target and couldn't resist teasing you when the opportunity presented itself. Unfortunately, one gentleman took it too far in the restaurant basement, and I had to increase Colin's participation to curb your suspicion. It was too soon for you to put it all together. I needed more time.'

'That's why you had him deliver Raina's necklace.'

'Exactly. Those security cameras were a brilliant addition, I must say.'

I watched the men and sirens below. Despite the elements hammering them from all angles, they talked and laughed like they were having a great time.

'So the goal', I said, 'was to show me how evil men could be by making them kill innocent women? So that I'd find our ability to stop them more noble?'

'That was part of it. The other part was to get you to

do what you did this morning. Paige, who turned out to be quite helpful in rallying the troops, even if she didn't know why, was the ultimate game piece. I assumed, correctly, that you'd do anything to save her. The chain of events wasn't quite what I planned, but no matter.' She paused. 'The end result was the same.'

'What do you mean?'

'I knew you'd follow Colin, which gave me time to secure Paige without you around. But I needed you back here to fight valiantly on Paige's behalf, so I sent Sam to get you. I assumed when Jaime went after your best friend, that he'd be the one you eventually . . . you know.' She peered past me to Simon, then looked at me and leaned closer. 'Don't worry. He'll get used to the idea eventually. They all do.'

I forced my mind past this last part and glanced over my shoulder. Sam still sat at the table, soaking wet. The deck was covered, and unlike the Jeep, whose top had been down while I drove, the truck had a cab.

'He was in the water?' I asked quietly. 'With Colin and me?'

Natalie followed my gaze. 'Considering the seaweed in his hair, I'd say so. A few minutes ago, when I saw how striking you were and knew what you must've done, I thought he was the one you'd done it to. That's why I

392

was surprised when he showed up. But again, these are details – and small ones at that.'

I turned back towards the harbour, gripping the railing so tight, small, jagged splinters pierced my palms.

Colin hadn't murdered anyone. He hadn't tried to strangle me in the ocean. Sam had. Which meant a completely innocent person had been killed . . . by me.

I was a monster. Just like the rest of them.

'You have to admit,' Natalie whispered, 'it feels amazing, doesn't it? The rush? The charge of life? And it never has to end. Just think of the possibilities!'

'Natalie,' I said evenly, hoping to buy more time for the police, 'what exactly do you want me to do?'

'Join me.' Her voice was excited. 'Help me find and train young, talented sirens who can then train others.'

'To kill?'

She shrugged. 'On occasion. That goes with the territory. But together we can *expand* the territory – geographically and ideologically. Ours can be the first siren community to cross state lines and control more members of the opposite sex than any group has before. We don't have to kill them all . . . we can simply mess with them, make them do our bidding, whatever that may be. Men have had the upper hand for centuries, and it's time they were put in their place.'

I wanted to ask another question to keep her talking,

but I was too stunned by what she was suggesting to form the words. For better or worse, she continued anyway.

'This isn't simply a request, Vanessa. It's an offer. An opportunity. If you agree, you'll become stronger and more powerful in ways you can't even imagine now – and your friends will live. I chose you because of your impressive lineage and abilities, but Paige can join us. You and Simon can be together. You'll have the life you thought was lost upon your transformation last summer, only better.'

'And if I don't accept?' I asked.

She laughed. When she realised I wasn't joking, her expression turned serious. 'Then you're not as smart as I thought. And . . .'

Her head turned slowly towards the scene below us.

The party had moved closer to the water. And the group had grown.

'Simon.' My heart stopped. Still bound and gagged, he struggled to break free of Sam's grip as Sam dragged him across the beach. Natalie's husband followed behind with Caleb, and Jaime with Paige. They'd moved them while Natalie and I talked.

'This can be easy or not,' she said pleasantly. 'The choice is yours. The party, which is in honour of you, will go on either way.'

With that, she put down her empty champagne glass, placed both palms on the railing, and launched herself off the deck. Her red skirt billowed around her as she fell to the ground, where she landed feet-first with a soft thud. She strolled towards the men and sirens, who continued to talk and laugh even as they entered the water.

The sirens were luring the men into the harbour. They were going to do what Raina couldn't, last summer. And if I didn't play along, they were going to take Simon, Caleb and Paige with them.

Vanessa, what's going on? What do we do?

Paige's voice was an alarm in my head. For a second, I didn't know whether I should answer. If Natalie was right, if Paige had known her newest hire was a siren . . . had she known everything else, too?

Sing, Paige. To Jaime. So he'll let you go.

I wouldn't do that if I were you, Natalie fired back. *Until we join forces, you're greatly outnumbered. On my signal, the ladies will switch targets instantly.*

That was all the answer I needed. Paige and Natalie weren't allies; Natalie had simply used Paige for her purposes. Not wanting to lose sight of them for even a moment, I put both hands on the railing and leapt from the deck. I landed surprisingly easily and ran.

As I headed towards them, I didn't notice I wasn't the only one in hot pursuit. Chief Green and another police officer had finally arrived and were bolting across the sand, too . . . as it turned out, in hot pursuit of me.

'Vanessa Sands!' a deep male voice shouted behind me.

I slowed, but didn't stop.

'You're under arrest! Anything you say can –'

'Under arrest?' Reaching the water's edge, Natalie turned towards us, one hand on her chest. 'Whatever for?'

I scanned the water behind her. The sirens and men were getting deeper. A few men were already kicking to keep their heads above the surface.

'For the murder of Colin Robbins.'

Now I stopped. But I didn't face the police.

I faced Simon. He stood with Sam, two feet from the water. At Chief Green's declaration, he shook his head and looked at me, eyes wide, confused.

'There must be some mistake,' Natalie said. 'Pretty, sweet, wouldn't-hurt-a-fly Vanessa Sands . . . a murderer?'

'I wish it was a mistake,' Chief Green said, stopping before us. 'Believe me. But we have the confession right here.'

My heart sank when he pulled out a digital voice recorder – *my* digital voice recorder, the one I'd taken out kayaking – from his shirt pocket. With everything that had happened, I'd forgotten all about it.

'We found it in the denim jacket she left with the victim.' Chief Green looked at me. 'It has everything – the underwater scuffle, the dragging of the body on the beach, your subsequent apology. Everything.'

Natalie clucked her tongue. 'Well. That was sloppy.'

For the first time, Chief Green looked past her. 'What's going on here? What are all those folks doing in the water?'

'Just a few friends having a small beach party,' Natalie said.

'In the middle of a storm?' Chief Green asked.

'We're very good swimmers.' Natalie smiled.

The other police officer – Sergeant Tompkins, according to his badge – came up behind me, took my wrist. Chief Green stepped towards the water just as a lightning bolt illuminated the sky – and the captives still onshore.

'Paige Marchand?' he asked. 'Is that you? What –'

He was cut off by an ear-splitting shriek. Once again, the world went white. My head went blank. But this single note lasted longer than the others had up on the employee deck, and after several seconds, my body seemed to adjust to the noise. My sight returned partially – I could make out the people and place before me, but they were soft, fuzzy, like I was viewing them through a grey screen.

It was enough. Chief Green stood perfectly still, his mouth frozen open in a startled O and both hands on his head. Simon, Caleb, Paige and their captors were also still. So were the sirens and men in the harbour, though the water continued to lap against them. Behind me, Sergeant Tompkins didn't move.

The only one who did was Natalie. She strode towards Chief Green, still singing. If she knew I could see her, she didn't let on. Certain this was the only chance I was going to get, I started to pull away from the officer – but was stopped by something cold and hard.

Handcuffs. He had one latched on to my wrist and held the other open in his right hand.

I know you're strong . . . now you just need to decide what it really means to be brave.

Charlotte's last words ran through my head.

And I knew what I had to do.

I tugged my arm until the other handcuff popped free from Sergeant Tompkins's fingers. Keeping one eye on Natalie, whose back was to me as she reached towards Chief Green's chest, I dashed across the sand to Caleb. He didn't seem to feel a thing as I untied his hands and ripped the tape from his mouth. I blinked back tears as I gave him a quick hug and moved on to Paige. I released her, too, and gave her a tighter, slightly longer squeeze. I considered shoving their captors away to give them a bigger head start, but I didn't know if the force would wake the men or alert Natalie. I could only hope Caleb and Paige moved fast enough once the spell faded.

And then I went to Simon. His eyes were still aimed towards Sergeant Tompkins, since that's where I'd been when Natalie had started singing. I couldn't keep the tears from rolling down my face as I undid his ties and peeled the tape from his mouth. I worked quickly, knowing I didn't have much time – and that I'd stop if I let myself think about how unfair this all was.

But then, wasn't this how it would've ended anyway? With us apart? And me as good as dead if not actually dead? Wasn't it better that it happened sooner rather than later, regardless of how, just as Charlotte had said?

I glanced behind me. Natalie was pressing her hands into the chief's chest, her eyes locked on his, her lips moving almost imperceptibly.

I turned back to Simon and pressed my lips to his one last time. They were still soft and warm, which made the tears fall faster.

'*I love you*,' I mouthed, careful not to say the words out loud or in my head. '*And I'm so sorry.*'

I stood, gently brushed his hair away from his forehead, and then started towards Natalie. My feet quickened beneath me, until I was sprinting. I slowed just enough to keep from ramming into her, slammed the other handcuff on to her wrist, and locked it shut.

'Vanessa!' she exclaimed, her spell instantly broken. 'What –'

She was cut off as I jerked her backwards, dragged her through the sand. Everyone around us came to, but slowly, as if they were waking from a long nap. I used their temporary, groggy confusion to my advantage; by the time they could remember where they were and what was happening, Natalie and I were already in the water.

This is touching but pointless, she screamed in my head. *You have no idea how strong I am.*

I guess I'll just have to find out.

As she kicked and squirmed, I tightened my hold around her shoulders. She wriggled from my grasp once, but I turned and was above her instantly, blocking her route to the surface. She tried to shoot past me, but I pulled her back and under my arm again in one swift motion.

Natalie was strong. But I'd just taken a life . . . and so was I.

What are you going to do? she demanded as we swam deeper. *Bury me in the sand at the bottom of the ocean?*

That's not a bad idea.

If you wanted to kill me, why didn't you just take the cop's gun and shoot me?

Because I *didn't* want to kill her. I didn't want to kill anyone, ever. But since that was the only way to stop her and save countless more people from dying under her command . . . I, at least, didn't want to live with having killed her. I supposed I could've shot myself, too, but I couldn't do that to Simon or my friends. Plus, this way seemed only appropriate.

We were going to swim. Drift. Surrender ourselves to the ocean without coming up for air. For hours, days or weeks. However long it took for our bodies to shut down from lack of oxygen, which we needed to survive as much as we needed salt water.

You're being foolish. How is this better than the life I offered?

That wasn't a life, I shot back. *And this way, no one else gets hurt.*

She laughed. *Maybe I was wrong about you after all, Vanessa Sands. Because if you think this ends with me, you're sorely mistaken.*

I kicked harder, dived deeper. She screeched, and the long, shrill note was temporarily blinding. Without thinking, I mimicked the sound, giving it my all in hopes of drowning her out.

Seconds later, we were surrounded by silver light.

You see? She patted my arm, which was still around her shoulders. *Look at how well I've taught them.*

The sirens. *Her* sirens. The same ones who'd just been luring in the fishermen now surrounded us, silver eyes gleaming. They formed a tight sphere, making it impossible to swim away. One by one they reached for us, grabbing our hair, our arms, our necks. At first, I tried to resist, to pull out of their holds . . . but there was no point.

So I stopped struggling. I relaxed my grip on Natalie and felt her float as far away as the handcuffs would allow. I closed my eyes.

And then, singing so softly only I could hear, I pictured Justine, told her I'd see her soon . . . and gave in to the light.

CHAPTER 27

The small room was on the top floor of an old brick building. The walls were white concrete, the floors grey linoleum. The ceiling was covered in glow-in-the-dark star stickers, left by a previous occupant. There were two beds, dressers, desks and bookcases. A single pedestal handbasin stood between two wardrobes. Above the iron radiator, a large window overlooked a cluster of similar buildings housing rooms identical to this one.

'Well,' Mom said, looking around, 'it's not the Ritz.'

'No,' I said. 'It's better.'

Her eyes watered as she smiled. Then, most likely to ward off the full-fledged breakdown she'd been fighting for days, she turned to the stack of folded linen on one desk, took a sheet and shook it out over one of the beds.

'Five flights of stairs,' Dad gasped, coming into the room. 'And not one elevator.'

'Which wouldn't be a big deal if someone hadn't insisted on bringing everything she owned.' Paige followed Dad inside and rolled her eyes playfully. '*Such* a diva.'

She was kidding. We'd passed several cars so stuffed

with belongings, the windows seemed to bulge, and mine had fitted neatly into the back luggage space of Mom's SUV – with room to spare. Paige had been so puzzled when she saw the packing job, she asked if we'd rented a removal lorry for the rest of my stuff. When I'd told her no, she asked if the car had been broken into. The teasing had continued since.

Dad hung up my winter coat, which Paige must've insisted he trade her for my suitcase when they realised there was no elevator, in one of the wardrobes. Paige rolled the suitcase to one of the dressers. Mom finished making the bed and then stood in the middle of the room, hands on her hips.

'We should put your clothes away,' she said. 'And what about your toiletries? Do you want them by the basin? On your dresser? How about your laptop and notebooks? We should organise your desk, too.'

'Mom.' I reached forward, squeezed her arm. 'There's not much to unpack or organise. I can do that later.'

She frowned. 'Then we should go shopping. You'll need a rug. And curtains. And maybe some more pillows, in case you want to read in bed.'

'Don't forget the mini-fridge,' Paige added. 'I'm definitely getting one of those when I move to San Francisco next spring. Maybe two.'

'That makes sense,' I said. 'You're going to a school for

restaurant management. You'll need them to store all the amazing dishes your future employees are going to try to bribe you with. I, on the other hand, am fine without. Really.'

'What about for snacks?' Mom asked. 'And water bottles? I should've thought of that. Why didn't I think of that?'

'Probably because you were busy thinking of everything else.'

Unconvinced, Mom bit her lip, drummed her fingers against her hips.

'I have a car,' I reminded her. 'If I change my mind, I can always go get one later.'

'But they're heavy,' she protested. 'And there's no elevator.'

'I'll help,' a familiar male voice said.

Mom turned around. I smiled.

Simon stood in the open doorway.

'I do plan to spend quite a bit of time up here,' he added. 'I'll make sure your darling daughter has everything she needs almost as soon as she needs it.'

Fresh tears filled Mom's eyes. She went to the door and pulled Simon into a tight embrace. When she finally let him go, Dad shook his hand and asked how the journey from Bates was. As the three of them made small talk, Paige caught my eye from the other side of the room and spoke so only I could hear.

You seem suspiciously calm. Everything okay?

Everything's great. Promise.

Good. And don't worry about your parents. I'll make sure the waterworks don't flood the entire north-east on our way to Winter Harbor.

I appreciate that, I said, thinking again how nice it was that Paige had come for the trip. She'd taken a train to Boston and spent the previous weekend with us, ridden in the Jeep with me up to Hanover, and would, I hoped, distract my parents when they left later this afternoon. They were going to Winter Harbor to prepare the beach house for winter, and had offered to drive Paige home to save her from having to take the train again.

By the way, she said, *this is so much better than e-mail. As long as I can hear your voice whenever I want, I think I just might survive the long distance and stretch between visits.*

I looked at her. *We've survived worse.*

It was hard to believe, thinking back, just how much we'd been through. Justine's drowning. Raina's and Zara's attacks, in both Winter Harbor and Boston, and their subsequent demises. Betty's near death and manipulation. The loss of Paige's unborn baby. Charlotte's unexpected introduction and equally unexpected passing.

Our physical transformations and the countless challenges they'd brought.

And, of course, Natalie.

There were so many reasons I shouldn't have survived the events of this past summer, especially considering how close – and often – I'd come to dying. Before I knew what it needed, my body had nearly failed me. A hypnotised fisherman might've killed me in the basement of Betty's if I hadn't accidentally interrupted him, and again in the ocean, when he'd tried to strangle me. And when by some small miracle I made it through all that, I should've died at the bottom of the harbour, handcuffed to Natalie and suffocated by vengeful sirens.

But I'd survived that, too. And for once, my Nenuphar powers had proved useful. Because the sirens hadn't heard Natalie's call and come for me. They'd heard my voice above hers . . . and they came for her. In a flurry of water and song, during which I was certain each breath I took was my last, they'd killed her. And when they were done, they'd looked to me for guidance.

When I realised what had happened, I acted automatically. I instructed the majority of the sirens to return to the men, make sure they were okay, and do what they could to soften the memories of that night. I asked two to take Natalie's body out to sea, where it would decompose long before it was found. When the handcuffs posed a problem, I took the chain between two fingers and broke it apart like it was made of seaweed rather than metal. And then I headed for shore, prepared to confess a second crime to Chief Green and Sergeant Tompkins.

Paige, however, had learned a thing or two from her time with Natalie. Before my feet hit sand, the police were gone – and apparently convinced they'd stopped by the beach to follow up on a noise complaint. The digital voice recorder, with my earlier confession, was in her possession. She'd also taken care of Jamie, Sam and Natalie's husband the same way I'd asked the sirens to handle the other men: by singing so sweetly they believed everything the sirens claimed, including my innocence. The only ones who still knew what I'd been accused of were Paige, Caleb, Simon and me.

The four of us talked for hours after that. They hadn't heard any of my conversation with Natalie up on the employee deck, so I explained everything she'd told me. When I was finished, I said I still planned to turn myself in to the police for what I'd done to Colin, but they talked me out of it. They were certain I'd simply acted in self-defence and that his death was ultimately an accident. They also thought that'd be difficult to explain to the authorities without trying to explain everything else.

I couldn't argue their logic, so even though I'd been – and still was – racked with guilt, I refrained.

As a visitor, Natalie wasn't known or missed outside our small circle, and her body wasn't found. Colin's death was deemed a tragic kayaking accident. The other mysterious deaths – Carla's, Erica's and Gretchen's – remained unsolved. Eventually, as weeks passed without incident, residents and life in Winter Harbor calmed down.

Paige even relaxed, although that took longer. Just as I felt guilty for my involvement with Colin, she felt guilty for hers with Natalie. Their friendship had started innocently enough, but Natalie had latched on to the fact that Paige wanted to increase business at the restaurant and, when the time was right, she confessed that she was a siren, too. She'd claimed she wanted to meet Paige after reading about everything that had happened the summer before and hoped to help her move on after such a horrific experience. Paige, desperate for business and curious about what a more experienced, seemingly trustworthy siren could teach her, quickly went along with Natalie's business propositions – including using her abilities to lure men to the new dinner contests Betty's hosted. She'd wanted to tell me but didn't, for two reasons. The first was that she was worried I wouldn't approve, and the second was that she didn't want to give me yet another thing to worry about.

She'd apologised endlessly, and each time, I told her it wasn't necessary. After all, considering what I'd done, who was I to judge?

I could go for some coffee, Paige announced suddenly. Then, 'Who wants coffee? My treat.'

My parents, miraculously picking up on the excuse to leave, claimed that they were in desperate need of caffeine. We agreed to meet at the dining hall, and they hurried from the room. When they were gone, Simon came all the way inside and closed the door.

'Hey.' He smiled.

I went to him, put my arms around his neck, and squeezed. 'Thank you for coming.'

'Are you kidding? I wouldn't have missed this for anything.'

It was true. It had to be. I'd certainly given him enough reason to stay far, far away for a very long time . . . yet here he was.

'Any sign of your roommate yet?' he asked, a moment later.

I released him reluctantly. 'Nope. But we e-mailed a few times and she seems nice. Her name's Sarah. She's from Nebraska.'

'Conveniently nowhere near an ocean.'

'Right.' That had been my first thought, too.

'Care for some friendly advice?'

'Always.'

He flopped on the bed. 'Ground rules. Lay them down as soon as possible – preferably after parental departures but before you go to sleep tonight. You don't want to wake up to a pre-dawn alarm clock or nude yoga or anything else that might get your relationship off to the kind of rocky start from which some roommates never recover. Trust me.'

I grinned and sat next to him.

'Also, are you sure about this side of the room? The unwritten rule is that the first one to arrive gets first pick, but I know you'd probably hand this side over if Sarah from Nebraska so much as smiled at it. So if you're sure, we should probably come up with polite ways for you to stand your ground. Another option is to wait till she gets here and discuss who gets which piece of furniture, but that's always more trouble than it's worth.'

Amused, I didn't say anything. A second later, he turned to me, eyebrows raised.

'Sorry,' I said. 'That was a real question?'

'Just wait. Tomorrow morning, when you open your eyes before the sun comes up and suddenly know your roommate *really* well . . . you're going to wish you'd taken this seriously.'

I leaned closer, bumped his shoulder with mine. 'What would I do without you?'

He lifted my chin, waited for my eyes to meet his, and spoke softly. 'That's one question, Vanessa Sands, you will never have to know the answer to.'

He pressed his lips gently to mine. As we kissed, I thought about how, for the first time, I actually believed this. I believed Simon and I would be together no matter what. Because he knew everything now. He knew about Colin. He knew that although Natalie had been technically killed by the other sirens, they'd been acting upon my distress call, making me at least partially – if not totally – responsible. He knew how I felt even stronger after her death than I had after Colin's. He even knew what I'd have to do if I were to continue to curtail the accelerated ageing process.

And he wanted to be with me anyway.

We kissed a while longer. When we finally pulled apart, Simon stood with a sigh and held out one hand.

'We should probably find your parents before your mother monopolises all the mini-fridges in a hundred-mile radius.'

I took his hand and he gently helped me up. 'Can I meet you at the dining hall? I just want to freshen up.'

'I'm happy to wait.'

'That's okay.' I smiled. 'I won't be long.'

He didn't press. He squeezed my fingers as he released them, kissed my cheek, and said, 'Take your time.'

I watched him go. When the door closed behind him, I surveyed the room once more. Besides the furniture and my bedding, it was bare, and my side would likely stay that way. As I'd packed during the days leading up to orientation week, I'd thought of Charlotte's home in South Boston, the guest room during her stay at the beach house. Her home had been simply furnished. Her bookcases had remained empty, the fireplace spotless, like it'd never seen a match. She'd stayed with us several days in Winter Harbor, but aside from her suitcase and slippers, the room always seemed unoccupied.

Charlotte had kept things simple. She hadn't wanted to settle in, to get attached. Because it was hard to feel comfortable in the present when your future could change at any time.

That was why I'd packed lightly. I didn't know what my future held. For now it was college. Simon. My friends and family. A relatively normal life.

But later? In a month? A year? Two years? When no amount of salt water or random flirting gave me the strength I needed to live a relatively normal life? When it was time to do what I wasn't sure I could ever do again?

I had no idea.

Still, I was hopeful. More so than I'd been in a long time. Which was why I'd brought a few things to help my dorm room feel like home.

My handbag was on my bed. I reached inside for the envelope I'd placed there the night before, went to the nearest desk, and faced the wall – and a brown cork bulletin board.

I did as Simon suggested. I took my time, working carefully, arranging thoughtfully. When I was done, I stepped back to survey the result.

The forest-green Dartmouth bumper sticker I'd received with my acceptance letter was centred at the top of the board. Beneath it were a dozen different photos – of my parents lounging in Adirondack chairs on the beach. Paige dancing with Betty as Oliver cooked in the background. Caleb grinning and pretending to attack the camera with a clam rake. Simon reading, hiking, and looking at the photographer like he'd be perfectly content to never look anywhere else.

These photos formed a loose circle around one other. It was a five by seven, and it was my favourite. In it, Justine and I are fishing in our red rowing boat. Her head's turned towards me and mine's tilted towards the sky. My shoulders are pulled up near my ears as I laugh until tears fall at something she's said.

'It's scary,' I whispered, gently pressing my fingertips

to her smiling face. 'But exciting, too. You would've liked it.'

I stood there a minute more – until a familiar voice called my name from somewhere outside. I went to the open window and peered down at the crowded sidewalk.

'*A cappella* in the quad!' Paige shouted, waving two iced coffees – one for each of us, I guessed. 'I have no idea what any of that means, but Fancy College Man assures me it's not to be missed. You coming?'

I grinned. My parents stood just behind her, examining the campus map. Simon stood next to them, hands in his jeans pockets, smiling up at me. All around them, my new classmates talked and laughed with each other and their families.

'Be right there,' I called down.

And then I grabbed my bag, took one more look around my new room, and went to find out what else today had in store.